The Pull

The Pull

A Novel

Summer Robidoux

THE PULL

iUniverse books may be ordered through booksellers or by contacting:

iUniverse
1663 Liberty Drive
Bloomington, IN 47403
www.iuniverse.com
1-800-Authors (1-800-288-4677)

ISBN: 978-1-4917-8860-8 (sc)
ISBN: 978-1-4917-8861-5 (e)

Library of Congress Control Number: 2016902112

Print information available on the last page.

iUniverse rev. date: 02/05/2016

For my family near and far.
—S.R.

Adventure is worthwhile in itself.
— Amelia Earhart

ACKNOWLEDGMENTS

First and foremost, I'd like to thank God for my many blessings! I cannot thank my husband and my three daughters enough! Thank you for all of your patience, love, and support. Jay, your encouragement and feedback kept my book alive. Aubree, Gracelyn, and Emma: your imaginations are amazing my little muses. Sending many thanks to Molly McCowan with Inkbot Editing and to Shannon Conner with Shannon Conner Photography. To my mother, Katherine, thank you for all of your input and encouragement. To my sis, Dara, you rock! Your support is like a boulder, and your friendship is priceless (also, thanks for letting me pilfer some of your life). Sending a very sincere thanks to Judy; I appreciate all of your ideas, feedback, and time. Special thanks to Sarah for letting me borrow *just* your name. To my girls: Skye, Misty, Karen, and Shannon, thank you for reading my subpar drafts and dealing with my relentless hounding. I appreciate all of your support and friendships. I am truly blessed!

PROLOGUE

*M*iss Jenni had her back to the third-grade class as she spoke. Her shoulder-length, curly blonde hair bobbed as she wrote all nineteen of the students' names on the board. "Okay friends, next week is career week. When I call your name, I want you to stand up and tell me what you want to be when you grow up. I'll write your answer on the board, and then we'll transfer your response onto a sheet for you to take home and give to your parents. They can help you find an adult to shadow at work one day next week."

Each student in the class took their turn. Answers varied: fireman, baseball player, ballerina, truck driver, teacher. Finally, it was my turn.

Miss Jenni's blue eyes shined. "Brit, what would you like to be?"

I stood, my eyes nervously skimming the class. I locked my gaze back onto Miss Jenni. "I'd like to be a famous explorer, and explore Mars."

Some of the other students snickered. My face flushed.

Miss Jenni said, "Brit, I think that sounds like a fine career, but your parents might not know an explorer. Can you think of another career?"

I thought for a moment. "I like animals."

Miss Jenni's smile grew. "Perfect. How about a veterinarian?"

I nodded. "That would be fun."

Miss Jenni wrote the word "vet" next to my name as I sat down.

I studied the three simple words: "Brittany Scott, vet." It sounded nice. But it still wasn't nearly as appealing as "Brittany Scott, explorer."

Chapter

O N E

My eyes wouldn't focus. I could hear whispering and see blurs of movement all around me. The gray colors altered into different shades, but I couldn't make out any details. After blinking several times I shook my head, trying to clear the pounding in my ears. I felt like I'd hit a brick wall.

I had hit a wall: a wall of thick fog.

I tried to sit up and the blood rushed to my head, sending the world swirling around me. I started to fall back, but someone broke my fall. The hand was large, engulfing my entire upper back. The palm and fingers were thick and strong, holding my frame with ease.

My eyes began to focus, and I was able to make out some details. The man leaning over me was unfamiliar, and he looked puzzled. He was older, maybe in his late fifties, with straight, mahogany hair that was salted near his ears. He had a strong jawline and small, narrow eyes that were cloaked under thick brows, making them appear even smaller.

I was sure he was a figure of authority, with broad shoulders and a presence that demanded respect. People were peering at me from behind him, but they kept their distance and didn't intervene.

After a couple minutes, my vision had almost completely recovered. I was baffled by my surroundings. The cavern I'd spent the last few days in was gone, and I looked up at the sky instead of the rocky ceiling I'd become accustomed to. The sky was gray and overcast, reminding me of my hometown in Oregon in the winter. Regardless, the dim sky seemed brilliant in comparison to the cavern.

How was this possible? Where was I? My heart rate increased as fright washed through me.

"Calm down. You are safe here." The man tried to speak reassuringly, but his voice was deep and intimidating.

Without thinking, I tried to get up, wanting to run away. His hand clamped down on my shoulder, and I struggled against his massive force. Effortlessly holding me in place, he waited for me to tire out. It didn't take long before I went limp in defeat.

"You need to calm down," he said. "No one is going to hurt you."

I was exhausted from the struggle. I nodded my head once with recognition, and he allowed me to sit up. He stood and reached out his hand. After taking a moment to register his intentions, I extended my hand up to meet his. He helped me to my feet, lifting my weight with ease.

The man's hands were in proportion to his body. He was enormous, standing at least six foot six. Dressed similarly to the others surrounding us, with dark cargo pants and a black T-shirt stretched tight across his chest, I deduced that they were all soldiers. His arms were thick and strong, ending at ample shoulders that engulfed his neck. I cowered at his size and air of confidence.

His mouth was narrow and moved quickly when he spoke. "Who are you and how did you get here?"

I froze.

"Who are you and how did you get here?" he repeated, asking the question slower this time.

I was torn between crying and fighting. I paused as I decided my next move, then squared my shoulders and exhaled. "That's exactly what I was going to ask you," I said aggressively, trying to present a strong front. Show no fear.

His lips twitched momentarily into a flash of a smile, and then his expression of confusion intensified. He looked around suspiciously before addressing me again. "You mean to tell me that you do not know how you arrived here?"

"I don't even know where *here* is. I was in the cavern, I got hit by a wall of fog, and the next thing I know, I'm talking to you."

His eyes narrowed to slits. "You have been sent by *them*, have you not?" Anger was brewing in his voice.

My panic started to resurface. "Sent by *them*? Who's them? No one sent me."

"The Sohrigs, that's who!" His face reddened as his voice boomed, making my stomach knot. Reflexively I took a step back, right into another onlooker who steadied me as I jerked away. This soldier was disinterested in me, never taking his eyes off the big one. The leader had his fingers and thumb spanning across his forehead with his eyes closed.

I looked at him blankly, mentally tracing over the events that had led me here, wherever here was. I carelessly said what I was thinking. "The man in the coffee shop."

"What man?" he ordered.

I took a breath and started to explain. "My friends and I were on a road trip and we stopped at a coffee shop in Boulder. A man approached us and gave us directions to the cavern that led me here."

"Their traveler," he spat, sounding disgusted. "Always meddling around. Boulder? What is Boulder?" His voice switched from anger to intrigue.

His question caught me off guard. "Um, it's a city near Denver." He still looked confused. "Colorado?"

He shook his head.

"Where am I?" I asked.

A new expression crossed his face. Not anger or frustration or confusion, but a sly look, as if he were playing a strategic game. "Sneaky. So *that* is their plan, to get to us through the back door."

He looked at the surrounding men and started blurting out commands. "Double the watch and shorten the shifts." He looked at two soldiers standing near him. "Go and inform the others of the situation, and put the camp on heightened security. No one enters or exits the camp without my consent."

"Yes sir," they answered in unison and several men ran off.

He looked back at me. "What is your name?"

"Brittany Scott . . . but my friends call me Brit," I squeaked.

"All right, Brit. Come with me," he said as he turned and walked away. I stood there for a moment, looking around at the remaining eyes staring back at me. Intimidated, I scampered to catch up with him as I gawked at the camp.

The site reminded me of something you would see in an old war movie. There were white, rectangular two-man tents in every direction, with a handful of larger tents that stood out. Looking more official than the others, these tents were spacious and had diagonal stripes of color on their doors. All the tents were arranged in circles, looking like miniature communities within the camp. He led me past several circles and then walked into a sizeable white tent with a thick, red stripe on the door.

I followed him, stepping through the tent flap. The interior walls were made of the same canvas material, looking much whiter than the tent's environmentally tormented exterior counterpart. The high ceiling was at least a foot over his head, and a thin, gray wool blanket was used as a rug on top of the dirt floor.

The interior furnishings were simple. A narrow green cot was placed against the far wall with what looked to be a bag of clothes tucked underneath. A small, square table with a few papers on it was positioned in the center of the tent. He walked over to the table and placed both hands on it, leaning forward with his head down.

He took in a deep breath and then spoke meticulously. "My name is Commander William Robb. I am heading this search party. We are trying to find them—and their base. And now you are telling me that they led you here? How did they know where we are?"

"Who are they and why—?"

He spun around. "The Sohrigs!"

I stepped back, alarmed by his outburst. He clearly had quite a temper, and somehow I kept saying the wrong things, igniting it.

He paused and collected himself. "They are a greedy, self-righteous people. They do not believe like we do. We appreciate other worlds and other cultures. We believe in balance and maintaining peace. The Sohrigs do not care about you or your world. They could protect you, but they choose not to. They would let others take everything—your land, your resources—and enslave your people. They would allow you to be thrown by the wayside!"

My chest felt heavy with horror and disbelief. Could people be so cruel? I was glad I couldn't answer the rhetorical question; it was easier to be unaware, living in my blissful existence.

"How do I know that you're telling me the truth?" I asked.

He looked down at me, meeting my scrutiny. Then he sighed and smiled slightly. "My father had a friend from your world named Little Bear—he was a great chief. Perhaps you have heard of him?"

Commander Robb paused so I could answer, but my mind was reeling. *A different world?*

He continued, jolting me from my thoughts. "Little Bear would often visit when I was a boy. You remind me of him." He seemed distracted for a moment, as if remembering his childhood. A thin smile crossed his face. "He told me your world was going through a similar transition, no?"

"The Arapaho! I can't believe the legends are true; Brody's going to freak out."

Commander Robb looked at me oddly.

"Oh, I'm sorry. The man that you spoke of, Little Bear, he lived way before my time—at least a hundred and twenty years, probably more."

He paused, and his shoulders slumped. "Time must pass differently in Boulder. Time has elapsed here, but not nearly that many years . . . not even close," he said sadly.

He pulled out a stool hidden under the table and sat down. With him seated, we were the same height. Confusion crossed his face once more. "How exactly did you make it to our camp? Little Bear would come directly to Trate,"—he paused, adding a soft sigh—"to our home. No one has ever found our camp, especially when we were on the move. He always traveled through the pull."

I gasped. "The Cleansing Pool. It really exists!"

Commander Robb had a strange expression. He spoke slowly, as if he were trying to put the pieces of the puzzle together in his head. "Ah, yes. I heard him refer to the pull by that name before, but you said you did not come that way."

"No. I was knocked over by a wall of dense fog and ended up here."

He looked at me with concentration, shaking his head, like the parts didn't add up.

Frustrated and perplexed, I decided to start at the beginning, seeing no other options. I didn't trust Commander Robb, especially with his temper, but my first priority was to find my friends. I had to unravel the mystery in order to figure out where I was and how I was going to return home. Reluctantly, I walked over to the cot, sat down, and began telling him the story that led me here.

"I'm from Portland, Oregon, which is a beautiful land far from here," I began, a quiver in my voice.

Chapter

T W O

Portland, Oregon was my home, born and raised. The area was a paradise full of thick, lush vegetation. With rivers in every direction, Portland glowed like emeralds. Contrasting shades of green gave the landscape depth, and the light reflecting off the water made it shimmer.

The rivers ran through the city like veins, twisting and curving before converging into the gorge. I was awestruck by the mass of these waterways. Although I saw them every day of my twenty-two years, I never grew tired of their grace and beauty. Their elegance pulled me in as if I were spellbound, and I'd watch them for hours. I sat on the grassy lawn at the river's edge, day after day, numbing my agitated post-work nerves with the water's peaceful essence.

I arrived at my river sanctuary early that Thursday. It had been a slow day in the critical care unit of the animal hospital, so I'd volunteered my shift to be cut early. Like most June afternoons in Portland, the weather was ideal, with a slight breeze warding off the sun's intensity. The air had a light and revitalizing edge. A few wispy clouds decorated the blue sky.

Heading straight to the riverfront, I walked across the soft, thick grass and tried to ignore the sights and sounds of the city around me. Portland was busy and full of energy, and the adjacent river was the opposite. Yet, making their presence known, cars scurried across the numerous bridges.

Although I typically sat and gazed at the water, today I plopped onto the grass and lay back. I let the sun caress my body as I stretched out and closed my eyes. My slow, deep breaths did nothing to settle my nerves. These feelings were not my typical post-work jitters. Self-doubt? Insecurity? Whatever it was, I felt inept and incomplete.

The scene from earlier continually replayed in my head: I had walked into the clinic with my coffee in hand and prepared to check in the surgery patients for the day. Around eight, shortly after admitting the last one, *she* walked in.

Dr. Eileen Straight was petite and slender, with deep-set brown eyes and mid-length, chocolate-brown hair. Her eyes were intensified by long, dark lashes that reminded me of a doe's. Her olive skin was radiant; she looked as if she had stepped out of a photo shoot and put on a white lab coat.

Dr. Straight was new to our clinic, and she was the most intimidating vet I'd ever dealt with. She wasn't cocky, but I found her confidence stifling. I couldn't focus and felt especially on edge, which made me mess up every time she was present. I looked incompetent. She seemed perfect. And the more I tried to push her to find a weakness, the more flawless she proved to be.

She was hip and trendy, down to her sassy red shoes. *Who wears red pumps to an animal hospital?* My head was full of callous thoughts as I tried to justify my insecurities. She must be from a storybook: she was too beautiful, too nice, too smart, too wealthy, too . . . everything. She didn't ask for anything unusual, but I found myself resenting her requests, as if I were merely a peasant in a noble's attendance. With each minute in her presence, I shrank, almost beyond recognition.

I was rattled to the core. My blanket of self-comfort and contentment was ripped off, revealing my shortcomings. I felt emotionally naked and vulnerable. Of course, no one saw the result—no one but me. How could I let this happen? I felt as if I were wearing a mask and had suddenly taken it off. I didn't recognize the person underneath.

Until now, I had considered myself a confident person. I was comfortable in my skin and dared to call myself cute. My long, caramel-brown hair hit the middle of my back, and I had light blue eyes and fair skin. My cheekbones were high, and I had full lips and straight, white teeth. Being tall and athletic, I felt healthy. My parents often said I was the ultimate depiction of the "all-American girl."

I was strong, mentally sound, and *always* in control. After hitting all the major life requirements my parents had deemed important,

I was independent and self-sufficient, and I excelled at my career. I was one of the top three vet techs at one of the largest hospitals in Portland, and I was frequently recruited because of my no-nonsense, get-the-job-done personality. I was often praised for my competence.

Secure in my existence, the world around me seemed predictable and controlled. But suddenly, there was a hole. Having Dr. Straight around was like having a mirror shoved in my face. There were major flaws. I had let my dreams and ambitions slip out of my grasp, leaving me on autopilot—moving *through* life but not *living* it.

Reflecting on my monotonous life made my stomach turn. Expectations and preformed notions had cut my path through life. Anesthetized and disoriented, I'd been oblivious to the path I'd followed for the last several years. I felt like a barn-spoiled horse, so conditioned to my normal setting that I would get anxious if I veered from my daily path. I always ran back to the comfort I was accustomed to, remaining stagnant. This corral of oblivious solitude now stood in shambles, all because of Dr. Straight.

She'd been in the office no more than an hour that day and had already made social arrangements with half of the staff. Her personality was magnetic; you couldn't help but be drawn to her. Dr. Straight was the life of the party, cracking jokes and building loyalty with everyone she came in contact with. After only a few hours, she had a tighter bond than I did with some of the girls I'd worked with for over a year. I felt like an outcast, even though she never alluded to such an idea. Of course not—she was *way* too nice.

But truth be told, she was real and engaging, and I wasn't—until now. My mind was set, and I was going to act. Dr. Straight had crossed into my territory, and I wasn't going to hide in the shadows anymore. The time had come to solidify my place at the hospital and with my colleagues.

* * * * *

The next morning, my palms were sweating as I waited for the best moment to present itself. I'd been assigned to surgeries for the day, which meant I'd be away from most of my colleagues. We had just wrapped up the last morning operation, and I had thirty minutes to burn until the afternoon round started. The break was technically scheduled as a lunch break, although I seldom used it as such. Usually I would get lost in a book or hang out with my favorite work acquaintances. The book usually won.

I didn't have a novel to read today. Plus, I was on a mission: this was a good time to check in with my colleagues. I walked into the treatment area and saw them in the middle of a procedure. Sarah and Rebecca were restraining an exceptionally angry nine-year-old orange tabby while Kat tried to place an IV catheter.

Suddenly, I heard the clicking of Dr. Straight's heels behind me. I kept my back to her, acting as if I didn't know she had entered the room. My nerves spiked, but this was the moment I had been waiting for: I could be just as fun as Dr. Straight!

Squaring my shoulders, I started to speak in my peppiest voice. "Mumford and Sons is playing next month at Red Rocks in Denver. Who's up for a road trip?" I knew if I used our favorite band as a carrot, I would have a better chance of getting them to join me.

The three of them paused and looked up at me, completely taken off guard. Then they turned their attention back to the irate tabby. I stood there edgily staring at the skilled vet techs, waiting for some type of response as they worked their magic. Once they wrapped up the procedure, I fidgeted with anticipation, ready to hear their verdict. I saw a slight smile flash on Rebecca's face.

Rebecca Jensen was my closest work acquaintance. She was shorter, with an athletic, stocky build and reddish-brown hair. Her face always glowed with a smile, making her green eyes beam. She had a wild side that made me feel free, yet she never pressed my boundaries.

She loved animals and had an overwhelming passion for her job. Rebecca thrived on the high-stress emergencies that the rest of us disliked. I respected her for more than her technician skills; I respected her for representing what I lacked—the truest sense of freedom.

Sarah Taylor was a close second. Sarah was the opposite of Rebecca, yet similar. She was what I would consider a type A personality with a type B disposition. Sarah was focused, both in her work and with the world around her, but she was lighthearted with me.

Sarah's intelligence was unparalleled, but she hid it under a cloak of blonde jokes, a great figure, and a flawless smile. Sarah came off as charming and naive but had a ruthless tigress underneath. I felt sorry for any man who dated her, devoured by his own desires and not seeing the predator waiting for him if he didn't live up to her expectations.

Katherine "Kat" Meyer was the romantic. She was a quiet introvert, often lost in her thoughts yet attentive to everyone around her. She was overly in tune with people and their feelings and was often the hospital's peacemaker. Outside of work she craved solitude. Kat was the only person I knew who could be stranded on a tropical island and flourish.

Rebecca responded first. She looked slightly shocked, but grinned eagerly. She acted as if this was a challenge instead of an invitation. "Really?" she asked, questioning my motives, I was sure.

I flashed a shaky smile. "Yes. Really."

"Really, really?" Her voice shot up an octave.

I sighed. "Yes, Rebecca."

She didn't say yes, but rather squealed with excitement, throwing her arms around me. It came off almost as if she were proud of me for taking the social plunge.

Sarah accepted my invitation with a bit more hesitation. "Um, sure, Brit. I'll go. Sounds like fun." Her expression was light, but like Rebecca, her voice was laced with skepticism.

I wasn't surprised when Kat rejected my invitation. "I wish I could go, but I can't. I'm sorry. But it was so nice of you to invite me," she said with a warm smile.

Sarah flashed her brilliant smile at me, and I mirrored it. I was ecstatic and terrified all at once.

* * * * *

Now here I was, lying in the grass, thinking of every possible way to get out of this trip. I'd made the offer yesterday, and I was still petrified. I thought that after a night of sleeping on the idea I would feel more resolved. Unfortunately, it didn't happen.

My nerves were tightly wound, and I was entirely out of my comfort zone. I was scared of being in the car for days, completely exposed and vulnerable with nowhere to run. I had an urge to invite Dr. Straight so I could hide behind her and keep the spotlight of interrogation off me. No. This is exactly what I needed: to get out of my monotony with a week of just living and connecting. Regardless of how I felt, I would have to live with my actions and overcome my fear. There was no way to back out now.

I took a deep breath, shut my eyes, and tried not to panic. I wanted to make a few changes in my life, and this trip was the key. My decision was made—I *needed* to go on this trip.

Chapter

THREE

arah threw her last bag into the trunk of my car. My poor
Accord was already protesting, the back end sagging a bit.
Sarah had packed twice as much as Rebecca and I—she was always
prepared for anything.

I had packed modestly, filling one large bag with clothes and
adding a tote with a few books to escape into just in case. This plan
B helped me rein in my anxiety as I stood ready to walk the social
plank and jump in with both feet. Three weeks had passed since my
initial invitation, but it felt like it had only been three days. The time
had passed in a blur.

Excited to begin our journey east, we piled into my white car.
Our trip was planned down to the minute in order to ease my parents'
minds. My mom, Mary, and my dad, Jed, demanded good planning.
My dad wanted us to be prepared, saying, "The only safe trip is a
well-thought-out one."

We were going to cut through Oregon and Idaho and then head
south into Utah. Then we planned to head east through Wyoming
and drop into Colorado. Our first stop in Colorado was Boulder, then
moving on to Denver and the concert. We wanted to hit Las Vegas
on our way home. The trip would take twelve days total, although we
had fourteen to play with. We wanted a buffer to spend a little extra
time at one of our stops. The other option was to come home early,
which was my parent's favorite plan.

My parents had worried looks on their faces as I pulled out of
my apartment complex. I waved to them reassuringly and yelled out

the window to thank my mom again for watching my cat, Edie, while I was away.

This was going to be an ordinary road trip—sightseeing, lots of food, and major bonding with the people in the car. Of course, I had a hidden agenda: to rediscover myself and figure out how I got lost in the first place.

I was almost shaking with anticipation, trying to keep my foot from slamming the gas pedal down to the floor. We were off to explore new horizons. My brain felt like a dry sponge ready to soak in as much of the experience as possible.

"I can't believe we're doing this," I said giddily, mainly speaking to myself.

"I know! Isn't it exciting?" Rebecca chirped.

Sarah smiled. "I have to say, Brit, I didn't think you had it in you." She watched me carefully as she spoke.

"Oh?" I inquired casually.

"I figured you were going to cancel our trip."

"Why would I?" Although I tried to look and sound surprised, Sarah was right. It had taken everything I could muster not to back out.

"Well, I didn't think road trips were your thing. Actually, I didn't think anything outside of the office was really your thing."

"I guess I'm into new things."

Sarah grinned. "Good. I'm glad. You're awesome, once you let that gargantuan wall of yours down."

Rebecca nodded in agreement.

Ouch. I wrestled back the sting—but she spoke the truth. I tried so hard to keep up a facade of perfection that I had isolated myself.

"Sorry," I mumbled.

Rebecca scolded me. "Oh please, Brit, we're way past apologies. What Sarah's trying to say is that she's happy you wanted to go. You usually avoid the social scene, so this is a treat. We're proud of you."

She looked at me and smiled with approval. My trepidation plummeted as her words, *"a treat,"* replayed in my mind. I sighed with relief and filled to the brim with happiness knowing these two girls thought of me like that.

* * * * *

I was the first to wake. Surprisingly, we had slept in—even Sarah had snoozed past eight. I was lying in bed stretching away the stiffness when Sarah jumped up and gasped.

"Oh no, we're late! Get up! We have to get to Boulder. Let's go!"

I laughed at her, and she glowered at me. Sarah loved tea and was excited to visit Celestial Seasonings, her favorite tea brand. Their factory was the one place she *had* to visit. We had more or less based our entire trip on the concert, a tour of Celestial Seasonings, and spending a few days in Vegas. Sarah had demanded the tour as one of our three big stops, and she was bursting with anticipation.

Sarah rushed us along. I barely had time to brush my hair and teeth, but with the crazed gleam in Sarah's eyes, I didn't protest. We threw our bags in the trunk, jumped into the car, and sped away from the hotel.

A couple hours later, we arrived in Boulder. Having Sarah at the wheel took thirty minutes off the drive. I held my breath the entire way, praying we wouldn't get pulled over in our haste. My father would've lectured us about safe driving, especially with us cruising at this speed. How would I explain the ticket? "But, Dad, the officer must have written it down wrong. We couldn't have been going that fast." He would give me *the look* and then lecture us on responsibility. I cringed as his typical speech crept into my thoughts.

We passed through several towns before we reached the edge of Boulder and pulled into the Celestial Seasonings parking lot. The factory was massive, with a restaurant and outdoor patio, a gift shop, and serene landscaping highlighting the front. I didn't notice much more of it because I was distracted by Sarah. She was so eager that she was bouncing in her seat like a child. Her speech sped up and a huge smile overtook her face.

I giggled at Sarah as she hopped out of the car almost before shifting it into park. We did everything good tourists are supposed to do: took the factory tour, bought every tea available—which I'm sure Sarah will be paying off for the next year—and ate at the restaurant. After a morning engulfed in spearmint, cinnamon, and peppermint, we decided to try another Boulder hot spot: Pearl Street.

Heading to our destination, we passed through Boulder, which was nestled at the base of the Rocky Mountain foothills. The town was beautiful, full of trees and streams. It smelled fresh and crisp with a hint of pine, and I found the aroma to be relaxing, regardless of the city's buzz. Bicyclists were everywhere, almost outnumbering the cars. I liked how active and fit everyone seemed to be.

Pearl Street was a pedestrian-only outdoor mall. It was full of character, almost tossing me into the 1960s. Buskers were playing several genres of music, competing for patrons' tips. Lively and fun, the street was lined with quaint cafés, coffee shops, and stores. These were not the typical franchises, but rather an eclectic arrangement of stores selling incense, trinkets, and toys. Even the clothing stores weren't typical, mostly appealing to the modern hippy's taste of hemp vests, long skirts, and head wraps.

After an hour of wandering, shopping, and gawking, we finished the Pearl Street tour at a local coffee shop. I sat with my latte and biscotti as we pulled out our trusty atlas, preparing for the next stop in our adventure. I heard the front door open, and I looked up.

A man wearing a perfectly pressed pastel-pink shirt and light-gray slacks entered, looking as if he had floated in. He was in his late twenties or early thirties, peculiarly handsome, and impeccably—albeit a bit oddly—dressed. Clearly, he was not from around here. His cleanly shaven bald head was as shiny as his white leather loafers. He was pale, refined, and graceful.

But there was something amiss about him that I couldn't quite put my finger on. What mainly caught my attention was his bizarre behavior. He entered the store, looked over his shoulder repeatedly, then sat quickly in the corner closest to our table. He didn't order anything or look up to acknowledge the stares addressed at him.

I glanced at him several times because his body language made me feel uneasy. He leaned in our direction with his head turned slightly and his eyes glued to the front door. His poorly concealed eavesdropping was irritating. Who was this guy? Regardless, he seemed to be overly interested in our conversation, especially when we were discussing our route.

I tried to ignore him and focus on the conversation at our table. Sarah was studying the atlas she had pulled out. "Okay. I've marked two routes we can take to Las Vegas. The one marked in green is our original plan through the mountains, into Utah, and down into Vegas. The orange line takes us south into New Mexico and through Arizona, which means we can see the Grand Canyon and the Hoover Dam before we head to Vegas."

We looked over her proposed routes.

"I think we should continue with our original plan and head west." I'd never been in the heart of the Rocky Mountains, and I wanted to capitalize on every moment.

Rebecca disagreed. "I think we should see the Grand Canyon."

In my peripheral vision, I saw the pastel-clad man shift in his seat, and I quickly looked over. His eyes locked onto mine. His lips curved slightly downward and he shook his head. Was he trying to tell me something? I didn't try to conceal the confusion and curiosity on my face. I shuddered and averted my eyes back toward Rebecca. I attempted to concentrate on the conversation and concurrently process the exchange that had occurred between us.

Because of my distraction, I had missed the final vote. Sarah had agreed with me to head west and spend a few days in the high country. Sarah and Rebecca had decided to stop in Summit County, which, according to the locals, or at least the barista, was another popular tourist area. Then Sarah wanted to go to Vail to look for celebrities. Searching was silly, but Sarah looked at us with her childlike enthusiasm and it was settled; we had to agree to the extended Colorado tour.

We finished our drinks and snacks. Refueled and ready to continue on with our day, we stood up, and the mystery man approached. His shoulders were squared and he looked determined. I felt uneasy as he stared at us, more so at me. I eyed him suspiciously, clearly in an unwelcoming manner.

He walked up and greeted us; his voice was as sophisticated as his appearance. He didn't greet us with the typical "hello," but rather a riddle: "Follow the trail on top of the ridge, until the land divides into two. Then go toward the resting sun until you come to a spotted meadow within the peaks. Here you will find the sliver of hope and the entrance into the cavern leading to the pull."

He looked at me and grinned, as if he knew I was on a personal quest and he'd just given me the clue to the missing piece. I was mentally miles away as I tried to decipher the riddle. By the time my wandering mind finally returned to the coffee shop a moment later, he had disappeared.

We stood in silence as we processed the interaction. Finally, Sarah burst into laughter. "What was that?"

Rebecca snapped out of her shock as well. "Uh, okay . . ."

"He was weird, even for Boulder," was all I could force out as I still quietly obsessed over the riddle. I felt like the puzzle was meant for me, particularly with his cunning smile. If anything, his smile added to the ambiguity of the situation.

We walked out of the shop reminiscing and laughing about the strange man and his message, and also about Sarah's unsteady hand being dangerously close to a precarious mound of tea at the factory. Sarah was still beaming from the tour, and she couldn't wait to get to Denver and find a hotel so she could sample her splurge before we had to leave for the concert.

We drove a short distance and found a hotel in a suburb west of Denver. After we settled in and Sarah had sampled at least five different teas, we drove west to Red Rocks Amphitheatre.

The massive sandstone rocks jutted high above the ground, forming enormous walls on either side of the stage. Another wall of stone was behind it. Because of the natural architecture, the acoustics were perfect. I was brimming with excitement knowing I would get to watch my favorite band play.

Around seven thirty, the clouds rolled in. A few sprinkles interrupted my daydream, and I looked toward the sky. The clouds were billowy and full of contrast—white, charcoal, and every shade in between. The sun's reflection made them shimmer as if they were lined with silver. They were anomalies compared to Portland's wispy puffs in the sky.

As I waited for the concert to begin, I kept thinking of the man dressed in pastel, his peculiar behavior, and his even more bizarre message. It seemed to be direct and focused—but why did he tell us? He must have known something I didn't . . . or maybe he was just a bit nutty. Something told me to listen to him, and that his message would soon have relevance.

I racked my brain for some time, trying to put the pieces of the puzzle together. Eventually I gave up, distracted by the crowd's screams as the band took the stage.

Chapter

FOUR

I woke to Sarah's relentless charge the next morning as she demanded that Rebecca and I get up. "We need to hit the road," she said. "You've slept long enough." Now I knew why Sarah was always scheduled for the morning shifts.

I chucked my pillow at her, hitting her square in the head. Quickly pulling the covers over my head, I hid. I felt like a little kid, hoping she wouldn't find me. Sarah grabbed a pillow and began hitting me with it through the safety of my covers. I could hardly hear Rebecca laughing at our display over my own bellowing laughter. Finally, I threw the covers off and stood up.

"Okay, okay! I'm up, sergeant," I said, adding an exaggerated salute. I quickly made my way to the bathroom, dodging a blow to the head from her feather-filled weapon. I was a night owl, so dealing with Sarah's circadian rhythm had proved to be challenging.

I felt stiff from dancing, and my voice was hoarse from cheering the night before. Nonetheless, all my aches were worth it because the concert was excellent. The band sounded great, and the acoustics were surprisingly precise for being in a venue with walls of rock. The weather was pristine for a summer evening—the clouds never dropped more than a few sprinkles of rain—and the company was exceptional. The night was magical, and all I had hoped it would be.

Even with getting back to the hotel late last night and Sarah waking us early, I felt fairly rested. However, my body was demanding its shot of morning joe. I was a certified coffee addict, so naturally a coffee run would be our first stop as we continued on with our road trip.

The morning was uneventful, full of eating, driving, sightseeing, and more eating. I wasn't sure where my insatiable hunger was coming from, especially since I'd been sitting down all morning. I suppose it gave me something else to occupy my time besides talking.

We gabbed about the sights of our trip, the concert, and our pasts. Rebecca and Sarah's tales were educational, and I felt like I finally knew them.

Rebecca had lost her father as a teen. I gathered that this experience was where she drew her passion from—she had pulled it from the hurt and loss and channeled it into her tenacious life. Rebecca never just went through the motions. Her voice was sentimental as she spoke of him, and it turned sorrowful when she told us about the day he never came home. She shared stories of her rebellious days, the days before she learned to draw on this experience and not fight it. She had no regrets, and seemed at peace when explaining why she chose to work with animals: she wanted to protect those who were constantly at the mercy of their environment and the will of others.

Sarah's childhood was like a storybook, somewhat reminding me of my own. She was close with both of her parents. Unlike me, she was well traveled, and her family was wealthy. She laughed as she told us the story of when she decided on her career choice. Her mother was appalled, wanting Sarah to bask in the country-club lifestyle. But anyone who knew Sarah would know that a lounging lifestyle lacked the stimulation she thrived on. After graduating from an elite tech school, she'd moved from Monterey to work in Portland; it was close enough to visit and be spoiled, but distant enough that she didn't have to deal with her mother's scowls of disapproval.

Sitting in the back seat as Rebecca took her turn driving, I looked at both girls and grinned contently. "Thanks," I said quietly.

"For what?" Sarah asked.

"For joining me on this trip. It means a lot that you came."

"Isn't that what friends are for?" Rebecca said, looking at me in the rearview mirror with a large smile on her face.

Suddenly, it hit me: these girls considered me a friend, and not just any friend, but a *true* friend. True enough to voyage clear across the United States with, even if I was traveling for my own selfish needs. It had only taken me a thousand miles to discover what they had already known—that I had more than acquaintances; I had friends, and ones I could count on.

This discovery made me smile, and I beamed with contentment. "Yes . . . but still, thanks."

"You're welcome, Brit," Sarah responded.

We continued west, taking the main road as it cut and weaved through the mountains. I was captivated as each turn revealed another gift for my eyes to unwrap. We soon came upon a pillarless bridge. As we drew near, the structure framed the most beautiful view of the distant peaks. Rebecca pulled onto a scenic pullout, and we spotted a herd of buffalo. I had to get a picture, and my company didn't protest. They were as excited to see these massive animals in their natural environment as I was.

After taking three-dozen pictures, we continued our journey, passing a few quaint mountain communities. The buildings looked worn from the harsh winters. There were old mines scattered along the mountainside with rusty trails leading up to them. I instantly imagined the days of the gold rush and the miners who scoured these hills.

Finally, I saw the first ski area. The ski lift stood still, resting, looking weary from the busy ski season. I studied the resort for only a moment before we came to a tunnel. The car was quickly engulfed, and I was fascinated; this was the longest tunnel I had ever driven through. I found it mind-boggling, being able to cut straight through a mountain.

The passageway opened up into another picturesque scene of mountain peaks. The road soon dropped us into civilization, which I hardly noticed because I was awestruck by the neighboring lake. The crystal-clear water, the abundance of trees surrounding it, and the rocky peaks reflected in it made me feel like we were descending into a postcard. The view was surreal.

We exited the interstate, arriving at Breckenridge. The quaint town was everything I had envisioned. The homes and buildings were made of logs, embracing the environment rather than competing with it. This town was better kept than the others we'd passed; it looked rustic, but not as worn.

The people were as natural as the buildings, and they also embraced the ruggedness of their surroundings. I didn't see anyone who was overly flashy or who seemed to be flaunting themselves; still, the area reeked of wealth. Nonetheless, I felt at home in my jeans, a Jimmy Buffett T-shirt (one of my favorite singers, thanks to my mother), and flip-flops.

Finding a hotel wasn't an issue; we passed several before picking one that appealed to us. The hotel embraced its rugged backdrop, looking like a large lodge. The lobby had dark wood beams spanning the ceiling and a massive stone fireplace in one corner that proudly exhibited an elk's head over the mantel. I scowled at the elk's head in disgust and then peered over at Sarah and Rebecca, who were each displaying a similar expression.

The front-desk attendant greeted us pleasantly. She was pretty; not wearing any makeup, she looked natural and fresh. Her demeanor was like many of the people here, calm and relaxed. After spending several days in the car, hitting rush hour at times, and trying to make our way through new cities, the peaceful mentality was welcoming.

We checked in, gathered our belongings, and proceeded to our room. It, too, was simple with an earthy ambiance. The green comforters and curtains blended in with the trees peering through the window. The walls displayed alternating glossy and matte cream stripes. Nothing hung on the walls except a mirror that reflected the abundance of light shining in from the afternoon sun.

I threw my bag on one of the beds and lied down next to it with a sigh of weariness. Sarah soon joined me. Rebecca called dibs on the other bed and fell onto it in the same breath. We were still, and I took this moment to reflect on the sights from the day, the peacefulness of our surroundings, and the serenity of the moment.

I abruptly opened my eyes. The room's bright lighting had been reduced to a soft glow. The sun was setting behind the peaks, highlighting them in a silhouette. I looked over to the clock on top of the nightstand and saw that almost two hours had slipped away. My lips twitched into a tiny smile. There was nothing better than an impromptu nap on a summer day.

I rose, trying to be quiet so I didn't disturb Rebecca and Sarah, and headed for the shower. The hot water pounded on my lower back, soothing its angry spasms. Next on my agenda was to tame my ravenous stomach. I came out of the bathroom and found my friends unmoved. An ornery grin danced across my face as I headed to Sarah's side of the room. I turned the lamp on, allowing it to shine directly in her face.

"Let's get this show on the road! Let's go, let's go, let's go!"

A moan escaped from Sarah's mouth. Laughing, I pressed on with my demands while Rebecca snickered from the other bed.

"What's wrong, Sarah?" I jested, hoping to get my point across.

She rolled over and pulled her pillow over her head. I couldn't help but laugh; using Sarah's antics against her was fun. I jumped onto the bed and shook her several times until she retaliated by hitting me with her pillow. She started laughing hysterically.

Once we were all ready, we headed to a bar and grill recommended to us by the hotel's concierge. Luckily, it was only two blocks away, so we could walk. Even looking at my car made me feel stiff, and my back would have protested. The walk passed quickly; I was distracted by the shops, which pulled my attention in different directions. I soon found myself standing at the restaurant's door.

The eatery's exterior was a rustic-looking log cabin, but a mouthwatering smell emanated past its doors, inviting us in. The inside was far more modern than the exterior. The decor was a blend of modern pictures and vintage metal logo signs hung on the log walls. The contrast was odd, but it added to the restaurant's quirky character.

We decided we were too hungry to wait for the dining room, so we headed toward the bar area and sat ourselves. I turned the corner and froze. Sarah bumped into me because of my abrupt stop and peered over my shoulder to assess the situation.

Our eyes locked, and I couldn't pull my gaze away from him. My brain felt stunned, like it had been jolted, and it refused to acknowledge the inquiries addressed to me from behind. I felt like I was in a movie and someone had slowed the reel. He was the most beautiful man I had ever seen. Sitting at the head of the table with his friends, I had a front-row view of a grace, beauty, and charisma that overwhelmed my senses. I was a realist, however. Lust at first sight, sure; love at first sight, a fairy tale. I stood there in complete lust for only a second until Sarah pushed me from behind, leading me toward our table.

I was interrupted by an unfamiliar voice. "Would you like a drink?" the waitress asked.

I sputtered, "Coke, please."

He was my definition of perfection. His dark-brown hair was a touch on the longer side, teasing his eyes. His eyes! They were forest green and amplified by his dark brows. He had a sharp, defined jawline and straight, white teeth; a smile that any dentist would be proud to claim. He was athletic, strong but not overly muscular, and dressed exactly like a model you would find in an outdoor clothing catalog.

Somehow food appeared in front of me, even though I didn't remember ordering it.

I secretly watched his elegant movements in my peripheral vision throughout dinner, brushing off parts of Sarah and Rebecca's conversation. He was laughing and carrying on. I had gathered from his friends' hand gestures that they were talking about fishing. He was enthralled by the story, but he glanced in our direction twice.

The first glance was in my direction. Again, our eyes connected for a split second, and I was mesmerized. My heart nearly leapt out of my chest. I quickly grasped the table's edge to steady myself while my breath restarted.

His second look was at our table's general bearing, and not at me specifically. It still brought a smile to my face and made my cheeks hot. I was so engrossed in my own obsession that I didn't notice that Rebecca had caught a fish of her own.

One of the men from the table stood up and walked assertively toward us. I sat in complete confusion, but I admired his boldness. The stocky blond walked right up to Rebecca and asked if he could buy us a drink.

Rebecca had a way with men. She was the cool girl, everyone's friend—she could talk sports with the men and fashion with the women. At the office, she attracted attention from just about everyone of the opposite sex. It didn't matter who they were: doctors, clients, the IT guy, or anyone else who ventured into her sights. It was impressive, although she seemed unaware of her allure.

She sat there, genuinely surprised by his gesture. She accepted with hesitation after receiving an encouraging smile from Sarah. He bought us a round of what we were already enjoying, which was a greyhound for me, and then sat down.

He introduced himself. "Hi, I'm Mike," he said, speaking quietly.

Mike tried to make eye contact with each of us, although you could tell it was hard for him to take his eyes off Rebecca. With his sheepish smile and limited conversation, I concluded that this audacious move was definitely out of character for him. His friends at the table looked in our direction with expressions of disbelief and satisfaction. This solidified my conclusion that Mike was a relatively shy guy.

"Are you from around here?" he asked.

Rebecca sounded casual. "No, Portland. We're on a road trip and wanted to spend a few days in the mountains. Are you from around here?"

Mike began to relax. "Yep, born and raised. So, here's the million-dollar question: does it ever stop raining there? Every time I've been to Portland, it does *nothing* but rain."

All three of us giggled. There were two seasons in Portland: summer and the rainy season.

Rebecca's smug smile matched her tone. "It's only sunny for the locals. When people visit, we do a rain dance to scare them away— population control."

Mike's laugh was deep and loud, making me smile.

After conversing for about twenty minutes, Mike invited us to go hiking in the morning with him and a friend or two. He was considerate enough not to volunteer his friends without asking them first—an admirable gesture, I thought.

He explained with a big grin, "You can't fully appreciate all that Breck has to offer without a local tour guide."

Rebecca quickly accepted, before even glancing at Sarah and me. I thought she might've been interested in Mike, but this confirmed my suspicions.

His table was starting to stir. One of his friends shouted, "Hey, Perry, you ready to go?"

Mike nodded at his friends and turned back toward us.

"Perry?" Rebecca questioned.

He shrugged a shoulder. "It's my last name."

Rebecca nodded. "Oh, okay."

He took our hotel information and told us to be in the lobby at eight o'clock sharp the next morning. Sarah smiled while I quietly sighed—eight o'clock was early, especially while on vacation. But hope flickered that I might get to see *him* again!

"Make sure you wear good shoes and bring plenty of water," he warned.

My smile faded slightly. His words were simple, but they made me nervous. My hiking skills weren't exactly polished. And if *he* was there, I might look like a fool. My heart sped up, and I thought briefly about faking an illness. I decided that I had to take my chances. Not wanting to waste an opportunity to see him again, I nodded compliantly at Mike's request.

Mike rose from our table, shot a smile at Rebecca, and left. He joined his friends, and all of the men exited the lounge together. I watched them, *him*, fade into the distance, and prayed that he would be joining us in the morning.

"Well done, Rebecca," Sarah praised.

"Why, thank you," she said, gloating. "Not too shabby, if I do say so myself. I think Breckenridge might be a good place to burn a buffer day or two. What do you think, Brit?"

I smiled stiffly, somewhat embarrassed about my recent display. Both Sarah and Rebecca looked at me inquisitively.

"Sure." I tried to look and sound nonchalant, but I couldn't hide my smile.

Quickly looking for a diversion, I reached for my Coke, but it was empty. I looked down at my meal and it, too, was missing. I had eaten a full meal in a coma-like state. Blood rushed to my face.

I stood up abruptly, demanding, "Let's go."

I heard them snickering behind me.

Admittedly, I had never acted like that before, and it was pathetic. But I couldn't help how I felt. I'd never seen a man like that before.

My nerves were in upheaval, and I was excruciatingly excited. I knew it would be a restless night. I had to see him again, somehow, and I prayed it would be in the morning. Tomorrow could not come soon enough.

Chapter

F I V E

struggle between being excited about the possibility of seeing *him* again and being nervous for our upcoming hiking trip occupied my every thought that night. I reviewed the scene from the restaurant at least a dozen times, flashing from one frame to the next like a picture flip-book.

Occasionally, fears about the hike would pop into my head, interrupting my memories of his sophisticated movements. I hoped that we would be on a calm trail, weaving along on flat ground and not challenging the steeper terrain.

Needless to say, I couldn't sleep.

Dying to see which of his friends volunteered to join Mike in playing tour guide, I felt like it was Christmas Eve and I was seven again. I tried to rein in my intense anticipation by attempting to focus on my brain's rational intellect and ignore my heart's giddy wishes, but it didn't work well.

Finally, it was six in the morning and I popped out of bed. I grabbed the most "Colorado" outfit I could find and almost ran to the shower. The steam from the hot water settled my nerves slightly as I shaved my legs. I quickly dressed and put on the most natural-looking makeup I owned. Going for the unnatural-natural look, I did my hair in the same manner.

I walked out of the bathroom and Rebecca rushed in. Apparently she hadn't slept well either. I turned the corner and Sarah laughed at me; I couldn't fool her. She and I both knew that the hike itself was the furthest thing from my mind. I glowered at her after she made a smart remark under her breath about "sightseeing."

When Rebecca emerged, after taking twice as long as usual to get ready, Sarah rose out of bed and headed to the bathroom to get dressed. Waiting for Sarah was excruciating. I sat on the bed and flipped through the same TV stations repeatedly, trying to dull my mind. My foot tapped rapidly due to nerves and anticipation. I looked at Rebecca, hoping for some type of reassurance.

Showing no emotion, she was staring at me with a more conditioned look. "A bit antsy?" she asked with an accusatory smirk.

Her expression made me shake my head, and I rolled my eyes as I answered. "I have no idea what you're talking about." Then I mirrored her smirk and giggled. "Mike seemed nice," I said, studying her face.

Her lips flinched upward before melting into a neutral expression. "Uh-huh."

"Oh come on, Rebecca. I saw how you looked at him last night," I nudged.

She scowled at me. "Like you have any room to talk."

Her expression softened as soon as my smile widened. "Okay, but you first," she gushed.

I was ready to spill when I heard Sarah rustling around.

The bathroom door opened and Sarah emerged, looking immaculate as usual. When Sarah walked into a room she was like a debutante—people were awestruck by something as simple as an entrance. I envied her confidence and control of every moment, including this one. She threw her belongings onto the floor next to her suitcase and headed toward the door. "Are we ready, ladies?"

The time had come.

The clock read eight past eight when we saw them walk through the sliding lobby doors. Why did men always have to be late? Trying to show off and prove how independent they are? Or to torture us women, knowing we were dying to see them? At any rate, I was still relieved, despite my irritation.

Mike was wearing a bright-blue T-shirt, longer jean shorts that brushed just past his knees, and hiking boots with socks pulled up to the mid-calf. He had a ball cap hiding his hair. Two others trailed him. The first was tall and thin, almost gangly, with brown hair and—

The room stopped, along with my breath.

There he was, looking perfect of course. I couldn't help the smile that engulfed my face as he entered the lobby. His wore a green T-shirt, making his eyes appear even brighter. They were a seamless contrast to his dark hair, which was hidden under a brown ball cap with an orange logo that I didn't recognize. The khaki shorts and brown boots polished off his look nicely.

Rebecca waved at Mike as the guys grew near. He reciprocated with a sheepish grin and introduced his friends. The taller friend was Jack Churchman, and *his* name was Brody Chandler. I tried to hide my excitement and sound nonchalant as I said hello.

Rebecca introduced Sarah first and then me, even though she said "Brittany" instead of "Brit." I corrected her and smiled, lifting my hand in a slight wave. Sarah reached out and shook each of their hands, but I was afraid my unsteady hand would expose my shaky state.

Mike smiled awkwardly and exhaled. "Are we ready to go? I could use a coffee run. Does that sound good to everyone?"

I nodded approvingly. I liked Mike already.

We walked to the coffee shop three doors down from the hotel. The nutty aroma filled my senses as I inhaled, and the pastries looked mouthwatering. Following the others to the counter, everyone took their turns until only Brody and I were left.

His eyes met mine. "Do you know what you want?"

My eyes widened and my brain went blank. "W-what?"

He frowned and turned his attention to the barista, clearly impatient.

My face heated up. What had I done? I had made myself look like an idiot, that's what. *Straighten up*, I mentally sneered at myself. I was going to prove myself to be a strong and capable woman. Before Brody could order, I stepped up quickly, almost cutting him off.

"Could I please get a medium latte and a blueberry scone?"

I handed a ten-dollar bill to the barista before I glanced at Brody. He looked amused. I gathered my change and my breakfast and made my way to the other members of our group. There were three open seats, two next to each other and one on the end next to Sarah. Still aggravated and somewhat embarrassed, I sat next to Sarah. I was hoping that Brody would take notice of the seating arrangement. Regardless, it made me feel better.

After breakfast, we piled into Mike's dark-blue Jeep Cherokee and headed south. Mike and Brody sat in the front, with Rebecca squashed between them. Sarah, Jack, and I sat in the back. I tried to pay attention to our route, but I found it hard to focus with Brody in my peripheral vision. Mike took a sharp turn onto a dirt road leading deep into the hillside. The road was full of switchbacks and potholes, almost making me feel ill. After fifteen minutes the road hit a dead end, and we parked. By this point I was lost, but we had reached the trailhead.

The area was saturated with trees and had a few boulders scattered sporadically throughout. The birds sang loudly, as if they were attempting to compete with the stream gurgling somewhere in the background. A light breeze filled the air with the smell of pine, which instantly calmed my nerves; the smell was like permanent aromatherapy. No wonder the people up here seemed so calm.

We threw on our backpacks. I wanted to come across like I was somewhat competent, so I had bought a new bag on the way back to the hotel last night. The backpack was royal blue, with a matching water bottle. The alternative was my old pink and brown tote, which usually held my books. I was happy to have a new bag, especially after looking at the complexity of their bags—they were obviously seasoned hikers.

A quick jolt of nerves shot through me. *What if I'm not good enough to keep up?* I pulled in a deep breath and regained my composure. The guys knew we weren't from around here. Surely they wouldn't do anything too intense, right? I blew out a breath of nerves. The mental prayers were abundant, begging for an uneventful, embarrassment-free morning.

We began our trek, following the trail that led into the forest. We walked for almost a half hour, seeing nothing but trees. I could hear a nearby brook, but it was hidden. I felt a bit claustrophobic and breathless, unsure if it was the landscape or Brody. Trying to enjoy the hike and the scenery was hard because I couldn't concentrate.

Brody was even more elegant in motion. His athletic gait was strong and confident. I wanted to speak to him, but couldn't muster up the courage. He didn't glance in my direction, which deterred me even further. He was obviously experienced, however, and I felt secure in his presence, even if he wasn't paying me any attention.

The tree-lined path went over a slight ridge and opened into a breathtaking view. The valley below gradually swallowed the stream that the path had been following. The nearby peaks were exposed, jutting high above the trees. The sun reflected off their white caps, and the blue sky was almost neon. I stood in awe as I took in the view. It looked like a painting.

A hand touched my shoulder, and I turned to look. I froze, surprised by his proximity. He was about six foot one, a few inches taller than me, and he smelled wonderful. His sweet scent penetrated my brain, like it was being etched into my memory. He flashed a brilliant smile at me.

"Are you going to join us?"

My stomach turned flips. I glimpsed past his shoulder and saw the group sitting on a nearby grassy patch. Flushing with embarrassment, I shook my head. I took in a calming breath and answered.

"Um . . . no, but thanks," was all I could get out. He looked at me with a puzzled expression. I would've joined the group, but I knew I wouldn't be able to sit still. I may not have been the most sociable, the trendiest, the most *anything* person, but I was curious. These surroundings made me inquisitive, and I wanted to explore. Plus, there was no possible way my nerves would let me relax. I needed to burn some of my excess energy.

"I think I'm going to take a look around down by the stream. I won't go far."

My voice broke, making me clear my throat. I flashed him a slight smile and turned, walking purposefully downhill toward the stream.

After weaving down the hill and ducking under a few low-lying branches, I came to a small part of the stream that had to be crossed in order to reach the main vein. As I started to cross it, I felt a hand grab onto my elbow. I jumped at the touch, instinctively pulling back, but the grip tightened. I spun my head around and saw Brody smirking sheepishly at me.

"Sorry," he mumbled apologetically. "I thought you heard me coming."

I offered a tiny appreciative smile in return. My heart leapt with delight, pulling the breath from my chest. I could see the color brighten in his face as he pulled his eyes away from mine and nodded his head toward the stream, motioning for me to continue. I stepped across the stream and he slowly dropped his hand.

"Thanks," I said as I quickly glanced back at him.

He responded with a sultry smile.

We continued silently for a few minutes. My heart fluttered and my stomach clinched. I was thrilled that he had decided to follow me, but now I was scared that I was going to trip and fall on my face. After my pulse slowed, I decided I had better speak so he didn't think I was being rude. "Are you from around here too?"

"Yep."

"Oh, so you and Mike grew up together?"

He shook his head. "No, we went to different schools. I didn't meet him until I was older."

"Do you come hiking here often?"

"You could say that . . . I hike up here a couple times a month. It's a place I come to think. You know, to get away from it all?"

Immediately flashing back to my river, I nodded. "Yeah."

We soon reached the shore of the second branch of the stream. I stepped onto a rock about a foot into its currents and stood firmly planted above the water. Here I had a good view of the stream in both directions. It wasn't deep, barely covering the rocks it washed over. Occasionally, the water came up against a bigger rock, folding around its edges and exposing slightly white turbulence. The icy-blue water was crystal clear, looking and smelling fresh.

Something downstream caught my attention—it looked like a large, black shadow moving through the bushes. I sat there staring, trying to decipher the riddle. Unexpectedly, Brody grabbed my arm, pulling me down to him. I stepped into the ice-cold water.

"Hey!" I protested.

He pressed his pointer finger over his lips, trying to silence me. He was in a crouch, looking directly at the same shadow, with alarm written across his face. He didn't say a word, but quietly turned around and pulled me away from the stream in the direction we had come, maintaining a semi-crouched position. My heart pounded; I wasn't sure if it was due to his touch or because of the situation and his strange behavior. We proceeded upstream as he constantly looked back to see if we had picked up a tagalong.

We were about fifty yards away from our original spot when Brody stopped abruptly. He turned around, eyeing me closely as if attempting to assess my feelings. Embarrassed by the intensity of his stare, I kept looking off to one side and then the other. He stood there for a moment and then lifted his hand and placed it softly on my shoulder. Although he was trying to be gentle, it felt like a burst of red-hot electricity.

"Are you okay?" he asked soothingly.

I was confused. "Yes, why?"

He smiled at me and began to chuckle. Then he let go of my shoulder and turned around to head uphill, back to where the others were. I was still baffled by his reaction.

"What is so funny?" I demanded.

"That wasn't just any animal. So unless you wanted to be an appetizer, a Brit-kabob, it was time to go," he said, laughing.

A smug smirk hit my face. "First of all, that was a black bear, and a small black bear at that. I think it was young. Second, there are two of us, and we're bigger. You know what they say: power in numbers. There's no way that bear would have bothered us."

Brody turned and looked at me with astonishment, completely speechless. This time I laughed, looking down at my wet shoe, and he quickly joined in.

"We should head back to the others," he said.

"Okay." I wondered how long we'd been gone. It couldn't have been more than ten minutes.

We began walking uphill again, wanting to rejoin the group. I quickened my pace, passing him as I trekked up the hill. Something came over me because my next words spilled out without me even thinking about them. "Try to keep up," I said with a facetious edge.

My lips curved into a smile as I glanced back to view his reaction. His eyes widened in surprise and he grinned approvingly.

"I'll do my best," he responded, chuckling at my challenge. "Okay, so are you going to tell me how you knew about the bear? Are you a bear whisperer or something?" he asked sarcastically.

I snickered. "Actually, I'm an animal expert," I replied with a touch of cockiness. "Sort of."

He looked at me with confusion.

"I'm a vet tech—a nurse for animals. I work at the same hospital as Rebecca and Sarah."

An ornery smile appeared on his face. "An animal lover, huh? Are you a vegetarian, too?"

"I'm an animal lover, not a saint."

He snickered. "Do you like Portland?"

"Yes, and no," I admitted.

His perplexed expression made me smile. "It's home and nothing can change that. But I would like to venture out, see new places, meet new people—that sort of thing."

"So why don't you?"

The question was simple, yet complex. "It's not that easy."

"Sounds easy enough to me," he challenged.

"Yes, but my folks are there and . . . and that's the main reason, I suppose."

"So you're close to them?"

I felt my face light up. "Very. They're amazing people. I enjoy hanging out with them, and I like having them close by. But you never know, I might travel the world one day."

"Really? Where to?"

"Oh, I don't know. I guess the question is who with, not necessarily where. I would like to see England and Australia. But the company is far more important than the destination." I shrugged. "I guess I would consider myself a 'go with the flow' kind of person, so I'd go just about anywhere."

"So when you're not caring for animals and 'flowing' with your friends, what do you like to do?"

I stiffened. "It's not like I follow the crowd like some spineless wimp." Satisfied with my stance, I looked over to him as I spoke. "I would call myself low maintenance."

His lips curved into a slight smile, but he didn't respond; rather, he waited for an answer to his original question.

I sighed. "I like to work out and I like to read. Actually, I *love* to read."

"What's your favorite book?"

I thought for a moment, but nothing popped into my head. "I like so many, it's hard to pick only one. I love sci-fi anything, but a good romance doesn't suck either."

He nodded in response. "What are you reading now?"

I began to summarize the book I was currently reading. It was a mystery with a splash of romance tossed in for good measure. He listened quietly and attentively, asking for more details in areas I had glossed over.

Before I knew it, we came upon our group still sitting on the grass enjoying the morning sun. They were almost oblivious to our arrival, laughing and talking like old friends. I gathered that they were discussing similar topics. I heard the words "bite" and "ER" in the same sentence and knew that Rebecca was telling the story of the psychotic calico, Peete.

No one could tell stories like Rebecca. She could tell the same story a hundred times and still make you laugh like it was the first time you'd heard it. Her dynamic personality shined when a good story was attached. After laughing hysterically at the end of the Peete story—more so at the way Rebecca told it—we gathered ourselves and decided to proceed.

We continued down the same path for some time. I felt like a pack mule, hauling my bag as I concentrated on the trail in front of me. Occasionally I would glance up, trying to take in the view, but then my eyes would drop right back down to the footpath in search of obstacles. Eventually it occurred to me to scan the path several yards ahead so I could enjoy the view—I was definitely a rookie.

Our group slowed when we came to a fork in the path. Brody didn't waver, leading us up the higher trail. Now having to face my original fear of steepness, my nerves tugged at me. The path began with a slight grade but then turned into a section that felt as if it were vertical. My anxiety began to blossom into a controlled panic.

Brody paused and reached for my hand. I grabbed it willingly, and he pulled me next to him. Not only did I appreciate the help, but I was also glowing with the knowledge that he had been keeping an eye on me. I normally wasn't into the whole "damsel in distress" routine, but I made an exception for this rocky terrain. Plus, I wasn't going to refuse any reason to touch this man. Energized by his touch, I felt like I was floating up the mountain, and I wished this uphill path would last forever.

We continued climbing as the path cut into the mountainside. I tried to take in the scenery, but between Brody's exhilarating touch and trying not to trip and fall down the steep grade, I didn't see much. We rounded a bend in the path, almost spiraling up, and stopped on top of the hill.

I stood there in awe as I savored the most breathtaking, panoramic view. Big, billowy clouds filled the sky, competing with the nearby white peaks. The blue of the sky matched the lake in the far-off distance, which had a town bordering its northern shore. Different shades of green were painted everywhere in between. I gazed at the scenery, the colors, and at Brody by my side. I imagined heaven looking something like this.

The serene landscape and perfect weather made me wish I had a hammock; I could have relaxed for hours. Looking around, I noticed the same contentment displayed on everyone's faces. We sat in silence, basking in the sun. It was the perfect silence, which seemed odd being that we had only met them last night. I was already comfortable with the new additions to our party.

The sun beat on my face as I lifted it to meet the warm rays. My mind was blank and my body completely relaxed.

"It looks like weather is rolling in; we should head out soon," Mike said.

I turned to look at Mike and saw him staring toward the western horizon. I followed his gaze, looking at the few harmless-looking clouds in the distance.

"That's a good call," Brody agreed.

I shrugged my shoulders and stood up. I didn't see the threat, but this land was foreign to me.

The return trip seemed quicker; we hiked back down the spiraling trail and continued following the hillside, which opened into a meadow. The field was full of color, looking like a paint fight had occurred with flowers splattered everywhere. The blossoms increased in intensity, feeding to a river of flowers that flowed down the valley and around the base of a neighboring hill. I almost tripped twice because I was so preoccupied with the divinity before me.

Once we crossed the painted meadow, we were back to our original path near the stream. I didn't want to leave, enjoying the tranquility of the meadow. Not wanting to fall behind, I lingered for as long as I could until I had no other choice but to move on. I took one last survey, a mental snapshot, and stepped into the forest. We followed the path toward the trailhead and were quickly engulfed, once again, in trees. We had completed a big circle.

After an hour, we made it to Mike's Cherokee. We piled into the SUV and started down the road. Soon, I heard a tapping against the windshield. A puzzled expression soured my face. Rain? I looked out the windshield to examine the sky and saw the far-off clouds light up, displaying a deathly tail of lightning. Mike was right after all. Unexpectedly, a monstrous boom rocked the truck. I jumped with surprise.

"Don't worry. If you don't like the weather, it'll change in about ten minutes."

A moment passed before I realized that Brody was speaking to me.

"If there's one thing I'm used to, it's rain," I said.

He nodded. "I'm sure you are."

"Portland's rain is pretty relentless at times, but I like the rain. It's refreshing, it smells clean, and the sound—the tapping on the roof at night is calming." I began to lose myself in memories but quickly gathered my poise. "But thunder and lightning are rare there."

"Really?"

I looked at Brody's inquisitive expression and nodded slightly.

I was disappointed that the tour and our time together were nearly over. I secretly hoped we would get a little lost or something to extend the trip.

"I'm hungry. How about an early dinner?" Mike's suggestion instantly lifted my mood. I glanced over at Rebecca, and she looked equally as pleased. I smiled.

Sarah started to plan, which was one of her specialties. "Let's clean up and meet in the lobby again at five o'clock."

I casually nodded in agreement, trying to hide the celebration going on within me.

Chapter
S I X

The clock displayed twenty after four, and I was already dressed in my usual fashion. My jeans had embroidered pockets, designed with dark thread, and I paired them with a red, feminine T-shirt and flip-flops. I reapplied my "natural" makeup and styled my hair, again going for the strategically natural, carefree look.

Rebecca dazzled in her typical vintage manner, anticipating the evening ahead. She wore lighter jeans with a flowing halter-top and sandals. She was a little more made up than me, and she had curled her hair, pinning one side up with a glass-cut, jeweled butterfly barrette. Her dark, smoky eyeliner added to her retro look.

Sarah slept until four thirty and then I woke her. I felt guilty, but I couldn't handle her peacefulness while I was stirring like a hurricane within. Rebecca and I urged her to get ready so we wouldn't be late. I wanted to be near Brody.

Sarah emerged from the bathroom looking like something straight out of *Vogue*. She was dressed in an eclectic shirt with one shoulder showing, jeans topped off with a wide, black belt, and fuchsia heels. Sarah always stood out in our group. She was trendy; she loved fashion, and eccentric fashion at that. Sarah was always made up, regardless of the occasion. Even to get the mail she would be complete, head to toe.

Sarah flashed a smile at us as she walked toward the door. "Are we ready, ladies?" Rebecca and I jumped to our feet, almost beating her there.

Brody and Mike were waiting for us in the lobby. They had made themselves comfortable in oversized chairs that looked miniature in comparison to the massive fireplace. The men were laughing and conversing, looking completely at ease. As we approached they stood up, displaying big smiles.

"Where should we eat?" Sarah asked.

I shrugged a shoulder. "I don't care. What do you all want?"

Sarah looked annoyed, probably due to our lack of planning and the fact she was hungry. For Sarah, that was never a good combination.

Mike grinned. "How about pizza?"

The group easily agreed, and Mike knew of the perfect local pizza parlor on the other side of town. We piled into Mike's SUV. Jack couldn't join us due to a previous commitment, so the Cherokee didn't feel as cramped this time. There was a noticeable change in the seating arrangements as we headed to the restaurant. Rebecca sat in the front, next to Mike. In the back, I was put in the middle, with Brody sitting on one side and Sarah on the other.

I peeked at Brody, trying to memorize his perfect profile. He glanced up, catching me in the act. I looked down quickly, feeling my cheeks getting hot.

I had hoped that Brody would speak to me on the ride over, but he didn't, at least not directly. Perhaps it was by chance that he was sitting next to me? I flashed back to the steep hill during our hike and how he had held my hand. Maybe he was only being polite then, too? I exhaled a frustrated breath.

The seating at the dinner table was similar to the car. I sat between Brody and Sarah. Again, I wasn't sure if it was because Brody wanted to sit next to me or if it was coincidental. Regardless, I could feel myself glowing from his proximity, and the smirks from Rebecca and Sarah solidified that I was not masking my feelings.

We began our meal with appetizers of cheesy bread and dinner salads. We ordered a cheese pizza for the vegetarians at the table, and a pepperoni pizza for everyone else. The group conversed effortlessly as we enjoyed our appetizers.

Mike stole the show with his stories of flawed camping trips and a whopper of a fish that escaped. During Mike's tale, Brody made his take on the story known by adding the adjectives "mythical" and "imaginary" to describe the fish, which added to our laughter.

The pizza arrived during the "mythical" fish story. Once the table had gained its composure from laughing, we reached straight for the pizza. I was ravenous from the day's activities, so I grabbed a piece of cheese pizza from the pie closest to me, added pepper flakes to it, and took a big bite.

The heat scorched my mouth and throat. Quickly reaching for my Coke, I guzzled it, trying to soothe the fire. The pizza tasted good. I ate it much too quickly and was soon on my second piece. Brody ate four slices of pepperoni. The entire group was silent as we ate, with only a few comments here and there about how good the pizza was. Obviously, they were as hungry as I was.

After dinner the conversation resumed, leading to a discussion about our road trip. We went state by state and took turns describing our favorite parts of each. I started, raving about Bend, Oregon, which was a favorite area of mine. Rebecca had loved Idaho and northern Utah. Sarah described the beauty of Wyoming.

Sarah talked about Laramie and then steered the conversation to northern Colorado; she thought it was flat and boring. I interceded, saying that I thought it was something that you would see in the Old West. The high plains butted up against the mountains in one direction and went on endlessly in the other. The natural grasses danced in the wind, quietly showing their graceful unity.

I steered the conversation to our stop in Boulder, and more specifically to Celestial Seasonings. Sarah grinned when I took a dig at her and her tea obsession; I said that I wanted to send her to a treatment facility to curb this unusual dependence.

She laughed lightheartedly and then took a jab at me, saying that I was the one who attracted odd behavior. "Any weirdo who walks through the door is instantly attracted to Brit. Seriously," she said.

I had to counter. "Oh, please. It's not like I somehow have a hand in drawing them to the clinic. It's that I *always* get stuck on their cases. I think you guys do it on purpose."

Sarah and Rebecca snickered.

To make her point, Sarah told the story about the man who had a second dog at the hospital—an imaginary one—and how I had to bring it to him before he broke into hysterics. I had indulged him, of course, but I was barely able to keep my composure. Next, she described the woman who was scared of any creature that walked through the door. I had to play bodyguard until we could get her and

41

her Chihuahua, Killer, out the door. The last example she gave was the mystery man at the coffee shop. Even though it didn't occur at the hospital, it was a perfect example of my unique exchanges.

Our interaction with him had occurred three days ago, but it seemed like a distant, faded memory. I had almost completely forgotten about the man dressed in pastels, and his message. I jogged my memory so I could remember his riddle. I giggled at how odd the encounter was, and shared the tale with Mike and Brody.

I told the story, possibly embellishing the pastel man's behavior—making him out to be more like a CIA operative—but not exaggerating the rest of it. I ended the story with his strange, cryptic message, and then I looked around the table, enjoying everyone's laughter about the situation.

My gaze made it to Brody. He wasn't laughing, and he sat there in what looked to be shock. I quickly stopped laughing, puzzled by his expression. I feared that I had offended him somehow, being that his jaw was almost hitting the floor.

"What's wrong?" I inquired, speaking quickly.

He leaned toward me and placed his hand on my shoulder before responding. "Were those his exact words?" he asked. "Are you positive?"

My mind went momentarily blank. He looked at me with a penetrating gaze, as if he were trying to pull the answers out of my head. Confusion washed through me, seeping into my voice. "Um, yes, I believe so, why?"

Brody slumped back into his chair with an astonished expression on his face. He raked his hand through his hair. Suddenly, he began to beam, as if the information I'd given him had answered one of life's great mysteries. It was as if I had unknowingly given him the key to a chest full of hidden gold, and only he was aware of it.

By this point, we had caught the attention of the rest of the table. Everyone looked baffled, like me. I sat there patiently waiting for an explanation while Brody was lost in his thoughts, still beaming.

Brody looked up at the four pairs of eyes staring at him, smiled, and began to explain.

"The pool he spoke about is known as the Cleansing Pool—it's from an old Arapahoe legend. According to the legend, if you entered the pool it would cleanse your soul. By doing so, the elder's visions were focused and clear. As if turning a dial on a radio, it would remove the static so they could hear, or rather *see*, clearly. Some records even state that the cleansing would let them communicate with spirits from other planes—their ancestors and so forth.

"You see, the Arapahoes lived near Boulder and would often hunt in the surrounding mountains. People have been studying their legends for years to try and find this pool; some have even dedicated their lives to searching for it. And now you're sitting here, telling me that some weirdo in Boulder gave you directions leading straight to it."

My jaw was hanging in disbelief. I was overwhelmed, not so much by what he'd said, but by the fact that he knew this information in the first place. I looked around the table, and both Sarah and Rebecca had similar expressions. Mike seemed unfazed as he nonchalantly grabbed his Coke and took a big gulp. They were best friends, and the fact that Brody knew this information probably seemed normal to him.

Brody must have known what we were thinking. A humble grin crossed his face. "I have a degree in cultural anthropology from Colorado State University. Native American cultures are sort of a hobby of mine."

I felt ridiculous. I had spilled things about myself during our hike, but I hadn't asked anything about him. Sarah and Rebecca seemed content with his explanation, but I was craving more.

"Any other minor details you've forgotten to share? Can you fly, too?" I said sarcastically.

He chuckled before indulging my request, revealing a few particulars. "Well, let's see . . . I played lacrosse. I like to ski and hike, and kayak. I teach, and sci-fi books are my favorite, too."

My lips curved slightly with the satisfaction that he remembered my favorite genre. "Do you still play lacrosse?"

He shook his head. "Nah. Mike and I played in college. That's where we met . . . seven years ago?" He looked over to Mike for confirmation.

Mike nodded. "Sounds about right."

Intrigued, I continued. "What else did you do in college?"

"Oh, just the typical stuff, I guess. I worked as a hiking guide during the summer months for a company up here. My folks are friends with the owner. Plus, it paid for my skiing habit during the winter."

"Do you still ski?"

"Yes, but nothing like I used to. At one point I would have called myself a junkie. I thought about making it a career, but after one season of being an instructor, I decided to go in a different direction."

"Didn't like it, huh?"

"I did . . . but I'm too selfish to teach it. I like to ski; it's sort of like a mental refuge for me. But when you're up there teaching, it's all about them. I couldn't let loose. So, needless to say, I only lasted one season."

"What did you do after college?"

"I took a short sabbatical and hiked for eight months or so."

"Hiked?" I asked incredulously.

"Yeah. I hiked all over the U.S., Oregon included, and backpacked through several European countries. Finally, I ran out of money and decided I'd better grow up and work. I couldn't find a job I liked, so I went back to school for my master's. One of my professors asked if I would like to teach a basic anthropology course at the community college while I was finishing my degree, and I decided, why not? One class turned into several classes. Now I teach classes online. It's a good career, and I get my summers off."

"What did you get your master's in?"

"Native American studies. They didn't have *Star Wars* as a choice, so I picked the next best thing," he said with a grin.

I giggled at his answer. "*Star Wars* is one of my favorites, too."

"And *The Matrix*. They're total classics." His face lit up as I nodded in agreement.

"What's *your* favorite book?" I was buzzing with anticipation for his answer.

He smiled. "*The Lord of the Rings* and *The Hobbit*; again, total classics."

"Oh, those *are* good."

I mentally compared our similarities. Our movie and book selections were similar. After today, I decided that I enjoyed hiking and would like to do it more regularly. I already adored skiing, though I was nowhere at his level. As for kayaking, I hadn't tried it before. However, rowing was a big deal in Portland, and it was a sport I'd tried. I presumed I would like kayaking, especially on a clear mountain lake.

The information he shared made me feel giddy, feeding my infatuation. He was handsome, smart, athletic, and he enjoyed the same activities I did. I beamed with satisfaction.

I looked over toward Rebecca and Sarah. Rebecca seemed content, but Sarah was slumped in her chair with a small frown.

"What's wrong, Sarah?" I asked.

Her grimace intensified. "I hope we can talk about something else, and soon, before I'm forced to shove this fork into my eye. I mean, really. *Lord of the Rings?*"

My face heated. Were we that boring? I giggled at her as I looked over at Brody. He reached for his beer and took a swallow, trying to hide his reddened cheeks.

Per Sarah's request, we changed the subject, and the conversation flowed effortlessly. I enjoyed everyone at the table, feeling a real sense of camaraderie. Ironically, it felt as if I had known these people forever.

Sarah and Rebecca had been colleagues of mine for a little over a year. I had learned more about them in the last week than I had over the entire time working together. This trip had definitely solidified my feelings about these girls—they were my best friends.

The other two at the table I had only known for about twenty-four hours. Mike and Rebecca seemed to hit it off, and as for Brody, he struck a chord. Sure, I'd had boyfriends in the past, but he had already reached deeper into my soul, piercing my desires, than any other man—and I didn't really even know him. I wasn't being rational, and I knew it. My parents would call it a silly crush. Regardless, I felt comfortable with him. I appreciated his youthful humor and demeanor. His entire outlook on life was optimistic and free, calming my conservative inhibitions completely.

We conversed for another hour. Afterward, we gathered our belongings and headed back to Mike's Jeep. Laughing about my "rusty" hiking abilities, especially in comparison to the local pros, I walked around the back of the Cherokee and heard music coming out of a bar from across the road. I stopped to listen.

Brody had been walking behind me, and he also heard it. He took one glimpse into my eyes and knew I didn't want the night to be over. He nodded toward the bar where the music was coming from. "Want to check it out?"

Hesitantly, I nodded. I felt like we should ask permission from the rest of the group. He turned and walked toward the bar, never looking back as he hollered, "Come on, everyone." I quickly caught up with him as I motioned to the others by waving my hand, urging them to join us.

They reached us before we walked down the flight of stairs leading into the dimly lit bar. The interior was set up like a coliseum, moving downward toward a center arena. There were tables on three sides, with the bar along the far side. Walking down a few more steps placed you onto the lower floor area, which was also arranged in a circular pattern. The majority of tables were placed there, having closer proximity to the band playing in the middle.

The band was loud and energetic. They played a diverse set, with songs from just about every decade and practically every genre. They won points from me when they played not only one, but two Jimmy Buffet songs. The group played for about an hour and a half, triggering memories as they traveled through time. I thoroughly enjoyed listening to them.

The atmosphere was electrifying, and with Brody sitting next to me, it seemed to be amplified. The round table allowed me to see the smiles and delight on everyone's faces.

Unexpectedly, a warmth encompassed my hand. A jolt woke me to the realization that Brody's hand was holding mine. I was immobilized, attempting to grasp the fact that that this time he was holding my hand not out of mere chivalry, but because he *wanted* to. I smiled at him approvingly, enjoying the electricity that flowed between us. I filed this evening away in my mind as unbelievable, never to be forgotten.

The band took a break and the bar quieted, at least by bar standards. I could finally hear myself think, with only a slight residual ringing in my ears.

Sarah stood up. "I'll be right back," she said. Then she turned, presumably looking for the restrooms.

"They're next to the bar," Brody said to her. He released my hand and stood up after her. "I'll show you and then get us another round while I'm at it."

He trailed behind Sarah through a maze of tables toward the stairs. I watched them until the crowd swallowed them up, then my gaze returned to our table, forcing me to acknowledge Rebecca's piercing stare. She grinned at me expectantly.

I looked at her innocently. "What?"

With a smirk on her face, she shook her head.

I justified my feelings by projecting my insecurities onto Brody. "Oh, please. I'm sure he's like this all the time. He's a total charmer."

The response to my statement didn't come from the direction I had expected; I'd been so enthralled with Rebecca's reactions that I'd forgotten Mike was also sitting at the table.

"Actually, I've never seen him like this. He seems to really like you," Mike said quickly and confidently.

"Really?" An ecstatic smile leapt onto my face, and Rebecca mirrored my expression. Mike shrugged a shoulder, nodded, and then took another drink, letting his eyes wander around the room. He acted like he was trying to be invisible, not wanting to interfere with the remainder of our conversation.

My heart fluttered as I processed this insider information for a moment longer before I suppressed it. I wasn't allowed to hope, even in the least. I knew this would go nowhere—how could it? Living hundreds of miles from each other was a recipe for relationship disaster. Add the fact that I had only known him for a day, and the word *pathetic* sprang to mind.

I was unexpectedly jostled from behind. I turned and saw a man getting ready to sit in the chair directly behind me. "Sorry about that," he slurred, a crooked smile on his face.

"No problem." I turned my attention back to our table.

Brody returned with five drinks. He had two bottles tucked under his left arm, and he was pressing the other three drinks against each other in his hands, creating a triangle with the glasses. I spoke quickly, barely making eye contact. "Thanks."

I didn't want him to see the redness in my cheeks—I was still blushing from Mike's comment. He sat down, put his arm up on the back of my chair, and started to play with my hair. I practically melted.

"Are you having fun?" he asked me.

I nodded with enthusiasm. "How about you?"

"Yeah, it's been a good day . . . totally worth passing on the tickets."

"Tickets?"

He grinned and answered with a touch of reluctance. "A buddy of mine had tickets to today's Rockies game."

"You passed up a baseball game to hang out with *us*?" I asked, shocked.

A surprised look flickered on his face as he answered. "You follow baseball?"

I shrugged a shoulder. "I like sports."

He smirked. "You know, that doesn't surprise me. It fits."

"It fits?"

His smirk widened into a large smile. "Yes, it fits."

"I'll take that as a compliment then."

"You should, because it was a compliment."

We smiled at each other. I was ready to dive into a conversation about baseball when I heard a voice behind me.

"Would you like to dance?" I turned and saw the man seated behind me who had had far too many spirits.

My cheeks flushed. "Me? Oh, no. But thank you."

"Just one? Come on, your friends won't mind."

"She said no," Mike barked.

The man's face turned smooth, and his voice followed suit. "No one was asking you."

Mike's laid-back persona completely shifted. He sprang to his feet, and his eyes turned into slits. "You better watch it, or I'll knock you into next week."

Brody cut in. "Come with me," he said to the man.

The man looked at him with a challenging expression. "Where are we going?"

"We're going to take a walk up to the bar."

Brody stood up and led the man away from the table. The two figures made their way to the bar. My eyes only left them once to sneak a glance at Mike, who was still standing, glowering at them. Brody stayed with the man, chatting, as the bartender handed a beer to him. They spoke for another minute, and then Brody left him at the bar and made his way back to our table.

"Why did you do that?" Mike grumbled.

Brody shook his head. "I didn't want to end up in jail when you knocked him on his ass."

Mike threw Brody a glare.

Brody smirked in return. "You're welcome."

"What did you tell him?" I asked.

"I told him he had good taste but that you were with me tonight. Then I bought him a beer."

"You bought him a beer?" I asked, skeptically.

"Yeah. I told him he had the choice of backing off and enjoying a beer on me, or I would knock him into next week myself. He opted for the beer."

"But what if he comes back?"

Brody's smiled smugly. "He won't come back over here—trust me."

Glad the altercation was over, I exhaled a breath of nerves. I wasn't sure what the conversation had entailed, but Brody had defused the situation nicely. Admittedly, I felt a bit smug.

The night grew late and I was getting tired. A day of high-elevation physical activity and excessive emotional stimulation had taken its toll. I tried to conceal it as best I could, but a yawn slipped out.

I didn't fool Brody. "Are we ready to go?"

I nodded, answering for the table. Everyone displayed the same glazed look as me, so there were no objections. We left the bar and headed back to the hotel. The drive seemed shorter than the first time we had driven this route. After pulling up to the front of the hotel, Mike cut the engine. We slid out of the Cherokee, saying our good-byes.

Brody wrapped an arm around me, and I could feel my heart trying to escape out of my chest.

"I'll give you a call in the morning, okay?"

I nodded. "Okay," I answered sheepishly.

I prayed he would, and mentally reminded myself to charge my phone overnight.

Chapter

SEVEN

$\mathcal{M}$y excitement from the night before led to a poor night's rest. I tossed and turned and checked the clock every three hours. Would Brody call me? Today was our last full day here, and I wanted to spend it with him. If he didn't call, I would be beyond disappointed.

I finally dragged myself out of bed at eight and took a quick shower. When I emerged, my roommates were awake.

"Morning," I chirped.

Rebecca stretched as she responded. "Morning, Brit."

"What do you guys want to do today?" Sarah asked, propped up on her elbow.

I shrugged a shoulder. I didn't care, just as long as it involved Brody.

"I feel like being lazy today," Rebecca whined. "How about seeing a movie? We could hit the outlet mall afterward if you want?"

Sarah and I agreed; a movie sounded nice.

After Sarah and Rebecca were cleaned up, we walked down to the hotel's dining room and ate breakfast. I scarfed down my eggs and toast, my phone silently burning a hole in my front pocket. I checked it twice to make sure it was on. It was. Unfortunately, it just wasn't ringing. I checked again after breakfast and again when we returned to the room. No change.

"If you check that phone one more time, I'm going to take it from you. You're driving me crazy," Sarah scolded.

My face heated. I hadn't meant to be that obvious. But why hadn't he called me? I blew out a frustrated breath.

Suddenly, Rebecca's phone rang, and she answered it quickly. I sat on the bed and waited patiently for Rebecca to finish her conversation with Mike. I was happy he called Rebecca, but I was disappointed that Brody hadn't called me.

When Rebecca hung up the phone, she looked at us, displaying a huge smile. "Mike and Brody are going to join us for the movie." She turned toward Sarah. "Mike wants to know if you want him to invite a friend for you?"

Sarah smirked. "As in a blind date? Only if he plays for the NFL."

Rebecca snickered. "That's what I thought."

Relief washed over me. I was thrilled that I would get to see Brody again. What I didn't understand was why he didn't call, or at least text. Either way, I would get to see him soon.

We pulled up to the movie theater at noon, planning to see the new romantic thriller, *In Brooklyn*. We bought our tickets and walked into the lobby. The guys had beaten us there and were playing air hockey in the little arcade adjacent to the entrance. As we approached, Mike glanced our way and grinned at Rebecca.

"Hey! Give me a second to kick Brody's butt, then we can get some popcorn."

"In your dreams, Perry." Brody tossed back.

The guys finished their game, with Brody winning seven-to-five. I felt a little smug that he had won, especially with all the trash-talking Mike had been doing. Brody looked at us and said hello. I could feel my face light up, even though his greeting was to all three of us.

Brody led the way to the concession stand. When it was my turn, I ordered popcorn and a Coke. We headed into the theater and found seats. Thanks to Sarah's nagging, we had arrived early enough to still find five seats altogether. Mike sat on the end next to Rebecca, then Brody, me, and last, Sarah.

I was exhilarated to be sitting next to Brody. I kept expecting him to take my hand, but it never happened. Ten minutes passed and he hadn't even spoken to me. He seemed to be completely enthralled in Mike and Rebecca's conversation and not the least bit interested in me. Thoroughly disappointed, I started chatting with Sarah about the author who wrote *In Brooklyn*.

"This might be Samantha Ledar's best book ever," Sarah declared. "I can't wait to see this movie!"

"I know, right? She hasn't written a book for a while, has she?"

I was expecting a response from Sarah, but Brody chimed in. "I heard she lost her husband and didn't write for a couple years."

I turned to look at Brody. He grinned sheepishly at me and then quickly turned his attention back to Mike and Rebecca. I looked back at Sarah and frowned in confusion. She offered a small smile and a little shrug.

Thankfully, the movie started and was a nice distraction from my growing irritation with Brody. Not only did he avoid holding my hand, he didn't even let his arm touch mine on the armrest. There were only a few centimeters between our arms, but it felt as if there were miles between us.

This sudden change was baffling and upsetting. The most confusing part was that I looked over at Brody and saw him staring at me two different times. When I caught him, he immediately turned his attention back to the movie. I wasn't sure if he was flirting or toying with me. I couldn't see his face well enough in the dark theater, but it was awkward nonetheless.

The movie ended and our group decided to go out to eat. We settled on a bar and grill with an attached brewery that was across the street from the theater. The lively, two-story restaurant was decorated with winter-sports paraphernalia. After we were seated, we discussed the movie.

We decided that the movie followed the book perfectly. Brody and I were the most insistent about this. I loved when a movie followed a good book to a tee.

"If you have a bestseller, why ruin it by changing it in the movie?" Brody argued.

"I couldn't agree more," I said.

Brody beamed at me, then turned away and changed the conversation.

The mixed signals I was receiving from Brody were ridiculous. He wanted to sit by me but not touch me. He chimed in on every discussion and seemed engaged, but then hastily retreated from the conversation. I caught him staring at me several times, but he always looked away. His behavior was odd, and I was officially irritated.

I hated playing games. Why did men have to make everything complicated?

Finally, the guys needed to leave because Mike had to go to work. Rebecca and Mike stood and talked to each other for several minutes. It was sweet to see Mike stumbling over his words, trying to feel out Rebecca's thoughts on extending their relationship. The rest of us stepped away, trying to give them room. I stood next to Sarah, and Brody was a few feet away.

"Are you going to get Brody's phone number?" Sarah whispered.

"I already gave mine to him. Plus, I don't think he's interested," I said sullenly.

She frowned. "I'm not so sure. For not being interested, he certainly is hovering."

I guess she was correct. He seemed distant in his behavior, yet he was always present and right by my side.

"Maybe I'll give him my phone number."

"I thought he already had it?"

"But he hasn't called or texted me. Do you think he lost it?"

Sarah nodded with encouragement. "Maybe."

I pulled out a small piece of paper and a pen from my purse. I paused for a moment. What if Brody didn't lose my number, and he just wasn't interested? What if he said no thanks? What if he laughed at me? I could wait to see if he tracked down my number from Mike, through Rebecca. But I knew that if I left it up to Brody I would be disappointed in myself for not being assertive, and I would regret my decision. I blew out a stabilizing breath and wrote down my email address instead. This seemed less personal; plus, if he did have my number, then I wasn't nagging.

I walked over to Brody, and he seemed surprised by my move.

"Hey," I said shyly.

He smiled at me.

"I wanted to say thanks for showing us around. It was fun," I said cheerfully.

He didn't respond. Now I was feeling uncomfortable. Did he have any feelings for me? My confidence was dwindling. I thrust the piece of paper into his hand. "Just in case," I said quickly and walked away.

* * * * *

I woke up early—too early. I looked at the clock and it read five thirty. I suspected it would be at least two hours until my roommates woke up, or at least until our rooster, Sarah, woke us up. I lay in bed for about twenty minutes, replaying the past two days over and over in my mind.

Admittedly, I was confused. One day Brody was holding my hand, and the next he avoided touching me. It seemed as if he were trying to give me a not-so-subtle hint. However, I caught him looking my direction several times, and he often stood next to me and chimed in during my conversations. He seemed interested, so why was he acting like he had a split personality?

We were scheduled to leave today. If we stayed another day, I wondered which Brody I would encounter: the attentive one or the elusive one? Regardless, I longed for another day with him; I would have liked the chance to get to know him better. I wondered if he felt the same way.

Granted, I didn't know him well, but I wanted to, badly. Was it even possible to get to know him better? My mind raced. We could try the long-distance thing? Or one of us could move . . . *Move?* Now I was just being ridiculous. Most likely Brody wasn't attracted to me and this was a frivolous fling for him. Which was possible after the signals from yesterday.

I envisioned his eyes, his smile, and the way his touch made my nerves spike. I was torturing myself, mulling over our time together. I had to get up.

Not wanting to wake the others, I snuck into the bathroom to brush my teeth and hair. I didn't even change out of the sweats and T-shirt I had slept in. I stepped into my flip-flops, grabbed a room key, and slipped out the door.

The breakfast bar opened at six. I walked past the selection of fruit, toast, cereal, and pastries several times before settling on a slice of buttered toast and a cup of coffee. I grabbed a newspaper and headed toward the cozy-looking chairs by the fireplace.

As I ate, I read the local news of the day: the mountain lion that was trapped by the rangers, the music festival happening this weekend, and the pine-beetle attacks on the local forests. I lowered the newspaper to turn the page so I could continue the article on the beetles, and saw Brody smiling at me.

He was sitting in the chair across from me. The same chair Mike had lounged in the night before, when the girls and I had interrupted their conversation.

I jerked back slightly as my heart stopped for a split second. I couldn't help but grin once my surprise subsided. Confused but ecstatic, I eagerly asked, "What are you doing here?"

"I'm so sorry! I was going to text you to see if you'd come down and talk to me. I just got here and you were already sitting here. I should have called or something . . ." He grimaced. "I couldn't sleep at all last night."

My lips curled into a small smile. "Me neither."

He sat there for a moment. His elbows were on his knees and he was leaning forward, as if he were trying to decrease the distance between us. Although he was smiling, his eyes looked perplexed, creating a slight furrow between his brows.

"This is going to sound crazy, and I'm not crazy, Brit. I promise I'm not," he said.

"What is it?"

He took a deep breath. "I like you," he blurted out. "I mean, I tried to back away, but it didn't work—actually, I think it made it worse. All I wanted to do yesterday was hold your hand and talk to you." He paused, looking disconcerted. "I'm more comfortable hanging out with you than most of my buddies, and you're leaving today. I know we barely know each other, and that's why this is so crazy, but what do you think of the idea of sticking around . . . at least for a little bit longer? I just met you and—"

He paused, flashing a stiff smile. I could tell he was trying to be optimistic, but distress seeped into his voice, exposing his true feelings. "I don't want you to leave so soon."

I wasn't sure if he was speaking to me or plucking the thoughts right out of my head. I'd had the same conversation with myself several times but wouldn't allow myself to entertain the idea. Now it was different.

I looked him in the eyes and reached for his hand. I didn't say anything for a moment as I let out a sigh of relief. We had a few extra buffer days, and I couldn't think of a better way to use them.

I tried to sound calm as I answered, "I think I'd like that."

"What about Rebecca and Sarah? Will they be okay staying?"

"I know Rebecca will want to. She moped around all night last night."

"What about Sarah?" he asked nervously.

"Don't worry, I know her weaknesses. We'll have to do a lot of shopping, but she'll stay. Do you think the hotel will have room for us for a couple more days?"

"It's the off-season, so that shouldn't be a problem." A huge, relieved smile covered most of his face and reached his eyes, making them crinkle. He looked elated, as if he had won a ball game and he was the star. He squeezed my hand, staring deep into my eyes, and leaned in closer than before.

I could feel the blood rushing to my cheeks. My breath became uneven as soon as I realized his intentions. I wanted to kiss him, but I felt like I was being tossed into the ocean's waves; my heart was being thrown about. I attempted to gather my thoughts, but with this emotional chaos, it was useless. I needed to slow down and allow my brain to catch up with my heart.

I wasn't ready for the next step, so I backed up and thought of a diversion. "Are you hungry? The toast is really something." I giggled timidly.

He nodded and grinned. "Yeah, looks real gourmet."

During our conversation, the newspaper had fallen to the floor. I released his hand, picked it up, and placed it on the small end table beside the chair. He grabbed my hand again and we stood up and made our way back to the breakfast area.

Chapter

EIGHT

Brody and Mike had heard about a rafting area called "The Float." After researching the spot, it seemed like a harmless run of river with a great view.

We pulled into the entrance, and at first glance, the name seemed fitting. Its crystal clear, deep-blue water was perfectly calm, like glass. All I wanted to do was steal a tube from one of the Cherokee's tires and float away.

After hauling the two small rafts off the roof rack, we dropped them into the water and crawled into them. Brody and I teamed up in one, while Mike, Rebecca, and Sarah situated themselves in the other. Satisfied with our arrangement, we headed lazily down the river.

Brody dipped his fingers into the water and flicked freezing-cold water in my direction. I tried to shield my face with my hand, but some of the water snuck past my defenses. A combination of a shriek and a laugh bellowed out of me. He chuckled, and then a yearning expression crossed his face.

Without warning, he leaned in and stopped a few inches from my face. My heart sped up with each closing centimeter. My breath caught and my stomach clenched as desire washed over me. I wanted to taste his full lips.

His hand reached out slowly and gently wiped the water from my face. He looked into my eyes, narrowing their focus so nothing else existed.

A yell broke through our moment. "Mike! No! Don't you dare!"

With a sheepish smile, Brody sat back up and rowed once to straighten out the boat. I wanted to scream at them for interrupting a pivotal moment as I turned to observe what was taking place. Mike was threatening to splash the other occupants.

"Mike!" Rebecca yelled, half scolding and half laughing during their standoff.

I tried to smile, but I was still irritated with them. I frowned, took a deep breath, and looked at Brody. He shook his head and shrugged his shoulders, as if apologizing for our broken moment.

We continued to float lazily down the stream until we rounded the second bend. The bubbles and turbulence looked harmless at first, but as we grew near, it was clear that we were approaching full-fledged rapids. A thrill of excitement ran down my spine, but my ignorant bliss dissipated when I saw the panic written on Brody's face.

"Hold on, Brit." His voice mirrored his expression.

I looked back at the other boat. Mike sported a similar expression as Brody, and Rebecca and Sarah were almost hidden by the boat, hunkering down. I followed suit, hiding behind the wall of the boat as it was engulfed by whitewater.

For the next seven miles, we toppled over rapids. The name of this part of the river was an ironic twist—we prayed that we would stay afloat. We blew right by our desired exit, located at the end of a set of rapids, forcing us downstream. When we finally found an exit, we were miles away from Mike's Cherokee. But as luck would have it, the exit was near a rafting company's headquarters.

Brody walked into the building and returned shortly with a man who had recently finished his shift. He was happy to give us a ride to our SUV, but his small truck could only fit one, possibly two, other passengers. We sent Brody while we sat, hoping the sun would dry out our soaked clothes.

Thirty minutes later, two men, one bearded with long, dirty-blond braids lined in rows on his head and the other with short, messy black hair walked by, gossiping loudly.

"Did you hear about the accident? It was on the highway, headed toward town. A car passed a truck and it lost control. I heard someone died . . . a guy."

My face went as pale as the snowcapped peaks. *It lost control.* What the hell does that mean? *What* lost control—the car or the truck? Horror flooded through me as the unknown reared its ugly head.

Sarah stroked my back. "I'm sure it wasn't——"

"Of course not," I stepped in, not letting her say his name.

I focused on remaining calm by slowing my breathing and tuning out the hearsay around me. But it was nearly impossible with Mike pacing back and forth in front of us. Every time Mike called Brody and received his voice mail, I sank lower. I had only known Brody for a short period of time, but his passing would strike deep and hard.

My world narrowed, turning into a small tunnel. I could feel the fog of despair creeping into my soul. Losing him would feel like a black hole sucking a part of me into it, never to recover. I was truly terrified, like never before.

My mind abruptly flipped. This—Brody and I—was intense, and I was now aware of exactly how intense. I needed him in my life. I didn't consider myself an emotional person, but an array of emotions danced when he was near: happiness, longing, contentment. They were like a drug to me, and the more I had, the more I craved.

I inhaled a large breath and a ghost of a smile crossed my lips as the reality of it hit me like a bulldozer: I *really* liked this man.

Could you fall for someone after only four days together? Apparently you could. My goal was to live life again and not coast on autopilot anymore. In the last few days, I had resurrected myself into the land of the living. Brody made me feel significant, appreciated, and, most importantly, desired.

Suddenly Mike's Cherokee came into sight, refocusing my thoughts. I jumped to my feet and ran over to the SUV as it pulled in. Brody stepped out of the vehicle with a solemn expression, and I almost tackled him as elation hit me like a tsunami.

"We heard there was an accident. I was so worried." The words spilled out of me like water from a pitcher.

"I know," his voice shook, "it was the car in front of us . . . one of the men died instantly. He wrapped his car around a tree . . . took the switchback too fast while trying to pass a truck." His arms wrapped around me tightly, shielding me from this traumatic news.

We all stood there for a minute in silence and sadness for the deceased, but we were relieved that it wasn't our friend. Moments passed until we peeled from our formation like layers from an onion and piled into the car. The excitement of the day had taken a somber turn.

Sarah refocused our thoughts in two words: "I'm hungry."

Mike nodded. "We'll grab some food in Vail."

I could feel Sarah's energy instantly rise, infecting us all. She'd had her heart set on hunting for celebrities, and even though this wasn't the touristy ski season, Vail was the perfect place to do it.

We took the Vail exit off of the interstate. The town was a cozy community overshadowed by a mountain full of ski runs. It was beautiful how the runs weaved, accenting the dips and caressing the curves of the mountain. And to think: in a few months it would be covered with people looking like ants on an anthill. The mental picture made me smile.

We started our tour of Vail at a little restaurant. The interior consisted of minimalist decor. One wall was made entirely of glass, from floor to ceiling; they were obviously proud of their mountain view. The peaks did have a calming effect, similar to the rivers back home. I also appreciated the distraction as we waited to be seated—I was starving.

After dining, we began our search for celebrities. Sarah decided to begin looking in the shops; it gave us a chance to nose around. Each shop had a unique character, some conservative and some eccentric. While trying to keep my shopping instincts at bay, I investigated each boutique. They teased my wishes, but I managed to get out unscathed. I exhaled a sigh of relief with each successful escape.

Sarah was comical with her wide, childlike eyes narrowing into frustrated slits with each celebrity-free shop. To Sarah's disappointment, the hunt was unsuccessful, but our trip to Vail ended the day on a positive note.

* * * * *

Brody and I sat under the starlit sky, captivated by its brilliance. The stars were vibrant, not having to compete with any city lights. They looked like hundreds of fireworks going off simultaneously but never fading.

The last four days had been bittersweet. We'd had fun, exploring new sights and sounds while ascertaining our feelings. Tonight was the most bitter; we both knew that the end was drawing near. We sat quietly, reflectively, both exhausted from our trying day.

Brody had his arms around me, shielding me from the chilling bite of the night air. I took in his sweet smell, deciding that its trace of muskiness was the key to its allure. He pulled me in tightly, and I memorized the contours of his arms and chest. His beating heart soothed my mind. I felt calm, completely tranquil. I was dreading the moment when I would have to say good-bye.

I would miss times like this—being held in his arms, feeling his warmth, and allowing myself to completely relax. I would miss our adventures, but mostly I would miss his company.

The conversations we had were random, sometimes pointless, but they were fun. I could be truthful, even if he didn't agree with my view, and he wasn't judgmental or demeaning. He actually tried to see my perspective and enjoyed the challenge of my quick-witted humor.

However, tonight we sat in silence. Feeling torn, I didn't know what to do. In twelve hours I would be in my car, leaving someone I could truly love. I was distraught that I had to leave the one man who was perfect for me—the icing on my cake. I could see my future self growing old with him, sharing our piece of the American dream ten thousand feet above sea level.

You have to leave, my brain argued.

But why? my heart retorted.

Animals needed to be saved here too; it wasn't like I couldn't find a new job. I could transfer, leave my family and friends, and move to a new town where I only knew three people. Everyone would ask why, and I would have to come up with a better answer than love— especially when I'd only known the man for a little less than a week. Perhaps I could say I fell in love with the mountains?

They would think I was foolish. I could envision the looks of disapproval and disappointment on my parents' faces as I packed my bags. I wasn't sure if I could handle their looks of anguish as their only child left them.

The whole scenario was not fair! I had to live my own life, without remorse. I would regret not following through with this relationship, which was chock-full of potential. The possibly of meeting your soul mate and then walking away to do what was expected of you made me sick. I *always* did what was expected. The thought of my previously forlorn and stagnant existence, my apartment in Portland, located only a mile away from my parents' house, and my same old job made me shudder.

Brody's fingers grazed my cheek. He looked at me with concern. "You okay?"

I tried to hold my emotions back and be strong, but it was useless. A single tear escaped, falling down my cheek and exposing my shaky state.

I started to look away, wanting to gain my composure. It embarrassed me to appear so sensitive and emotional. Before I could turn away he grabbed me, pulling me in closer and hugging my head to his chest. I shut my eyes and inhaled.

I felt safe and warm and my overwhelming sadness eventually subsided, allowing my brain to gather my feelings and translate them into verbal communication. I took a moment and then responded with a simple "I'm sorry." My voice was tinged with embarrassment and shame.

"Don't you dare apologize," he scorned lightly. "That's what I'm here for." His words were soothing and sympathetic, as if he already knew what was bothering me. Was he feeling the same? I was terrified to expose my feelings to him, and terrified not to.

I had to know his thoughts. I had to take a leap, even if it meant a broken heart. I looked up at him and blurted out, "I don't want to leave. It's not fair!" My cheeks began to redden. This was a bold move for me, to talk about my feelings and wants so freely. "Now do I sound like the crazy one?"

I sat patiently waiting for his response; it felt like an eternity. I prepared myself for a possible rejection, not sure my heart could handle much more. I winced when he spoke, as if I were shying away from an attack, because I knew I could be mending my wounds for some time.

"No. I know exactly how you feel," he said softly. His response made my heart jump with delight.

"What should we do?" I mirrored his tone. "I wish we could . . . I don't know . . . run away."

His next look was unfamiliar to me. It was a mix of exhilaration and astonishment. "Why can't we?"

"Run? Where to?" I could hear the panic in my voice. I wasn't exactly being serious when I said we could run away.

"How about to find gold?"

I was baffled by the turn in the conversation, not understanding where his thoughts had come from. I waited patiently for an explanation.

There was silence for about ten seconds before he presented his proposition to me. "You were given directions to a major piece of American history. If we find the Cleansing Pool, we would be given a fat finder's fee. Plus, that would give us a couple of weeks to figure out what *we* are going to do. Think of it as a diversion while we buy ourselves some time. I wonder if Rebecca and Sarah would want to go? I'm sure Mike would go."

He spoke as if he were explaining this plan to himself, walking through each scenario out loud.

I felt excited—especially with how he used the word "we." His plan could actually work. I could move to Breckenridge when this was over, telling my parents the real reason. They couldn't protest something I truly loved. Plus, this gave me almost a month with Brody, which sounded much better than a measly week. The thought of more time with him sent my heart into a whirl. My mind was made up, but I was unsure of Sarah and Rebecca's responses.

"Well, I do have vacation time. I could call the hospital and tell them I'll be gone for a little longer. I think Rebecca and Sarah have plenty of vacation time, too. I don't know if they'll go for our plan, though." Visualizing their reactions made me a little nervous. "We'll have to talk them into it. And you're sure Mike would go with us?"

Brody nodded his head with a cunning smile. "Yes, I think he would go, especially if Rebecca went."

I knew that if Mike joined us, I could convince Rebecca to go. She acted indifferent, but she couldn't fool me. She liked him; in fact, she couldn't wait to see him. She beamed when he was by her side and moped when he wasn't around. Her sulking expression was amplified this afternoon when we packed our bags for our return trip. I could see the pain in her eyes, even though she acted strong and unconcerned. Rebecca always acted strong—I wouldn't expect anything less from her.

She felt the same for Mike as I did for Brody, I would bet a month's wage on it. I was ready to place my wager and pray for a win.

Rebecca had more vacation time than I did. She'd been at the clinic for three years, and this was only her second vacation since I had started. However, Sarah would prove to be problematic. She took many more vacation days than either of us. She enjoyed taking a day off here and there to visit the spa or go to the beach and relax. Adding time to our trip would use the remainder of her vacation time, which she held dear. But if I convinced Rebecca first, the two of us together might stand a chance against Sarah.

My job didn't pay the best and the hours could be tedious, but the benefits were exceptional. Not only did I get medical benefits (and free veterinary care for my pets), but I also got three weeks of paid vacation. This was huge in my line of work because it was stressful and emotionally draining, and the burnout rate was so high.

It would be unfortunate if my friends chose not to stay and join us on this adventure. Even so, my mind was made up. I was going to stay with Brody no matter what my boss, parents, or friends said or did. I hoped that Rebecca and Sarah would stay by my side, but my path was decided.

I looked at Brody, bubbling over with self-satisfaction and excitement. "I'm in!"

For the first time in years, I felt free. I could take a deep breath, even at this elevation, without constrictions. I felt like I could see a dozen paths, like branches stemming out from a tree trunk, and I got to choose which one to follow. Each path was owned by me and me alone, I had to accept the awards and consequences of the one I chose. I could no longer hide behind what was expected of me or use others as a crutch. I was free to explore my own life. The possibilities were endless.

I blamed no one but myself for relinquishing my power of choice, but I was ready to resume my role as director of my own life. From now on I would do exactly what I pleased, with my supporters where they belonged: behind me, cheering me on, rather than in front of me, forging my way. Assuming I would still have supporters.

Brody flashed an incredulous, yet ecstatic, smile. "Let's go recruit the others."

He jumped up onto his feet, lifting me to mine and kissing my forehead in the process, making my heart skip a beat.

"Let's go." He pulled me by the hand toward the parking lot. "Mike will still be up."

Soon we pulled up to Mike's house; it was a smaller, wood-paneled ranch-style home. Trees surrounded the house, giving it an isolated feeling even though there were neighbors on both sides.

It was ten o'clock and every light was on. Energy conservation was obviously not a priority to him. The front door was unlocked, and to my surprise, we walked right in. Brody rapped on the door and yelled his name loudly. "Hey, Mikey?"

Sounding muffled, Mike responded, yelling from deep within the house. "Hey! Grab a drink and relax. I'll be out in a few minutes."

My cheeks heated as it dawned on me that he was in the bathroom. I felt uneasy, like we were intruding. Brody seemed unfazed, so I found the closest sofa and sat down. Brody came over to join me, putting his arm around me and smiling with an edgy expression. I was nervous to hear Mike's response, and it seemed like Brody felt the same way. I reciprocated with an anxious smile and he squeezed me, acknowledging our unstated feelings.

The inside of Mike's house was modern, sporting a limited color palette of grays, black, and a splash of red. His decor was classy and elegant; I could envision it in a New York City penthouse. The furnishings weren't typical of the mountain taste, which initially surprised me, being that Mike dressed with an outdoorsy edge.

Mike joined us eventually, grabbing a Coke from the refrigerator before he sat down. I felt shaky, as if I were getting ready to give an opening statement to a jury, argue our case, and wait for a verdict once the evidence had been deliberated on. It was silly, because I didn't need anyone's permission. I was an adult. Even so, I felt the need for someone to justify our crazy decision, someone who didn't care about how irrational this escapade may look—someone like Mike.

I think that was why Brody and I meshed so well. We were both a bit irrational and spontaneous, or just plain crazy, but at least we had each other in our delusional little worlds. God had led me to water, and it was time to take the plunge.

I loved being with him. No, I *had* to be with him. Desperation filled me, and at that moment I knew I loved this man. And for the first time, I actually knew what that meant. More than lust, or practicality, or familiarity—it was faith. I had confidence that God had made our paths intersect, and that I was meant to be here. God had led me to Brody for a reason.

Brody pitched our treasure hunt, and Mike raised his eyebrows in disbelief. Brody began to look tense and he took another angle, focusing on Rebecca's possible involvement. Mike looked at us with puzzlement, questioning our mental state I was sure, and he burst into laughter.

"What about work?" He laughed.

I interceded without letting Brody respond to his friend. I couldn't allow Mike to talk Brody out of our trip and our time together.

"Vacation days. I have almost two weeks left to burn. Of course, that means I'll have to work on Christmas, but hey, I might get to retire if we actually find the pool, right?"

Mike must have seen the angst in my eyes. His approval could possibly be the life or death of Brody's decision to move forward with our trip. He looked at me with empathy and said, "Sure, why not? I could use a vacation. It's been a long time since I've had one . . . too long."

I bounced up and hugged Mike without even thinking. His eyes widened with surprise, not expecting this reaction. He resumed his laughter, shaking his head with incredulity. His involvement would be the key to Rebecca's commitment. One down, two to go.

Mike walked over to the coat closet and grabbed his shoes and jacket. He made his way back to the chair and put his shoes on. While reaching for his jacket, he looked up at us and said "Ready?" Both Brody and I nodded, smirks plastered across our faces. Mike insisted on tagging along on our recruiting expedition. It seemed that he, too, had made it his mission to make sure Rebecca joined us. He was obviously interested in Rebecca, which made me smile for my friend. We all loaded into the car and headed to the hotel.

Rebecca was sitting in our room watching a sci-fi action movie. I ran over to her and jumped onto the bed, blocking her view of the TV. She looked at me with slight annoyance but still laughed at my random act. Her laughter was instantly silenced when Brody and Mike walked in. She and Mike had made plans to hang out tonight, but she had told him that she wasn't feeling well and wanted to lie down. Her face paled, clearly exposing her excuse as exactly that: an excuse not to see him. I knew precisely what she was avoiding. No one hated good-byes more than Rebecca. She wanted to keep Mike perfect in her memory, and not face the ache of valediction.

My words poured out quickly; I wanted to say everything before she could refuse. "We're going on a treasure hunt, looking for the Cleansing Pool. You *have* to come. We're all going and using our vacation days so we don't miss work. It wouldn't be the same without you. So, what do you think?"

A long moment passed as she processed my request. She looked up at the three of us, taking in our anxious expressions. Her eyes lit up.

"No way!" she shrilled animatedly.

I nodded, exhibiting a huge childlike grin that engulfed my face as I waited for her answer.

"Your parents are going to freak."

I chuckled, mainly due to my nerves. "I know." I sighed loudly. "I know . . . Oh, well. They'll get over it," I retorted matter-of-factly.

Her smile was grand and infectious. "Okay, I'll do it!"

I had a feeling that this would be her answer since Mike was joining us. Nonetheless, I threw my arms around her, ecstatic that she had said yes.

Now that Rebecca had accepted, it was time to face the wrath of Sarah. In the worst-case scenario, I would buy her a plane ticket home. But I would be disappointed, and I would miss her fun, sassy presence.

Sarah hadn't been able to handle Rebecca's sci-fi movie any longer, or more likely her brooding, and had gone downstairs to check out the local scene. We found her in the lounge, sitting at the bar talking with a couple of guys.

The men all exhibited the same expression: wishing they would be the lucky chosen one, the man who actually received the time of day from her. Sarah wasn't a snob, but a realist. She knew exactly what she wanted and didn't waste her time, or his. She loved the attention, but this wasn't her scene. She needed to be wowed—really wowed—and the typical mating games didn't appease her.

Readying ourselves for the ambush, we walked in and created a semicircle around her. She looked up, grinning at the formation.

"What's up?" I could hear her smooth, competitive edge rising to the challenge.

Again, I was the one who spoke up. I knew that I would have to appeal to Sarah's business side, because unlike Rebecca, an outdoor adventure was not her forte.

"Sarah, we need your help." She raised an eyebrow, making me speak quicker. "We're going to try to find the Cleansing Pool. There will be a *huge* finder's fee. And since we have directions, we'll only use up two weeks of vacation—tops. Of course, we'll have to skip some more of our road trip, but it'll be worth it."

Her brow furrowed. She didn't appear overly convinced. I had to up the stakes.

"I'll owe you big. How about if I do your kennel duties for a month? What do you say? *Please?*"

Her face grew serious, almost sour. "You want me to go hiking for two weeks? Are you serious, Brit?"

"It'll be fun, you'll see. Did I mention there's a finder's fee? Think about it—unlimited massages and facials." I began to whine. "Fine . . . I'll do your kennel duties for three months. Please, Sarah, we need your help." Begging was not becoming, but I was desperate.

Despite the odds, Sarah could elevate above any situation. She was like a hovercraft, floating around while the rest of us staggered along, enduring life. She was lively and canny, and with Sarah around we could accomplish anything. Once her mind was set, events would happen exactly the way she said they would, as if she'd willed it. I would do almost anything for her to say yes.

Sarah must have read my mind. "Make it six months of kennel duty. And we'd better find it, because I'll need some major pedicures and a few chiropractic adjustments after this trip."

I chuckled as I let out a sigh of relief.

The smiles were contagious. Tomorrow we would embark on our new mission instead of leaving for Portland. I was soaring with exhilaration—now I would get to spend even more time with everyone, especially Brody. I had come on this journey hoping to have two friends by the excursion's end, and now I had four—and then some.

I had found friendship, independence, and love. I felt free, like a bird flying high above the world's worries.

Chapter

N I N E

Far too excited to sleep, we all sat in the lounge for three hours, discussing what we needed to pack and buy.

My eagerness was intense, making me almost tremble at the future prospects. Two weeks! The thought of two more glorious weeks of being near him made me smile. Our little plot was perfect, and we both knew it. Hidden under the table, I squeezed his hand, making him grin halfway through a sentence as he spoke to Mike.

At last, my pragmatic side took hold and brought me to back to reality. The clock read one thirty, and I was exhausted. Yes, I was eager, but even I had limits. "I'm going to be a zombie tomorrow without at least one REM cycle. Especially if we're going to be hiking as much as you say we are."

Everyone, now realizing the time, agreed. We stood up, ready to part for the night.

Rebecca looked at Mike. "You guys might as well crash in our room tonight—it's too late to be out driving."

My heart skipped a beat. Even the thought of this remarkable man sleeping only a few feet from me made my cheeks glow and my heart race.

Brody turned toward me and smirked. "Well, I am pretty tired."

He said his house was a fifteen-minute drive down a narrow road with several switchbacks. The commute could be dangerous in certain conditions, and I would consider being tired as one of those conditions.

71

"I agree with Rebecca: you shouldn't be driving this late." I tried to sound calm, wrestling the enthusiasm out of my voice.

Brody looked at Mike, who nodded once with approval.

Rebecca brightened. "Good, it's settled then."

We headed upstairs to our room. Distracted by my mission of persuading Rebecca to join in our expedition, I didn't realize the state of the room the first time I was there. It looked like a mild disaster, to say the least.

The clothes from yesterday were thrown in the corner, and snacks were strewn across the dresser. The beds were in disarray even though they had been made earlier in the day, and the bathroom looked like a war zone. As soon as I saw our room, I regretted our decision . . . sort of. They could have as least given us a five-minute head start.

Brody and Mike seemed unfazed by our heap and grabbed the comforters off the bed, leaving the sheets.

Brody looked at me and asked, "Which bed is yours?"

I answered sheepishly. "Um, this one," I said, pointing to my side of the bed.

He took his bedding and laid it on the floor next to where I would be sleeping. My heart leapt with excitement; I would get to be next to him for hours on end.

I spent a few minutes readying myself for bed: I brushed my teeth and hair and put on a new T-shirt, tossing the old one onto the accumulated pile. Lastly, I took a few calming breaths before I stepped out of the bathroom and rounded the corner. Brody was lying on the floor next to my bed. His hands were folded behind his head and his ankles were crossed. He looked relaxed and beautiful. I couldn't help but beam with satisfaction.

Everyone assumed their sleeping positions, and Sarah turned off the lamp next to her bed. I turned on my side toward Brody and breathed deeply. I lay there quietly, content as I thought about the upcoming day.

All of a sudden, Brody's fingers caressed my face, sending my body into a whirl. I couldn't move, nor did I want to. I shut my eyes and focused on how his electrifying touch felt red-hot on my skin. The flame of desire nestled in the pit of my stomach grew into a bonfire. My breath pulled deeper, feeding the fire.

I opened my eyes, surprised to see his face in front of me. I reciprocated by caressing his cheeks with my fingers, feeling him smiling at me. He leaned in slowly, pausing for only a moment, and brushed his lips over mine.

I had continually dreamt of this moment, and it didn't compare. His lips were sweet and soft, feeling even fuller than they looked. His hands were gentle as they stroked my cheeks and arm. He turned his head, changing the angle of his kiss, making me feel like I could explode. I moved my hands into his hair, holding onto the thick mane for dear life.

At that moment I knew Brody was made for me. Connecting with someone like this was epic, and I didn't think I could ever recover. Whether he chose to stay or leave, he was engraved into my soul. This moment would be forever etched into my mind, and only time would dictate whether it would become a haunting memory or not. I prayed that he felt the same way.

His lips broke away from mine. I lay there completely breathless, and I was forced to gasp for air. He let out a small chuckle, and my cheeks turned red. I was glad that the room was dark; I didn't feel quite as exposed. He gently grasped the back of my head and pressed his lips to my forehead. I shut my eyes, memorizing the contour of his lips on my skin once more. He released my head while I took in another jagged breath. I was floating.

"Good night . . . sleep well," he whispered.

"You too." I brushed his cheek with my hand before he lay back down. I felt like I was in a dream, never wanting to wake.

The next morning I sprang up with a childlike enthusiasm, excited to see Brody. I looked around, but he was gone. My worst fear of this actually being a dream was rearing its ugly head. I could feel the scowl growing on my face as Sarah burst into laughter.

"They left about an hour ago, sleepyhead. Brody sat on the edge of the bed and played with your hair for about five minutes as you slept."

Horror crossed my face. "Oh no." I was sure I looked like a mess. Plus, I could have been dreaming, or worse, drooling. My cheeks flushed. "I feel like such an idiot."

She shot me a look of disapproval. "Oh, stop it. It was sweet," she said. "Mike wanted to start packing, so they left. They'll return soon, don't worry. They wanted us to pack—lightly," she said with a sour grimace. "And to tie up loose ends while they're gone."

"Loose ends?" I questioned.

"Well, we have to call work, and don't forget your folks. You'll have to fess up sooner or later," she said with a parental undertone, adding to the sting of reality.

Loose ends. That's not what I would call it. I had talked up my newfound strength, but really, I was petrified. This would be the first time I had ever stood up to my parents, other than telling them exactly what type of nurse I would be. They had wanted me to be a "real" nurse—a nurse for humans—and I'd wanted to work with animals. I fought tooth and nail, and finally they gave in when I adopted my cat, Edie. Knowing this would be the first of many, they figured I would save a ton of money on my animal expenses if I worked for a vet.

I dreaded this conversation, but I knew I had to do it. I wouldn't truly be free until this one step had been completed. It was like when Luke Skywalker fought Darth Vader—if I didn't face this challenge and succeed, I would never be the Jedi of my own life.

After cleaning up and packing, I couldn't procrastinate any longer. I walked over to the dresser and grabbed my cell phone out of my purse. I looked at it for a long moment. I pressed the speed dial to call my mom and ended it immediately. I sighed, releasing a breath of nerves. I decided to take the easier road—baby steps—and called the hospital first.

It rang twice before someone answered. I had a speech all prepared, but the voice on the other end surprised me.

"Kat? Is that you?" I asked. Kat was a certified vet tech, so to have her answer the phone was a bit unusual.

"Yeah . . . Brit, where are you? Why are you calling? Is your trip going okay?" I could hear the concern intensifying with each sentence.

"Yes, everything's fine, don't worry. We're in Colorado. Where's Karen? Why didn't she answer the phone?"

"She had to pee, so I'm covering for her. She'll be right back."

My plan of dancing around the truth and using car issues as my excuse went right out the window. I couldn't lie to Kat. She would see through my phony story in an instant.

I took a deep breath and began to explain. "Kat, I need you to talk to the docs. The three of us are going to be at least a week—make that a week and a half—behind schedule."

"What? Are you kidding me? What is going on, Brit?" she demanded.

"Kat, settle down. I met someone." This information calmed her immediately.

"Oh?"

"He's . . . incredible. You'd really like him. He's so nice and gorgeous and . . . perfect." I could feel myself glowing. "And he needs my help. We want to stay and help him, Kat. Will you talk to them for us please?" I pleaded.

She giggled as she spoke. "Tell me everything and don't leave anything out," she insisted.

I told her about how we met—more so how I couldn't even function when I first saw him—our first hiking trip, and the rafting trip. I gushed about what he meant to me. I explained about the Cleansing Pool and our mission. Lastly, I told her that he was someone who I could see myself with, and that I needed more time with him.

Kat was so ecstatic that I could almost hear her grinning through the phone. "I'll take care of it for you, don't worry. I'll fib and say you had car trouble or something." I could hear her mentally scheming while she spoke. "But you have to promise me that you'll keep me posted, okay?"

"Of course I will. We're going hiking for a little while, so I'll be out of cell phone range. But I'll call you as soon as we get back, I promise." I was suddenly wishing that she were here too. "Kat, I owe you one, thanks."

"I'm happy for you, Brit."

I knew Kat would take care of work for me. She understood that this time with Brody was exactly what I needed. I was pleased that I had told Kat the truth; she was a romantic at heart. She would help any new love blossom, especially a friend's. I could count on her.

I hung up the phone. Sarah and Rebecca had huge grins plastered across their faces. Sure, they knew I liked Brody, but this was the first time they had heard me acknowledge my feelings. Now they realized that Brody meant something more to me than a simple crush. They seemed giddy with this news, as if they'd made the match themselves. Rebecca jumped off the bed and threw her arms around me. Sarah was next in line, and she squeezed me tightly.

Sarah took a step back and gave me a scrutinizing look. "Okay, now the hard part. Brit, you *have* to call your parents."

I sat on the edge of the bed, almost hyperventilating. She was right. I had to do this and make my big stand. Rebecca and Sarah could see the panic in my eyes and quickly sat next to me, one on either side. Both silently offered their moral support as I picked up the phone. If I had to face the fury of my parents, these were the people I wanted by my side.

I hit the speed dial, number two, and then put the phone to my ear. My hands trembled with dread, praying that no one answered.

One ring . . . two rings . . . three rings. Her voicemail picked up.

My prayers had been answered—they had already left for work. I had never appreciated technology more than at this moment. I could hear my mother's voice in the background. My mind raced until I heard the beep, breaking my train of thought.

"Hey, Mom, it's me. I wanted to check in with you and Dad and let you know that everything is going great. We're in Colorado. You would love it here; it's beautiful, and the mountains are really something. Actually, we're having so much fun here that we've decided to stay an extra week . . . or possibly two. I've already called work and they said it wasn't an issue. So, if you wouldn't mind, I'd appreciate it if you would watch Edie a little bit longer. We've decided to go hiking, and we'll be out of cell phone range. I'll call you as soon as my phone works again, so don't worry. I love you, and tell Dad hi for me. Bye!"

My eyes were wide and I felt stunned. I had done it—theoretically. I'd made my decision and was sticking with it.

All three of us sat there quietly enjoying the moment. Suddenly, Rebecca shrieked with joy, and I joined her. Sarah wasn't far behind. We were all squealing like schoolgirls—thrilled because of the potential of our mission, our friendships, and my newfound love.

There was a knock at the door, and Rebecca ran over to open it. Judging from her expression, Brody and Mike had returned. Mike unquestionably captivated her. Even having him nearby changed her mood completely.

They walked around the corner and Brody looked up, locking my gaze. My eyes lit up, and my heart pounded with joy. Would I ever get tired of this? He was picturesque in every way. He was beautiful, and his smile made my knees weak. I wanted to run over to him and repeat last night. My hands craved his warm skin and wanted to get lost in his thick locks. My lips begged for another magical kiss. My stomach knotted, and my body tingled from head to toe.

Beaming a smile at me, Brody walked over and brushed my hair back behind my ear. His touch was electrifying. I shoved my hands into my pockets, trying to oppress my instincts. I had to distract myself and speak to him before I lost control and kissed him in front of everyone.

"Did you get everything packed?"

"Yeah, we're about ready. We still need to swing by the grocery store, and I need do a quick inventory on what you've packed."

"Me? Why me?" I asked, slightly defensive.

"Well, you and the others. I want to look over what everyone packed and make sure you all have everything you'll need."

"Oh, I see." I smiled wryly. "Make sure the rookies aren't going to starve."

He looked at me for a second and then sprang at me, tackling me onto the bed. I loved being wrapped in his arms; they were strong and defined, yet gentle as they engulfed my waist. I laughed and put his head into a headlock under my arm, messing up his hair with my free hand. We were in our own world until I heard a sigh.

"Let's go, you two." Sarah stood with her arms crossed and her eyebrows raised, tapping her foot. Mike and Rebecca stood grinning, holding hands. A sheepish grin crossed my face and my cheeks turned hot, exposing my embarrassment. Sarah shook her head and giggled at me.

"All right, all right. Let Brody look in our bags," I ordered.

Brody stood up and then helped me to my feet. He grasped me by the waist, pulling me into him. The proximity of our bodies created sparks that lit up the room like fireworks. I exhaled a deep breath before I let him go and retrieved my bag.

We threw our backpacks on top of the bed and displayed our packing attempts. Rebecca and I packed perfectly, while Sarah had to discard at least three outfits and a pair of heeled boots. Reluctantly she did what she was told, pouting more with each item discarded. Rebecca and I stood there snickering as Sarah stared daggers at us.

Once our packing and Sarah's repacking were approved, we gathered our backpacks and luggage and checked out of the hotel. We loaded the extra suitcases into the trunk of my car, got in, and drove to Mike's house, following Mike and Brody in the Cherokee.

We were free! A content smile was glued onto my face, reflecting the happiness that touched every aspect of me.

Chapter

TEN

I left my car parked in Mike's driveway and we piled into his Cherokee. We retreated the way we'd originally come, heading back toward Denver. Our route confused me; I had expected to journey deeper into the mountains. Before I asked where we were going, we turned off, heading north.

The road ascended the mountainside swiftly, making my ears pop in protest. We quickly passed the timberline and hit the top of the pass. I was eye to eye with the surrounding peaks. Everything below was small and insignificant; it felt like I was soaring, but with my feet planted safely on the ground.

Rebecca's eager voice pulled my gaze. "Look, a fox! Can we stop for a quick picture?"

Mike chuckled under his breath. "Sure, why not?"

He pulled into a gravel parking lot and we all exited the vehicle to stretch our legs, knowing that her "quick picture" would take a while. A single ski lift sat lonely and undisturbed, leading to the top of the closest peak.

"I bet the view from up there is awesome," I said.

Brody wrapped his arm around my waist. "It's pretty spectacular. I'll take you up there sometime, okay?"

I smiled. "It's a date."

I felt giddy, excited to be by his side on this adventure. I hoped he would take me on many more, so we could see new sights and hear new sounds together. Of course, that was assuming that he would *want* to be together after all this.

You're being silly, I reprimanded myself, but convincing my nagging doubts was difficult. He was perfect, and I was just . . . me. I knew it was a defense mechanism trying to protect my heart, but I recognized deep down that it was too late. I had already fallen for him, hard.

"Ready?" he asked the group.

I flinched, exiting my thoughts and jumping back into reality. Rebecca had captured her picture and was still beaming about her photographic success. I nodded and followed Brody toward the SUV.

We drove for about an hour before we turned off again. Looking through the windshield, I could see that the road headed straight toward a set of intimidating, massive peaks. I instantly hoped that this wasn't the area we were supposed to conquer. I could feel my nerves building up.

Brody must have sensed my reaction, because he tightened his grip on my hand. This settled my worries some, knowing that we were in this together. I smiled at him reassuringly.

We drove for some time and then came to another town nestled in the mountains. It was serene, and the buildings were reflected in the small lake they were adjacent to. A trickle of a stream escaped from the lake, weaving itself through the town and into the neighboring valley. The town had mountain charm and an authentic demeanor, displaying a few diverse shops along its main street.

We decided to take a break from driving and take a walk around the town, allowing our muscles to stretch out. Within seconds, I noticed the name Grand Lake plastered everywhere: hats, shirts, cups, and more. The name was fitting, being nestled next to a truly grand-looking lake.

We walked slowly, without purpose, peering through shop windows and allowing them to showcase the treats they held within. Finally stopping for ice cream, I realized that the lure of the previous windows was successful; we'd lost members of our group because they had wandered into the shops that interested them. The main street was small, so getting lost wasn't a concern.

While Brody and I finished our sweet treats, we decided to sit on a lonely picnic bench and bask in the sun. The day was ideal, with a slight, crisp breeze, and the pines overpowered any other aroma. It was a perfect day to relish in each other's company.

Across the street, on a little grassy patch, I saw a small family. The mother and father were enjoying the sunshine while watching their baby chase something. The baby was about a year old, with blond hair and blue eyes, and was dressed in pink from head to toe. She focused on what she was chasing, laughing with each miss of her hand. It looked like a grasshopper, but I wasn't sure.

I barely even noticed eating my ice-cream cone because I so preoccupied with the little girl. Her hearty laughter was contagious, making me giggle each time she missed what she was after. She soon grew bored with the bug and ran back over to her mother. The mother could never deny the little girl; they looked almost identical. Preoccupied, she handed the baby a bowl filled with some snack, and the baby began to shove it into her mouth.

I ate my cone mindlessly, observing the scenery. Occasionally I would check in with the little family before something else would catch my attention. After watching a hawk pass by, awestruck by its grace and control, my gaze found its way back to the little girl.

Something was wrong: her eyes were wide, her hue was too bright, and there wasn't a trace of glee on her face.

I jumped to my feet, dropped my ice-cream cone, and sprinted across the road. I grabbed the little girl and flipped her so her head pointed downward. Then I thrust my hand down firmly onto her back. Before the parents could even react, the baby had coughed up Cheerios all over the ground. I turned her right side up and handed her to her mother. The baby was now screaming—a good sign—and Brody was by my side. The mother had caught up with the moment and threw her arms around the baby, clearly distraught.

"Thank you! Oh my goodness, thank you. Thank you!" Both parents displayed the same expression of relief, terror, and embarrassment.

"No problem," I answered.

I turned from the family and walked away quickly. I could hear Brody's footsteps behind me, gaining distance with every step. He was soon by my side and he grasped my arm, swinging me around toward him. He looked at me for a moment with his deep, green eyes and then kissed me. This kiss was unlike the kiss at the hotel. It was strong, powerful, and passionate. I took his lead and grasped his hair, intertwining my fingers in it, letting his passion send currents through my body.

Brody broke away, keeping his face inches from mine. "Brit, you saved that little girl from choking—you're a hero."

I shuddered at that word; I was hardly a hero. "It was only a reaction. I deal with emergencies at the hospital all the time."

He didn't look convinced.

"Please, Brody. Her parents would have figured it out . . . leave it alone." I said, frustrated.

I had never enjoyed or sought out attention. I liked excelling at what I did and being one of the best, but I shied away from the attention that followed. The only attention I wanted was from Brody, but even this was making me uncomfortable.

He shook his head in disagreement, ready to continue with his argument, when I saw a store that looked interesting. I looked back at him and interrupted.

"Look, a Native American trading post. We should go check it out."

My diversion worked. Brody's attention shifted to the shop, which was around the corner from the main road. It was slightly hidden, sitting between a run-down cottage and the back of the shops we had already browsed. We wouldn't have seen it if we hadn't crossed the street.

We walked across the remainder of the road and approached the shop. The window decor was simple, full of dream catchers and a single tomahawk. We entered, the door shutting behind us. The shop was small, dim, and smelled like incense. The music in the background was mostly drumming and chanting, and items were laid out all over the counters.

Brody was like a kid in a candy shop, animated and easily distracted. I looked around while I tried to keep up with Brody's explanations. He was well educated in many of the customs and traditions of numerous tribes: he spoke of the Cheyenne, Pawnee, and Ute nations. As he began talking about the Arapahoe nation, a voice spoke from behind us, making me jump.

"Your knowledge is impressive. How do you know of these legends?"

I spun around and saw a man leaning against the far counter. He was older, with straight, mahogany hair reaching past his shoulders. He dressed youthfully, wearing jeans and a tee, but his face had many wrinkles, exposing his age.

I wasn't sure why, but I instantly didn't trust him. There was a gleam in his eyes that made my hair stand on end. He looked at us for a moment and continued while we stood there silently.

"What is it you seek?"

"Information," Brody responded. "We want to know about an Arapahoe legend."

"Oh?"

"What do you know about the Cleansing Pool?"

The man stood motionless, eyeing us with distrust. I was sure he was wondering what our intentions were. Then he began to mindlessly cite familiar textbook information: "The Cleansing Pool is a fictional legend. It was said to be a source of great power, allowing the elders to focus and communicate with others from the spirit world."

It sounded to me like he was downplaying his knowledge. Brody was scowling.

Brody seemed insulted by the man's answer, because his next words were sharp, surprising me. "You know just as well as I do that it *does* exist and that the legend is true. I don't want to hear quotes from textbooks. I want to know if you have any *real* information on its whereabouts. Of course, maybe you don't know anything."

I didn't understand the source of Brody's frustration. The man's answer was sparse, but it seemed legitimate to me.

Anger flashed across the man's face as he snapped back. "It's a local hot spring. The heat intensifies the effects of the elder's ceremonial tools used to experience a vision quest. And that's it— the pool is nothing special." His once-narrowed eyes widened and he redirected them immediately. Abruptly, his expression shifted into a wry smirk, as if he were saying we would never find it. "Good luck with your search."

"Thanks," I said, trying not to gloat. Little did he know that we had directions.

I glanced at Brody and melted at his smug grin. "It's time to go," he said, adding a wink.

We left the shop and gathered our friends. After loading back into the Cherokee, we drove north toward the peaks. I was mesmerized by our surroundings; as the peaks grew near, they dwarfed us. I was intimidated.

"Do you know where we're going?" I questioned as Brody gave Mike directions.

Brody's childlike excitement was barely contained. He beamed. "Sure. Well, close enough. You said he told you to follow the trail on top of the ridge until it divides the land in two. Then go toward the resting sun and you come to a spotted meadow within the peaks, and that's where we'll find the entrance to the cavern. Do I have that right?"

"Yep, that's what he said."

"The directions basically say to go to the top of Trail Ridge Road, which runs into the Continental Divide. The divide separates the flow of water—water west of the divide flows west and water east of the divide flows east, ending at one of the two oceans. So it's dividing the land in two. The intersection is called Milner Pass, and then we'll head west until we find your spotted meadow. The cave's entrance should be there."

"Cave?" My eyes grew large.

Brody's lips twitched into a small smile. "That's what he said."

I was pleased that Brody had deciphered the riddle, which now sounded elementary if you knew what to look for. However, I was still perplexed that no one had discovered this historical landmark if it had always been so close to civilization.

"How come it's never been found before?"

Brody grinned at me and then kissed my hand. "Because no one has ever had directions before. The passages in textbooks only brush over it, like it's purely mythical. But our friend at the shop confirmed that it does exist in a physical form."

Impressed that Brody had taunted an acknowledgment out of the Native American man, I nodded with a smile.

We drove toward the top of the peaks, almost reaching the summit, until we came to a turnout. Mike pulled over while Brody grabbed his map. Once the car was unloaded, Brody laid out the map on top of the hood. He and Mike looked it over while the three of us hovered, taking turns peering at the map over their shoulders and gawking at the peaks surrounding us.

Brody pointed to a few areas that could have a hidden meadow. "We'll look for the meadow when we reach the other side of the mountain. Hopefully the clearing will have a panoramic view of the landscape. That'll be our best chance of finding this spotted meadow."

Mike agreed, and Brody tucked the map into his bag. It was time to begin our journey. I stood there with my pack securely on my back, looking at the terrain I had agreed to tackle. I peeked over at Brody—my ultimate motivation—and gathered my confidence. I took my first step forward, signifying my independence, and followed my friends westward.

Chapter

E L E V E N

I could almost feel its hot breath on my face as it growled. The whites of its eyes matched the full moon in the sky, and its teeth seemed to glow in the moonlight, amplified in size.

I was captivated by its size and grace. Its massive paws sunk into the needles covering the forest floor, yet it looked as if it were floating as it took one last approaching leap. Its muscles flexed and rippled under the thick blanket of fur until they, too, stopped.

It was momentarily silent: the calm before the storm. I couldn't hear the typical forest inhabitants that filled the night with their bustling as they scurried around to find food.

My mind screamed at me to do something—anything. But I didn't care. I watched the massive grizzly out of my peripheral vision as I stood there, devastated by the two figures running away from me, hand in hand.

He had chosen her.

Brody could take only one, and he had chosen her over me. I wasn't concerned about the fate I was about to endure because nothing could hurt like this. I wanted to yell in protest, but I could only manage a whispered "no" as I stood there in shock and disbelief.

I loved him.

Brody glanced back at me only once before they faded into the distant light.

Suddenly, the light flashed. It was so bright it blinded me. I put my hand up, trying to dim its attack. I heard a cracking sound and felt pain against my skull. Did the bear strike me? It must have. This must be what dying feels like.

I was cold, so cold, and the light was gaining ground. It was blinding, but I still walked into it until I was completely engulfed.

I blinked as the sun's blinding rays assaulted my eyes. I pulled in a jagged breath as relief and rage toiled against each other.

It was only a dream.

The dream—the nightmare—was about something I feared and anticipated. I agonized over the thought of losing him, especially after we found the pool. What would happen then? Would Rebecca, Sarah, and I go back to Portland, with Brody and Mike staying in Colorado?

I would lose Brody to "her" one day, and the worst part was that I didn't even know who she was. Regardless, it was the beginning of a new day, and I should capitalize on the time I did have with him.

The air was crisp and cold. I yearned for the clouds that draped the skies back home and tamed the relentless sun—then I could have a few more minutes of sleep before I faced another tedious day filled with hiking, searching, and hoping.

A sigh broke through my lips as I stirred in defeat. I rolled over, attempting to ignore the demands of the morning, but guilt washed through me. I procrastinated for ninety more seconds until I finally surrendered to the inevitable.

I dressed in my sleeping bag, pulling out the clothes I'd shoved into the foot of it the night before in an attempt to keep them close and somewhat warm. I reached for my jeans first. The fabric was unmistakable, but putting them on was comical. I wrestled to find the legs, contorting myself until my foot was enclosed in denim. Luckily, the long-sleeved T-shirt was less work. Officially dressed but still groggy, I lay motionless for a moment, trying to motivate my coffee-less body to face the morning chill head on.

A chuckling outside of my down-filled cocoon caught my attention. Anticipation swept through me, knowing that he was up and that he would be the first thing I would get to connect with. Brody's presence intoxicated me. His eyes wrapped me in a blanket of adoration and desire. This connection made mornings more than tolerable; I decided that I actually liked them. Of course, I had a reputation to maintain, and not sharing this secret often led to extra sleep.

"Good morning. How did you sleep?" he asked, trying to suppress his laughter as he greeted me.

I looked over to him, embracing my slight irritation. "Ugh."

Brody's laughter could no longer be suppressed. I glared at him but couldn't keep the corners of my mouth from turning up. I could imagine the spectacle he had just witnessed.

"Come sit with me." He patted the area of sleeping bag next to him. "Are you ready for some breakfast?"

I nodded. Grabbing my dark-blue backpack, I crawled next to him onto his red sleeping bag and sat down with a rebellious thud. I rustled in the front pocket of my backpack and pulled out my plastic bag full of food. My days usually began with a breakfast of a few almonds, a protein bar, and tea—we had an abundance of tea.

I handed a generous helping of almonds to Brody and then snagged a handful for myself. As I ate, I mentally prepared myself for another day of hiking and wondered if today would be the day.

Brody began to play with my hair, smoothing out the disarray. His hand brushed over the back of my scalp and I winced in pain.

"Are you okay?" he asked with concern.

I rubbed the back of my skull and found a bump that was sore. "Ouch," I whined.

His eyebrows shot up. "I take it you didn't look for rocks before you laid your sleeping bag down?"

My expression soured. "Actually, it was a grizzly," I mumbled.

"What?"

"Nothing." I sighed, still sulking about my nightmare.

I popped the last almond into my mouth, but my stomach was still protesting, begging for a real meal. I never thought I would miss bacon this much.

"All right, let's get this show on the road." Sarah started each morning with a similar phrase, but this morning it made me cringe more than usual.

I giggled at her relentlessness. "Yes, General," I said, adding a salute.

A sly smile broke across her lips. "That's right, Private."

I shook my head at her as she patted me on the shoulder. "Don't forget, you wanted me on your mission. You asked—actually, you *begged* for this."

"Can I change my mind?" There was snickering around me.

"Very funny. Plus, if it weren't for me, we would be behind schedule," she tossed back, grinning.

"All right, give me a minute." I succumbed to her argument.

My body accepted the work graciously, but my feet were a different story. They were blistered and had calluses that any true hiker would be proud of. I had put my delicate skin through hiking boot camp, and I was finding it harder and harder to ignore the pain.

I had come to the conclusion that "no pain, no gain" must have originated from a similar trip before it was adopted into our everyday motivational language.

I dug into my trusty backpack and found the only salvation for my feet: my lined hiking socks. I plucked out a pair and put them on. I laced my boots and paused, building up the courage to assault my feet. I winced as I stood up; the pain was always worse in the morning.

I turned and looked back at Brody. His expression was a combination of empathy and helplessness. I knew that nothing I said would help, so I flashed him a reassuring smile and held out my hand. He smiled as he gently grabbed my hand, kissed it, and let me help him up.

"Need some help packing?" he asked.

"Sure," I responded with a chuckle. "It's hard work packing up *all* of my belongings."

I threw on my coat and hat to get them out of my way as I put the rest of my belongings in their appropriate places. After rolling up my sleeping bag and tying it onto my backpack, I placed my blue water bottle in its designated pocket on the side of my bag and tucked the almonds into the front pocket.

I was happy I had brought such a hefty supply of almonds—it had allowed me to use them to barter for other treats. Our food supply was limited, so I felt rich, being able to buy treats like a kid in the cafeteria. "I'll give you a handful of almonds for one of your chocolate granola bars." The flashbacks to elementary school made me snicker under my breath.

Water was an easier commodity, since the mountains were full of streams. We collected water when we came across rapids. The turbulence made the water taste fresh, better than any water you could purchase in a bottle—or at least until we added the water treatment tablets. Because my dark blue water bottle was fairly new, the plastic smell masked the smell of the tablets. Sarah's tea was another nice cover up; I had learned to appreciate it.

I felt like I was in some sort of survivalist boot camp. Besides almonds and water, the other luxury I had learned to appreciate exponentially was matches. It amazed me how something as simple as a match could give us a touch of control in this wild terrain. And although this control was fickle, it still presented hope when things seemed bleak.

Our trip was balancing on a razor's edge, like on one of the surrounding peaks that engulfed us. We had been hiking for a couple of days, and I wondered if we would be forced to walk away. I knew the group would be disappointed, but all I truly cared about was what would happen to Brody and me after this trip. I obsessed about it, thinking about it day and night.

However, I decided that this trip had inspired me. I had tapped into a hidden treasure of self-discovery and empowerment, and I thirsted for more. With every step I took and every obstacle I faced, I learned something new about myself: new emotions, new strength, and a new internal force. And surprisingly, it was a force to reckon with.

We had been hiking for a few hours when we decided to take a water break. More so, it was a break for our aching feet, but no one would admit to this reasoning. It was more gallant to pause for water than for pain. We sat for ten minutes or so, rehydrating, and then decided to continue onward.

Through the trees, I could see a clearing in the distance. I enjoyed each clearing. It was more of the anticipation, like a fortune cookie about to be opened, foretelling the upcoming fate. I had been in this situation at least a dozen times but had not lost faith.

As we walked into the clearing the view opened up nicely, giving us a bird's-eye view of the topography. The horizon was decorated with white peaks and a deep-blue sky—the color of sky that you would see in paintings, or that someone would sing a song about. It was stunning.

I turned toward Brody. "It's beautiful, isn't it?"

Brody looked at me and smiled before he answered. "Sure is." His eyes didn't leave mine. My face began to flush at his compliment, forcing my gaze to retreat back toward the view.

I stood motionless, memorizing the peaks' jagged edges cutting into the blue velvet. Suddenly, Sarah's voice broke my concentration.

"Look! Over there," she said as she pointed to a distant area. "Do you think that's it?"

I immediately turned and looked toward the area she pointed at. It looked like it could be a meadow, but I was unsure. It was hidden under a blanket of boulders that had a touch of green sneaking past them. From our view, it reminded me of the fur from a leopard. It could definitely be the spotted meadow.

"Yes, Sarah, I think you've found it!" Mike exclaimed.

Brody led our party downhill, our pace quickening as we descended. I could feel the thrill and hope radiating off everyone, lifting our moods so high that they competed with the surrounding mountains.

It felt as if the hike down to the meadow took all day. For every step I took forward, the meadow seemed to take three steps back. I had walked for days—my feet made it feel like months—to find this meadow. Nonetheless, I savored this moment, and every step of our current success. Overjoyed and exhausted, we finally made it to the edge of the meadow.

We wandered aimlessly through the boulders, looking around in awe. I tripped once, catching myself on Mike's unexpecting shoulder. He took a staggering step forward and stopped, regaining his balance before he looked back.

"Oops! Sorry, Mike." I grimaced.

He laughed at my clumsiness. "No problem, Brit."

I could hear Sarah giggling behind us.

"I need a water break," Rebecca whined quietly.

Brody nodded in agreement and walked toward the higher-lying land. "Let's rest up there. Hopefully it will give us a better view and we'll be able to see something."

We chose a boulder that was about the size of a minivan to rest on as we eyed the surrounding terrain. The boulders were arranged as if they had been scattered like sprinkles on an ice-cream cone—they had no organizational pattern, yet they were perfect in their disarray. The green grass was now visible, looking almost neon against the drab color of the rock. The velvety blue sky proudly displayed thick and billowy white clouds.

I sat for some time cloud-watching; they transformed before my eyes, making one picture after another and mostly imitating animals. Occasionally the sun would escape from behind the clouds and expose its rays, which temporarily blinded me. Then the clouds would mask them again, allowing the sky to continue on with the cloud parade.

Once again, the rays edged past a bulky cloud disguised as a whale, and I turned my face toward the sun, wanting to soak in as many rays as possible. As I shifted, I accidentally knocked my bag off the front of the boulder and it landed below with a small thud.

"Aw, man . . ." I didn't want to stand up on my poor, aching feet.

Gingerly, I jumped off the backside of the boulder, which was closest to the ground. I walked downhill, following the contour of the boulder, and reached down to retrieve my bag. While in my stooped position, I saw an entrance into the earth.

It wasn't a hole like the one that Alice's white rabbit had jumped into, but rather an oversized slit placed under an enormous boulder. You couldn't see the slit from a standing position because it was well cloaked under the boulder's shadow. But from a crouched position, you could see the sun sneaking under the slit, exposing the shadow's secret.

I tried to be rational and not jump to conclusions, but in my heart it was too late. The entrance! It had to be the entrance leading to the pool. His exact words were "a sliver of hope," and this was definitely a sliver. This discovery validated the pastel man's message and my sanity. The pool was not just a fabrication in the history books.

The Cleansing Pool had to exist—I'd just found the door.

Chapter
T W E L V E

I stared at the sliver for what seemed like an eternity, frozen in surprise and the realization of my discovery. The "sliver of hope" was literally that. The opening wasn't large, especially in comparison to the boulder covering it, but a person could easily fit through it. The sliver lay at an angle, and was wider in the middle due to the slope of the land. It reminded me of a half-shut evil eye, staring at me, glaring, daring me to enter.

This was the door. I didn't know how or why, but there was no doubt in my mind. I felt a pull from this sliver, as if we were destined to meet. I was meant to be here, at this time, and with these people. God had willed these events, and I accepted my role and the surprises that accompanied it. I was thankful, yet nervous, that I'd been chosen for this path.

I was startled when Brody approached from behind, checking on me.

"Brit?" His voice was full of concern and curiosity. He placed his hand on my back and crouched over to make eye contact with me. I quickly shared my disbelief by looking into his eyes and then back at the sliver.

"Brody," I whispered.

He looked down to see what had gained my attention and froze, mirroring my stance.

Before I knew it I was wrapped in Brody's joyous arms, fighting back tears. I gasped for air due to his tight embrace and electrifying touch. We had come such a long way to reach this door within the earth.

A mixture of emotions swirled through me: happiness that we reached the goal, anxiety from the unknown waiting for us, and relief that our trip would get to continue.

I yelled at the rest of our entourage to join us. Rebecca and Mike reached us first, with Sarah trailing closely behind. We all crouched there, speechless and amazed, as if we'd won the lottery. In a sense, we had. We knew the pool existed, thanks to the inadvertent response from the shopkeeper, but finding it, even with directions, was something else entirely. Wishful thinking had turned into factual reality, and my mind was having issues wrapping itself around the possibility of the legend being true.

Sarah stood up and cautiously walked toward the entrance. "Whoa, Brit, I can't believe you found it. Good thing your bag fell."

"Yeah, it's a real coincidence——" I stopped, thinking about my feeling of being drawn to this place. "Or maybe not," I said, letting my voice fade into a whisper. At first I was going to share my feeling, but I was sure they would think I was losing my mind. I decided to keep it to myself.

Sarah turned her head, giving me a suspicious glance, and then resumed her path toward the sliver. I wondered if she had heard me. I joined her, peeking over her shoulder. We paused at the entrance, leery of the unknown.

"I'm going to take a look," Sarah said to me, glancing over her shoulder.

"I'll go with you."

"Don't go far," Brody warned.

"We won't. I just want to see what's on the other side," I said.

Sarah looked back at us, flashed a shaky smile, and took a step inside to get a better view.

"Careful, Sarah," I whispered, as if not to disturb the cave's inhabitants.

Although the boulder was the size of a small camper, it looked strategically positioned. It was as if someone had picked it up and deliberately placed it there, hiding the piece of history hidden underneath. I could imagine how big the opening was without its umbrella of stone——it would have been easily seen, and therefore discovered, making our trip unnecessary. I felt as if this moment had been meant for us.

The boulder was decorated with rays of sunlight. Sarah ducked under its rocky lip and stepped into the shadow that had kept the cavern hidden. I followed closely behind, mimicking her steps. Every surface my hands and feet touched was made of cold, damp stone, and the entrance was so narrow that I could barely extend my elbows out to the sides. However, once we cleared the belly of the boulder, the passageway opened up, widening into a poorly lit corridor.

The path leading into the earth dropped down, causing the ceiling to reach high above our heads. The walls were decorated with linear designs made up of different earth-tone colors, looking like a rainbow. The designs were smooth and precise, as if someone had painted them on.

My curiosity was piqued, so I took a few steps forward. Once I descended through the last hint of light on the rainbow walls, the path took a sharp right turn. This area looked like an entrance into a stereotypical cave, full of darkness and mystery. I shivered and retreated back to Brody to report my findings.

Brody and Mike stood at the entrance, discussing their strategy. They reached into their backpacks and each pulled out a foreign-looking object. It was round with straps matted up in a ball, like dirty laundry on the floor. They unraveled the chaos and strapped the objects onto their heads, over their trusty ball caps. The objects were simple head flashlights, like what you would see on top of a miner's hard hat. I smiled at their competence; I never would've thought to bring something so ingenious. I stood there with an increased sense of security, even more than I usually had when I was with Brody.

Feeling smug, I looked at him and smiled, wondering how I had scored "that guy." He reminded me of the flawless, untouchable boy from high school. I was sure that he still had his faults, although I couldn't seem to think of any offhand. Brody was perfect in so many ways: gorgeous, intelligent, strong, sensitive, and athletic. He was a dream, and I was petrified of waking up.

Mike's voice raced with exhilaration. "Brody will lead, and I'll take up the rear. It's going to be dark, even with the headlamps, so we'll have to take it easy."

Brody nodded in agreement. "All right, are we ready?"

Rebecca sounded characteristically confident and extremely motivated. "Let's go!"

Brody led the way into the rainbow cavern. I followed, with Sarah, Rebecca, and Mike behind me. As we approached the right-hand turn, I paused at the bend, taking a deep breath to steady my nerves. Then I took a step forward into the black shadow. I was leaving one world—one I was familiar with and comfortable in—and entering another. This step forward invigorated me; I wasn't sure if it was the adrenaline weaving through my body or the excitement of finding the pool, but this was the scariest thing I had ever done.

We hiked deeper and deeper into the earth. The headlamps were no match for the blackness—they would give us a slight glimpse of the path ahead. The uneven terrain seemed like it was grabbing at our feet, trying to trip us up. Occasionally, I would use the wall for support, but it was a false sense of security.

I stumbled over a ridge in the path and fell. The stone was cold, which added to the stinging sensation in my hands as they slapped onto the ground. A disgruntled moan escaped. "Dammit."

"Are you okay?" Brody asked from several yards ahead.

I was irritated with myself for being so clumsy. I was *supposed* to be athletic, so it embarrassed me that I was the first to go down.

"Yes, I'm fine," I grumbled.

Blood rushed to my cheeks as I braced for the upcoming attention. "All right, then let's go."

I was taken aback by Brody's response. Admittedly, my parents coddled me by giving unneeded attention to my actions or my health. I appreciated Brody letting me assess my own situation and trusting my judgment.

I stood up and brushed my knees off. I took another deep breath, preparing to refocus my hiking efforts, and almost choked; the air was stale and stagnant. I coughed once to clear my throat and heard Rebecca masking laughter under a cough of her own. It didn't surprise me that Rebecca would find me falling on my face funny.

I threw Rebecca an elbow. Laughter erupted, echoing off the cavern walls. I couldn't help but join in until Mike reprimanded us with a hushing; we instantly silenced—or we at least attempted to. By this time snickering had become a big part of our hiking trip, and our camaraderie made me smile.

We continued on, like baby ducklings following their mother. The pathway's outline was relatively straight, with only a few stray trails along the way. We chose to stay on the main path. Plus, this plan would guarantee a safe exit.

Our group rarely spoke as we made our way through the tunnel, so I thought intensely about our goal and the unknowns at the end of our journey. The Cleansing Pool was our physical goal, our pot of gold at the end of the rainbow. I was hopeful that we would find the pot of gold, but I didn't care as much as I should have. I came to the conclusion that my pot of gold was time with Brody. Each minute I had with him added to my riches, and this trip ensured me days of wealth.

After walking for several hours, we decided to stop for the night. I suspected that we hadn't made it far, even though we'd been hiking for the better part of the day. Our cautious pace on the uneven terrain had slowed our advance.

Ecstatic to give my feet a break, I plopped down. The ground felt damp and cool, with a chill in the air that penetrated me to the bone. I disliked the cold, but the dampness made me feel at home. Sarah and Rebecca joined me without hesitation, but Brody and Mike were more leery as they shined their lights around before sitting. Brody found his way to my side, with Rebecca on my other side. We nestled in tightly, trying to share warmth, while we dined on gorp and rehydrated.

I didn't even bother spreading out my sleeping bag. My body felt heavy and numb. I sat in stillness and exhaustion, leaning on Brody's shoulder. My eyelids followed suit, drooping under their own weight, but I couldn't tell if they were closed. The blackness didn't change regardless of what my eyes did.

I woke to the same darkness, finding shelter in Brody's arms. His embrace kept me warm, protecting me from the chilly dampness of the stone below. Even with the stagnant air, Brody smelled sweet. I was content, happy that I got to wake in his arms—at least for now. When I stirred, he squeezed me tightly.

"Good morning. How did you sleep?"

I returned the embrace. "Actually, not as bad as you would think."

He chuckled.

"How about you?"

"You were in my arms, so I'd say it was a good night."

My breath caught and my heart pounded, making me feel slightly light-headed.

"However . . ." he continued.

My heart stopped. I had been anxiously waiting for a "however" moment. My breath went from staggered to nonexistent as I braced for his news.

"My butt is killing me," he said.

I burst into nervous laughter. I was relieved that his news was not actually news, but this was getting ridiculous. My fear of rejection and losing him was getting out of control. It was almost consuming my every waking thought and restless night. I was afraid when he spoke, and when he did, I often wondered if this was going to be it. He was remarkable, while I was just . . . me.

"Are you hungry? . . . Brit? What are you thinking about?" he inquired.

"Oh, nothing. Hungry? Yeah, starving."

I quickly fished a protein bar out of my bag, and we began our day the same way we had ended yesterday.

After we had eaten our assorted snacks, I reluctantly rose to my feet and lifted my backpack onto my shoulders. "Come on, guys. Let's go."

We walked and walked, making me feel like a hamster in a wheel. Occasionally we would discuss odd smells in the cavern or the foods we missed the most (mine being a combination of olives, cheese, bread, and wine). But mostly we were silent. My mind wandered, and it was surprisingly nice; I felt alone with my thoughts but safe among friends.

We hiked to what seemed to be the middle of the earth. I was constantly hearing noises that didn't transpire into anything. I imagined that this is what it would feel like to be lost in the Sahara, seeing mirages. The hallucinations seemed real, yet I was aware of their lies. This time I could hear a waterfall in the distance, but I couldn't see it. Its thunderous applause teased my body's desire for water: a drink, a bath, or a swim. I could feel its cool, wet mist on my skin and smell its refreshing scent in the air.

"What is that?" Rebecca asked.

Her three simple words broke me out of my trance and brought me back to reality. Was my mirage real?

We turned a corner, and there it was. The waterfall wasn't as colossal as it sounded from the echoes off the cavern walls, but it was beautiful. There was a small flow of water falling out of the adjacent wall through a spout-like opening. Below it was an area of shallow water, three feet deep at best, which accumulated before flowing out through an opening in the back wall. The path continued on past the waterfall.

Oddly, there was a soft pink glow reflecting off the rocks in the cavern. It was coming from an unknown source within the pooled water. After two days of enduring darkness with little headlamps, it seemed as bright as the sun.

"Oh, wow!" Sarah was rarely amazed.

"Come on!" Rebecca shrilled.

I snapped out of my shock and chased after Rebecca, with Brody and Mike following. We took off our packs and threw them in the corner. Then we hurriedly took off our shoes and socks and rushed to the water's edge, jumping in carelessly and soothing our poor feet.

After a joyous celebration in the pink, glowing pool, which ended in a water fight, we decided to make camp. I changed into dry clothes and crawled into my sleeping bag, waiting patiently for my neighbor. He quickly followed, got into his sleeping bag, and then pulled me in close to him.

Nights were my favorite time. It was our alone time; so far it had been dark enough that I couldn't see anyone, feeding my illusion of being alone with him. Even with the glow ruining this fantasy, I cherished the time regardless.

I felt warm and protected, but more so, I felt wanted. Brody would hold me tightly. Sometimes we would talk about random topics, and other times we wouldn't say a word. Nonetheless, I felt comfortable. And like tonight, I would lay next to him, content, until I drifted off into a deep sleep.

I woke early. Although I didn't know what time it was, my body sensed it. I looked around and saw that everyone else was still sleeping soundly. I rose silently and walked to the pool's edge. It, too, looked peaceful.

Relaxed, I sat silently as I studied my surroundings. The pool was oblong and slightly deeper toward the back, where the waterfall fell into it. My gaze moved to the rest of the room. I saw the path we had conquered and the path that lay ahead. The pink pool, as perfect as it was, was not *the pool.*

The Cleansing Pool, so the legend stated, was a single, shallow pool that was gray in the middle with gold around it, like an eclipse. It wasn't a grandiose object to behold; in fact, I would imagine it being like what you would expect when discovering the Holy Grail— simple. Plus, the shopkeeper said it held hot water, and the water in the pink pool was ice cold.

The smooth walls looked polished as they reflected the pink glow of the pool. I looked toward the area where my faux family lay sleeping, tightly grouped in the corner. I felt, for the first time in weeks, complete.

A stirring in the corner disrupted the stillness. I waited to see who might be joining me. It was Brody. I saw his arm move, feeling around the area where my sleeping bag lay. A jolt of satisfaction hit me: he was searching for me. His head popped up and he looked around. Finally, his eyes met mine and a large smile grew across his face. He rose, stretched, and then he weaved his way from the sleeping camp's chaos to me.

"Good morning." He sounded rather taken aback. "I'm shocked you're up this early. How did you sleep?"

I flashed him a reassuring smile. "Great."

He grinned at me and then pulled me into his arms. I sighed with satisfaction. My draw to Brody was so much deeper than superficial lust. Our essence connected and longed to be near each other at all times.

We silently held each other until the rest of the group began to stir. "Everyone's starting to wake up," I said.

He kept me wrapped tightly in his arms. "Okay," he said nonchalantly.

"Do you want to start packing up? Get an early start?"

He pulled away and looked at me.

"I think we should stay for the day and explore. We could all use a day off. What do you think?"

The answer came automatically, without any thought. "I don't care. Whatever makes everyone else happy." Then my words registered, and I scowled. This was a perfect example of how placid I had become, and how I succumbed to everyone else's wants, especially my parents.'

Brody chuckled.

"What?" I demanded.

As if he could hear my reprimanding thoughts, he said, "I don't care what everyone else wants. I want to hear what *you* want."

I appreciated his insight, and smiled. "I would like a day off—a day with you."

He pulled me into his chest and whispered, "Careful, you keep this up and you won't be able to get rid of me."

I hid my face in his chest, trying to conceal my giddiness and the flushing of my cheeks. "I'm not going to get rid of *you* . . ." My words faded away; I couldn't finish my sentence.

Brody pulled me off his chest and looked at me. I couldn't meet his eyes, and my cheeks were still flushed with embarrassment.

"What were you going to say?" It sounded like he was on the brink of irritation.

I looked up at him and bit my lower lip. I couldn't speak. What was I going to say? That my heart was at his mercy and his rejection would break it? I winced at the thought of it.

"You don't think *I* would leave *you*?" he said.

I didn't answer; the depth of his response surprised me.

"Aw, Brit." He shook his head with disapproval. "You're stuck with me, so deal with it."

A huge grin covered my face. He grazed his fingers slowly across my cheek, and my smile faded as desire consumed me. My heart raced and my skin quivered under his touch. He leaned in slowly and froze at the sound of Mike clearing his throat. We simultaneously looked toward our friends, who were trying to appear preoccupied. I laughed in embarrassment. Brody wrapped his arms around my shoulders and pulled me into him. He smiled broadly as Mike walked over. The rest of our group soon joined us.

After breakfast, we decided to leave our backpacks behind and explore the path that continued on past the waterfall. The decision to walk around was unanimous, but we weren't willing to travel far from our newfound riches of water and light. Plus, we knew that tomorrow we would have to continue with our search.

We explored the path for about half an hour and then decided to head back to our belongings and relax, enjoying our day off. As we rounded the last bend, I saw the pink glow highlighting the final leg of the path. The air began to feel thicker and wet—a welcome change from the stale air deeper in the tunnel. We entered the pink cavern and walked toward our camp, located in the far corner next to the pool.

Without warning, it appeared. And it was a sight to behold.

I couldn't breathe. This wasn't like when I'd first started trekking in the higher altitudes and my lungs couldn't pull enough oxygen out of the deprived air. This felt like the oxygen was gone, and a weight was placed on my chest that was so heavy it crushed any remaining hopes of a breath.

I stood frozen at the sight of the approaching haze. It was a wall of dense fog, steadily advancing. Although the enormous gray mass moved slowly, it engulfed everything in its path like a tsunami.

My heart leapt out of my chest and my hands shook in protest as adrenaline pumped through my body. My feet didn't move, however—they were firmly rooted in fear.

Determination overcame the fear. Without thinking, almost as if I were on autopilot, I sprinted to our belongings. I fumbled with my bag, opening the front pocket, and found my small knife. I wasn't going down without a fight, and I sure wasn't going to let anything happen to my friends. I looked up toward the gray haze encroaching and noticed the brilliant contrast in the cavern: pink and gray. The colors looked like two polar opposites colliding in the air.

I had an epiphany.

I screamed the only viable solution. "Run into the water! Run into the water!"

I saw Brody register my words. He began herding the group, and they ran.

Relief came over me for a split second until I heard Brody's panicked voice. "Brit! Run!"

I sprang from my crouch and sprinted toward the pool. I saw my friends in my right peripheral vision as they jumped into the pool. The haze was to my right, and it was alarmingly close. I took one last step, making it to the edge of the pool, but I wasn't fast enough. I was forcibly knocked onto my back.

The haze hit me like a wall of bricks instead of a wall of fog, and I lay there, dazed. I felt numb and disoriented, looking up into the dense fog as it encompassed me. I reached out, trying to ward it off, but it was useless. The haze faded from gray to black as I closed my eyes in defeat.

Chapter

THIRTEEN

*C*ommander Robb listened intently, not showing any emotion. After my explanation, we sat silently. I was worried about Brody and the others, wondering where they were and hoping they were safe.

I tried not to think about their situation in depth. Every time I allowed my thoughts to wander, my fears would take over. I was petrified to lose any of them, especially Brody. Just the thought of him being away from me felt like someone had stabbed me in the heart. Denial was my best defense. I averted my focus onto my faith, and told myself that everything was going to be okay.

"How does the Cleansing Pool work?" I broke the silence, interrupting Commander Robb's thoughts.

"I was told that if you enter the pull completely, you end up in Trate. I am uncertain, but it is a portal of some kind between our worlds."

"Have you ever used it? You know, to go to our world?"

"No. We only have enough power to send one person to travel between worlds. If we send any more than that, it weakens our supplies and leaves us vulnerable."

I was baffled by his answer.

"You see," he paused, trying to simplify the explanation, "a sizable amount of energy is needed to send someone through a pull into different dimensions, and we cannot risk sacrificing that much energy. We have to remain strong enough to protect everyone from the Sohrigs."

A moment passed as I processed the information. Doors started to open deep within my brain.

"These dimensions, is it like string theory?" I was trying to jog my memory on the subject while I spoke. I had taken physics and had touched on the subject lightly.

"I have no knowledge of that theory," he said, a perplexed look on his face.

I spoke slowly, trying to remember what I'd learned. "It's the theory that we live on parallel strings." His puzzled expression didn't waiver, but I pressed on. "Um, planes? Dimensions? And there are millions of strings laying next to one another. And if there are bends in the strings, the adjacent strings intersect, and you can potentially travel to other dimensions—or even through time. Of course, you would need the energy to be able to travel at the speed of light, but it sounds like your world has the capabilities to do it."

His puzzlement dissipated, and he nodded his head in agreement.

I continued. "So, the cavern is a bend or weakness in the strings. The pool must be one too. And if the Cleansing Pool is the portal from our world to Trate, I'll bet the pink pool is a portal leading to *their* base." I gasped. "Brody's a prisoner . . ." my voice faded away, lost in my own internal panic.

My friends were possibly caught in this world, unable to escape and in the hands of the enemy. Alarm struck. "I have to go back and get to the pink pool—I have to find my friends!" I rose quickly. "How do I get out of here?"

Commander Robb grabbed my arm, turning me toward him and almost shaking me. "You don't know if that is another portal, and even if it is, you will join your friends as a captive. Calm down and we will find a solution. Together."

I stood there for a moment, unsure of my next move. I was torn between following my brain and following my heart. I took a deep breath and decided to be rational. I looked back up at him, gave a small smile of comprehension, and sat down on the cot.

My smile faded and tears began to stream down my face as feelings of worry and helplessness crept into my thoughts. Commander Robb sat down beside me, not speaking but waiting patiently for me to exhaust my frustrations. I slowly gathered control of my feelings and began to ponder my next move.

"I'm sorry." I sniffled as I wiped the tears away with the back of my hand. "I still don't understand how I ended up here . . . not using the pool, I mean."

He looked at me with a comforting smile.

"I think you stumbled onto a door—sort of a random hole, or a bend as you called it—that led you here. A small search party had just returned to our camp for the night when you appeared. I believe our movement must have sent ripples through the weakness in your cavern. When you walked through the weakness, or in your case were hit by the weakness, you arrived. Our doors must look like haze in your world. You obviously didn't come through the pull or you would be in Trate right now instead of our camp."

His hypothesis made sense to me—sort of.

"Wait. So this isn't Trate?"

"No. This is just a temporary camp we've constructed to search for the Sohrigs and protect Trate, our homeland." He paused. "What I do not understand is how you obtained the power to get through the door. And how did you find enough of it—"

"—Why did they give us directions to the cavern in the first place? It doesn't make sense."

He looked away briefly.

"I think the Sohrigs sent their traveler to you, hoping you could find the pull and, consequently, our home. They have never been able to find it. I am certain that their traveler has been following you and your friends.

"The Sohrigs approached the Arapahoe people once, but the Arapahoes saw right through their intentions. Little Bear told my father of the incident and said this would be our last meeting, because he did not want to place us in danger. That was our last encounter with him." He sounded livid. "The Sohrigs underestimated the Arapahoes. Perhaps they waited for a few generations to pass, so there would not be any knowledge of them. Once you found the pull, their traveler would tell the others of our location, and a war would be inevitable.

"If the Sohrigs take control over us, they will have free rein of the pull and will be able to control everyone. They will be one step closer to universal domination. That is why this camp is here in the first place; we had a lead on the Sohrigs' location. Regardless, it is our job to protect Trate and its pull, and to locate their base.

"We have never been able to find the location of their base; however, it seems we could put their plan to good use and exploit it, using their tactical maneuvers against them by forcing the location of their base from their traveler." He smirked.

I shook my head. "I still don't understand how they can take over other worlds if they can only send one person through the portal at a time. I would hardly call that a tactical maneuver."

"*They* have the energy to send as many people as they wish through the pull."

The reasoning still seemed sparse. "If they have the energy to send more than one person, why would they care about our land and our measly resources?"

His head snapped up. He gave me a perplexed, almost angry stare, and then looked back down. "They probably want to use your world as a base."

Abruptly, he stood up and started toward the door. "Are you hungry? Would you care to eat?" He grabbed the flap to the door and held it open, motioning for me to follow.

I was confused by the sudden shift in our conversation, but I didn't care. The possibility of a real meal sent my stomach into celebration. I jumped to my feet and trailed after him, passing through the door and only peeking behind me once as the white flap closed.

I followed Commander Robb to the center of the camp and into a large, open tent. The setup reminded me of a summer picnic in the park. There was bustling all around, with most of the commotion located around the food. The faux pavilion was full of tables and people conversing loudly—at least until I walked in. I peered beyond Commander Robb's mass and saw a roomful of curious eyes looking at me. I froze for an instant, but quickly forgot my audience when the smell of food struck me.

The aroma drenched my senses and pierced my stomach; I hadn't eaten a real meal in what felt like weeks. I followed Commander Robb to a table decorated with plates of food. Each plate held a roll and a brown square of something resembling a firm block of tofu. The food looked foreign but smelled delightful. Plus, factoring in my exuberant hunger, I would consume about anything.

Commander Robb picked up two plates of food and led me to a table off to the side of the mess hall. I began to sit down for our meal, but my hunger got the better of me and I snatched the roll from my plate. I shoved half of it into my mouth, only slightly glancing up to address the smirk of disapproval and amusement on his face.

Before he sat down he walked over to another table and grabbed two white cups, then returned to our table. I took another large bite of the roll and washed it down with the water he placed in front of me.

After almost engulfing the entire roll, I paused. "I'm sorry. I'm starving."

"I can see that." His eyebrows lifted.

My cheeks warmed, exposing my embarrassment.

His hearty laughter instantly calmed my humiliation. "Would you like my food? I am not starving."

I shook my head, although his roll did look appealing.

"I have some work I need to take care of. You stay and finish your meal, and I will leave my plate here if you change your mind," he said, flashing a large smile at me. "I will have someone stay with you and escort you back to your tent when you have finished."

I nodded and watched Commander Robb walk gracefully out of the meal area and disappear behind a neighboring tent. I had already accepted his invitation by grabbing the roll off his plate. I looked around as I shoved his roll into my mouth. The rest of the room had watched his exit with interest. His presence was not only authoritative; it was also intimidating. He reminded me of a father figure, offering guidance with a healthy amount of fear.

A movement in my peripheral vision made me jump. I spun around and faced a young soldier. His bright red hair matched his freckles, and they were both a significant contrast to his pale skin. His uniform was the same dull gray that most of the soldiers wore, but it was well pressed and spotless. His face looked as if it were made of stone—cold and unwelcoming. He was obviously not happy to have been put on my detail.

"I have been instructed to escort you back to your tent." His tone mirrored his expression.

"I'm almost done." I spoke over a forkful of mush.

He frowned and turned away. I shrugged a shoulder and turned my attention back to my meal. The mush tasted much better than it looked. It was an interesting combination, tasting like a maple-sweetened rice pudding at first with an aftertaste of whey protein.

I devoured my mush and both rolls and suddenly felt ill. My stomach felt like it could explode, so I decided to walk off some of my gluttony. I glanced over in the redhead's direction; he was immersed in conversation with another soldier. I stood, stretched, and walked out the back of the mess hall, almost positive that I could remember the way back to my tent.

The camp was larger than I expected. The miniature communities were plentiful. Each circle of tents encompassed a campfire, a meeting place filled with laughter and lightheartedness. I enjoyed watching the camaraderie, but it made me miss my friends even more. I longed for our campfire bonding.

I wandered for almost an hour. I enjoyed the smell from the campfires as they filled the air with an aroma of wood and leaves. The green grass had worn flat along the path, snaking through the camp like a stream, but it was lush along the sides. I had missed the green. It surprised me that I could miss something as simple as a color, but its presence instantly calmed my nerves.

Waltzing aimlessly around the camp, I passed numerous rectangular tents. I came across an official-looking one and halted in my tracks, recognizing the voice within.

"You need to control the situation, sir."

"There is no situation," Commander Robb said.

"She's probably a spy and is lying about her knowledge!"

"She does not have any information," Commander Robb said calmly.

"But, sir, what about them? And the pellets?"

"She does not have access to either. She did not even know they existed until today. My theory is that their traveler sent them to find a door."

"I still do not like it. Let me interrogate her; I bet I can get information out of her."

"No, that is not necessary."

"But, sir—"

"I said no," he barked.

There was a moment of silence before Commander Robb continued. "I realize the situation is unnerving, but she is not a threat. In her world, the people are bold about their objectives."

"You know people of her world, sir?"

"I have met one from her world before, yes." He paused. "Regardless, keep an eye on her. Maintain your distance, though—I *do not* want her spooked."

"Yes, sir."

My mind began to race as I quietly strolled away from the tent. Their conversation was clearly about me, but thankfully Commander Robb didn't perceive me as a threat. If he had, my welcome would have been drastically different.

A hand clamped down on my shoulder. Startled, I spun around and saw the redheaded soldier. His face was red with anger, matching his hair.

"It is time for you to go back to your tent," he snapped.

I sheepishly nodded, trying not to smirk at the frazzled soldier who had lost his detail for the past hour. I was thankful that he didn't catch me eavesdropping on Commander Robb—he surely would have told him, and I wouldn't want to see Commander Robb's fury released. Even the few times he'd seemed irritated with me were unnerving. And judging by the other soldiers' caution around him, I suspected that lighting his fuse wasn't hard to do.

I walked quickly, heading back toward my tent. The trip was short and quiet. The redheaded soldier opened the flap and said nothing, but I could feel his relief as I walked past him, making me chuckle.

* * * * *

I had an uneventful afternoon. Sitting motionless in the tent's doorway, I observed as the buzz of the camp passed me by. I tried to relax and enjoy the scenery, but stress emanated off the soldiers, making me feel slightly on edge.

Seeing the sky was a nice treat. Although the sunlight was nonexistent, hiding behind a veil of gray, the sky still felt open and fresh. The dull-green grass was a colorful contrast to the brown-and-pink world of the cave. The view made me homesick, although I couldn't believe I would actually miss the gray of Portland's rainy season.

After several hours the hidden sun fell, dimming the gray into a glowing blackness highlighted only by a sliver of moonlight. I began to feel tired, but knew I wouldn't be able to sleep. With each passing hour, I grew more and more uneasy. I decided I wanted to be alone, isolating myself from the relentless bustle going on around me. I left my post and made my way into the tent.

I paced around trying to quiet myself, but it didn't work. My mind raced, reviewing my options. I had to do something: staying here was a sure path to madness. I wasn't about to sit here, safe and sound, while my friends were going through God knows what. I was going to hunt them down, and then we would escape from this world—together. But how could I get out of here undetected? I needed a plan.

Commander Robb said we were leading the Sohrigs' traveler to the pool because the Sohrigs couldn't locate it themselves. They could give us directions to the entrance, but they couldn't locate the pool itself? It didn't make sense. Directions weren't my forte, but the path seemed pretty cut and dried to me. And how could these groups hide entire cities from each other?

The traveler kept creeping into my thoughts. I wasn't sure, but somehow I knew he was the key. My heart fluttered with hope as a more aggressive plan snuck into my mind. The time had come to take matters into my own hands.

I almost jumped to my feet with exhilaration. A trade! I was going to find Trate, or more specifically, Commander Robb's house, pass through the pool to my world, catch the traveler, and ransom his life for the life of my friends. This was going to be a hostage exchange.

"Brit, may I come in?" Commander Robb's voice boomed through the wall of the tent, making my heart race.

"Of course," I said, trying to sound calm and relaxed.

I was hoping for some answers, and this was my opportunity. I hadn't had enough time to work through my plan completely, so I would have to improvise. But this was it, my chance to get what I needed: directions to Trate.

He opened the tent flap, and once again I gawked at his size. He was enormous, looking even larger than before. His hair disappeared into the blackness of the night sky. His brows were more defined, brought out by the black background, and they overpowered his eyes.

He examined me with concern as he stepped into the tent. "Are you well?"

"I'm thinking about my friends. I'm worried about them. Once we find them, are we all going to be able to go home?"

"Yes, the return is not complicated. Little Bear would leave by walking through the wall in my house; he would just disappear."

"The wall?" I spoke with surprise.

"Yes, in the living quarters."

"Hmm, it must only be a pool in our world," I mumbled.

Commander Robb flashed me an odd expression. "I think we need to find the Sohrigs, and then we will find your friends. After we have captured them, we will proceed back to Trate, you and your friends can exit through the pull, and then you will be home."

"Is Trate far from here?" I asked innocently.

A smirk spread across his face. "It is approximately a ten-day trip, due north." He nonchalantly pointed in a northerly direction.

I tried to sound natural, to test his intentions. "Maybe I should go home first to see if my friends have escaped. They might already be there. I could check the cavern quickly and return if they aren't."

"No!" he barked.

I flinched.

He recovered quickly. He sounded superficial, like he was hiding something from me, and his smile was forced.

"That is what their traveler wants you to do. You could lead him to the pull and ultimately to us. We cannot risk your return. It is better if you stay with us. We will find your friends, I can assure you."

I exhaled a large breath of nerves. I was officially a prisoner, but not for long. Plans on how to save my friends were swirling in my mind. I was going to save them, and no one could hold me back. Commander Robb and his army had been searching for the Sohrigs for a while, but I didn't have time to be patient. I would be more efficient and less detectable alone, so if I had to escape from this camp first, so be it.

I smiled, speaking evenly. "Of course. I was only trying to help." I added a theatrically impressive yawn at the end. "Oh, excuse me."

"You look tired. Try to get some sleep. I will send for you in the morning." He turned his back to me and headed toward the door. "Good night, Brit."

"Good night."

Commander Robb exited the tent. I sat there for a moment and then tiptoed to the front door so I could peek out. I saw a soldier sitting there, unaware of me spying on him. I went back to the cot and sat down.

I waited there tensely for an hour, trying to conjure a plan of attack before I rose again. The camp was next to mountains, which happened to be nestled due north. I had picked up enough survival techniques to last a week, which would get me to Trate. Then I would escape this world through Commander Robb's home (hopefully someone in Trate would point out the way), catch the traveler, and get my friends back. But first, I had to make it to the mountains safely, and running at night was my best shot.

I peered out the front flap and saw the same soldier sitting there, so I decided to try the back of the tent. Grasping the canvas, I pulled hard trying to lift it, but it didn't budge. It was stretched tight and reinforced. Panic began to surface, but I repressed it. I knew if I couldn't get the side of the tent up, I would have to go to plan B, which was to bolt through the front door and run for it.

I grabbed the stool, held it with the round seat against my torso, and tucked the two top legs under the canvas. Using all my body weight, I pushed the stool downward, lifting the canvas and exposing my escape route. I pushed down until the stool was flush with the ground, and then pushed the stool forward until the round seat was all you could see, securing my escape hatch. The hole it created was just big enough for me to skim under.

I walked back up to the front of the tent and peeked at the soldier again. He sat with a relaxed stature, obviously unaware of my imminent escape. As I waited for a couple of minutes to gather my courage, I plotted my most probable route.

I took a deep breath and concluded that the time had come. I slithered on my belly, barely clearing the door I had created. I slowly crept around to the front of the tent, peering at the unsuspecting guard. Nightfall had quieted the camp, calming the buzz and allowing me to execute my plan undisturbed.

Exhaling, I turned to make my way to the edge of the camp. As I turned, I smacked directly into another soldier. Luckily, my force knocked him back and he tripped, falling to the ground. I tore into a sprint.

Although I didn't get the details of the soldier's face, his look of surprise was unmistakable. I ran hard, never looking back. I could hear shouting and footsteps behind me. I ran like my life depended on it—no, like my friends' lives depended on it—and sprinted toward an invisible finish line.

As the edge of the camp grew near, the air began to thicken into a mist. With each step, the mist blocked my view, making my escape a blind getaway. It began to weigh on my chest, making me feel light-headed. I staggered through the fog, tripping occasionally, until I could go no farther. I felt like I had been drugged. I widened my eyes, trying to focus them, but it was useless.

The mist engulfed me, blinding me completely and taking my breath away. I took one last trudging step and fell into blackness.

Chapter

FOURTEEN

"*B*rit? Brit, baby? Come to me, hon." I could feel warmth brushing over my cheek. "Come on, I know you can do it," he begged.

Brody? Yes, it was his voice—an unmistakable voice coming from the heavens. It sounded like silk caressing my ears, sending a jolt through my mind and awakening my senses.

But how? Where was I? He was supposed to be captured, and I was supposed to save him from the enemy. I wanted to show him my dedication and devotion, sacrificing my own safety for him—for all of them. But here he was, sounding concerned for me instead.

I tried to open my eyes, but they refused to respond. Dazed and confused, I tried to sit up, but my body wouldn't budge. Panic momentarily swept over me as I realized I couldn't move or see, but my hearing seemed unaffected.

"Look, Sarah, she moved!" Rebecca shrieked.

Rebecca? Sarah? You're both safe too! My panic instantly turned into cheer as I rejoiced in their presence.

A hint of light began to break through. My eyes were hazy and unfocused, and my head pounded. It felt like déjà vu. Luckily, I knew exactly what to expect this time. I lay there patiently, waiting for my eyes to show me my surroundings, while my friends were happily speaking around me.

Brody's face was finally coming into focus. I reached up slowly and touched his cheek. He gazed at me affectionately and the corners of his lips turned upward. Without warning, he leaned in and kissed me.

"Careful, Brody. She might have a concussion," Rebecca warned, speaking softly.

Brody pulled away. "Can you sit up?"

I paused for only a second. "I think so." With his help, I sat up slowly.

"What happened?" I could hear Sarah's voice breaking through the commotion. I looked up at her and noticed that she was soaked. I glanced around; they were all wet.

"What do you mean what happened?" I questioned. "I went to the other world . . . didn't you?" My bewilderment increased with each passing second. "And how did you guys escape?"

"We didn't go anywhere; we've been here the entire time. We've been busy looking for you." Sarah raised her eyebrows at me. She looked fatigued and stressed.

"Didn't the pink pool take you to the other world?"

Sarah shook her head. "No, but I ruined another change of clothes."

I was more confused than ever. "Where was I?"

Sarah's responded impatiently. "We were hoping you could tell us. That wall of haze came and you disappeared into it. You were gone an hour and then you returned . . . after I had to jump in the pool again to dodge the wall of *whatever*. What happened? Where have you been?"

"I went to a parallel dimension—another world." I smiled at Sarah, ecstatic to see her, regardless of her irritation.

Sarah looked at me with wonder. "No way."

"I know—it's crazy, isn't it?"

I began to explain everything I'd seen. I told them about the camp, Commander William Robb, and the redheaded soldier. I described what their world looked like, which was easy because it looked like Portland in the winter months.

I told them that the pool existed and that it was a portal that led to Trate. I explained what the Sohrigs and their traveler wanted. I talked about Little Bear and how time passed differently there. Lastly, I told them how I had escaped my courteous captors, and I explained my plan to spring them free by capturing the traveler.

"I vote that we stick to your plan," Brody interceded.

"What?" Rebecca and I spoke in unison.

"Everything happens for a reason. I think we've been brought here to stop the Sohrigs and save our world. We have to catch the traveler and send him back where he belongs." He spoke as if he was giving a motivational speech, making eye contact with each of us. He ended with me, gazing deep into my eyes while grasping my hand, pleading to do what was right.

I squeezed his hand in affirmation and then looked toward the remainder of the group. "He's right."

Sarah's face soured. "I think you both have a concussion."

Mike interceded, rebutting Sarah's protest. "We can't just sit here and do nothing."

I turned back to Brody, meeting his eyes. "What did you have in mind?" I asked.

"We need to set a trap." He looked away, staring at the pink, glowing pool.

His eyes narrowed and he turned back toward the group. He began to whisper. "If the traveler is following us, we'll lead him down the bend. When he turns the corner, we'll catch him by surprise. We have more people, and we have knives to protect ourselves. It's the only way to ensure everyone's safety." He smiled at the simplicity of his plan.

We all nodded our heads in agreement. It was settled—we had to protect our world.

* * * * *

Traveling between worlds had taken its toll on my body, and I had to take a nap. It felt as if I hadn't slept in days and had traveled around the world. The combination of exhaustion and the feeling of jet lag were unbearable.

I opened my eyes, feeling refreshed from sleep.

Brody was smiling down at me. He sat near my head and brushed his fingers through my hair. He leaned down and kissed my forehead. I shivered from the warmth of his lips in contrast with the chill of the rocks underneath me.

"Feel better?" he said between kisses.

I nodded enthusiastically.

"Good."

I slowly rose and noticed we were the only two in the cavern. "Where is everyone?"

"They went to find a good spot to trap our friend," he whispered. "I sent them ahead while I stayed behind with you. There's no way I'm letting you out of my sight again." He pulled me into his chest, wrapped his arms around me, and held me tightly.

I leaned into him, taking in his sweet scent. Reaching up, I held his face between my hands, studying his lustrous eyes. He brushed his lips over mine.

Suddenly, his lips pressed into mine. His hands traveled upward, getting lost in my hair. Our bodies sparked with electricity and mine screamed with desire. Our kisses began to turn instinctive.

A strobe of reality flashed: we wouldn't be alone for long, and this moment was leading down a path I wasn't ready to travel. I pushed away, needing space before I imploded. He chuckled before he gently pulled me back in, lightly touching his lips to my forehead. His hands swept my hair out of my face and he touched his forehead to mine, releasing a long, passive sigh.

"Are you hungry?"

"No, not really." I wasn't hungry because I had gorged myself at Commander Robb's camp.

I tucked myself into Brody while we waited for the rest of our party. Being engulfed in Brody's arms made me hope they wouldn't return for hours. Every inch of my body was satisfied.

We sat silently, lost in our own thoughts. Once again, I found myself obsessing about the aftermath of our adventure. What would happen when this was all over? Would I return with my friends to Portland? I didn't think I could. I had to be in his arms forever. Even the thought of being separated from this man made me cringe.

"What are you thinking about?" he asked casually.

Blood flooded my face. "I was thinking about what was going to happen to us when this was all over."

He quickly looked at me and a nervous expression flashed on his face. "And?"

I took a deep breath, ready to spill it all: my desire to be with him, to move to Breckenridge, and to pursue this relationship to the next level. "I think that—"

A faint noise echoing along the rock attracted our attention, instantly silencing the conversation. I waited for my friends' voices to come closer, filled with laughter and lightheartedness. It didn't happen. However, we were not alone—it had to be the traveler.

I pulled my knees into my chest and didn't say a word, afraid my voice would expose my shaky nerves and blow our secret plan. Brody looked down at me and squeezed me tighter. We continued in our silence, knowing that we would revisit our conversation, and waited.

It was Rebecca's voice that traveled to us first. She was carrying on, laughing and impersonating someone.

"Very funny." Sarah sounded like she was moping.

The voices grew nearer until I saw them all round the bend.

"Brit, you should have seen it. Sarah was leading our group and went down a new tunnel, not the main path. The tunnel didn't go very far until it opened into a little room. She slipped on something, face-first of course, and landed on a poop mound—bats, I think!" Laughter seeped through her words, increasing as the story continued. Rebecca found this even funnier than I did; she was almost in hysterics.

I looked over at Sarah, who was already at the pool's edge washing off what looked like dirt. I giggled at the thought of her being engulfed in bat poop. Sarah was far too prissy to be involved in anything dealing with feces. She left that to the rest of us peons. Even at work, the rest of us would be covered in unmentionables and Sarah would walk out looking perfect, without even a spot.

The profession Sarah had chosen seemed like an odd one until you knew her. She was compassionate and stood up for those who couldn't stand up for themselves. Sarah was usually sent into a room to deal with the clients. She educated them, basically steering them in the direction of her choice. After the clients were done gawking at her, they followed her recommendations like a religion.

Rebecca was the complete opposite of Sarah; she was a magnet for anything dirty. She was always the first one on the scene, and with Rebecca, the more gruesome the better. She loved the hands-on, adrenaline-rush scenarios: pumping a dog's heart with its chest wide open, holding in a cat's innards after a car accident so it wouldn't bleed out, or any other flat-line scenario was her idea of enjoyment. Rebecca's downfall was the client—she didn't like to deal with any human unless she chose to do so. Dealing with clients was her idea of torture.

Today, Rebecca was the clean one for once, and the irony of the situation was the funniest part of all.

After we'd had a good laugh at Sarah's expense, we resumed with the matter at hand. The group had found a promising ambush site not far from our current location.

Rebecca stated loudly, "Come on, Brit and Brody. I think we found a tunnel that leads to the Cleansing Pool." We left our sleeping gear behind, only grabbing our daypacks and headlamps, and began toward the faux pool. I followed, trailing behind a bit, with Brody by my side. I still felt tired and a little woozy from my trip.

We walked along the main path until we came to a three-way split. Our current path was the largest, and it continued straight. The path veering left was the smallest, and the path that cut to the right was somewhere in between. We turned right and walked for a long way. The path dropped down, almost as if there were a small flight of stairs, and rounded a corner into a small opening. The opening was filled with crevices and boulders—plenty of hiding places for an ambush.

Everyone found a hiding spot except Sarah and me. We were to continue down the tunnel and talk naturally so the traveler would be lured into the trap.

I fought their decision to turn me into bait because I wasn't one to avoid the action. I wanted to be a part of the team and help where I could, not just hear the excitement from afar. But between my earlier adventures and still feeling a bit unsteady, Brody made it clear that he had worried about me enough for one day.

I appreciated his protective stance. I always played the role of the levelheaded protector, doing what was needed to keep everyone happy and safe. To relinquish the role to him was welcoming, so I didn't put up too much of a struggle.

Brody's eyes met mine. I could feel the anxiety building up inside me. I tried to put on a strong front, but I was terrified. The thought of Brody challenging the traveler, who was armed with unknown weapons and skills, made me tremble. I hated the thought of him in any type of danger. Although the odds were definitely in our favor, my luck had been good—too good—and I was scared it was going to run out.

He cupped his hand under my chin and grinned. It was if he could hear my thoughts. "Don't worry about me. Everything will be fine," he whispered.

I frowned. He sounded a little too confident to me.

His grin widened into a smile. "I promise."

The corners of my mouth turned up. This faint smile was the best I could give him under the circumstances. He leaned down and gently pressed his lips to mine.

"Please be careful," I begged.

"I will. Quit worrying," he said softly.

"Ready?" Sarah asked hesitantly.

I nodded once before Sarah and I headed down the tunnel. I was nervous for the ambush party, but Sarah babbled on about the last time she'd watched MTV, trying to distract me. It worked; I felt better with every tidbit she educated me on. She started many conversations this way: "This one time on MTV, I saw . . ." I giggled at her, feeling composed for the moment.

We walked for about ten minutes and sat down, still discussing topics we'd seen on MTV. We tried to decrease the volume of our voice over a period of time, as if we were walking away from the ambush room. Finally, we were silent, sitting and waiting.

After what felt like an eternity of silence, we heard it. Mike urgently yelled commands, there was a commotion that sounded like a struggle, and then . . . nothing.

Chapter

FIFTEEN

*M*y heart pounded with distress. I sprang to my feet and ran, sprinting to see the outcome.

"Brit!" Sarah yelled from behind me, but I couldn't wait for her.

As I grew near, I could hear Rebecca speaking sharply. "Sit there and don't move."

My anxiety instantly started to settle. I turned the last corner and saw a flashlight beam along the wall before I entered into the room where the ambush had taken place. My heart rejoiced at the sight of Brody, who didn't appear to have a single scratch on him. Fueled with relief, I hurried across the room, threw my arms around him, and kissed him fiercely.

He broke away. "It's been a rough one today, hasn't it?"

I nodded. The emotional burden of the day was finally taking its toll. Brody wasn't the only one who'd had a day full of worrying. I could feel my eyes beginning to well up with tears. I blew out a breath to steady myself. I wasn't going to cry.

He looked at me with concern at first and then began to chuckle under his breath. "I told you everything was going to be fine," he said sweetly. It seemed as if he was enjoying my emotional fiasco.

I let out a small sigh of relief and broke out in a faint smile as he brushed his fingers over my cheek.

Finally, Sarah entered the room and stopped next to Rebecca and Mike. They, too, looked untouched and had triumphant smiles plastered on their faces. The traveler was sitting quietly on the floor in front of them.

I looked down at the traveler, and his expression took me by surprise. He didn't seem frightened at all. He was calm—almost too calm, as if he'd expected this. I was puzzled. As I studied him, his eyes met my scrutinizing gaze.

He hadn't changed a bit since the last time we had met. His outfit was exactly the same. He was smothered in pastels, looking perfectly put together. His clothes didn't even have a wrinkle. His skin was pale and flawless, highlighting his rosy cheeks and vivid blue eyes. I was surprised I hadn't noticed them before.

It was time to find out some answers, and apparently Brody was thinking the same thing. Brody released me and slowly approached the traveler, eventually crouching down next to him. I could hear Mike protesting under his breath, wanting to take a more aggressive approach by forcing answers out of him instead. Mike had probably seen one too many "tough cop" movies. Brody ignored him and continued.

"What's your name?" Brody began, speaking softly and calmly.

The traveler looked at him blankly without answering.

"Do you understand me?" Brody was a patient man and would sit all day if need be.

Mike interceded. "We know about your plan, and it's not going to work. We won't let you take over. This is our world!"

Rebecca grabbed Mike's arm and he instantly calmed down. Although they were a quiet couple, they seemed deeply connected. I could see the electricity between them and the craving in their eyes when they looked at each other. Rebecca floated when Mike was around.

Brody glowered at Mike before he looked back over to the traveler, attempting to continue with his interrogation. He was interrupted again.

"What do you mean *take over*?" the traveler said curtly, clearly disgusted by the accusation. "That is exactly what *we* are trying to prevent." His face was stern.

"We were told by a reliable source that your people want to take over our world—our land, our resources—and that you even want to enslave our people," I said, trying to suppress my suspicion and resentment.

The traveler began to laugh. I could hardly see humor in the situation.

"What's so funny?" I snarled.

The traveler looked at me, took a deep breath, and began to explain.

"My feeling is that William Robb was your 'reliable source.' That lunatic would do anything for revenge, and that is why we have to stop him. The only problem is that we cannot find his camp." He scowled.

I took over the conversation. Commander Robb had been nice to me, even though he wouldn't let me go. Clearly, his story had several holes in it. And since I was the one who had dealt directly with him, I was determined to get to the bottom of this.

"According to him, the Sohrigs are the 'lunatics,' and—"

The traveler's laughter interrupted me mid-sentence. He shook his head, and his face grew solemn.

"William Robb *is* a Sohrig," he said. "That is the name of our people. We are peaceful and do not intervene in the affairs of other worlds. Robb disowned his kind when his father was told to choose between our world and yours."

"Little Bear!" I gasped.

"That's right," he said, nodding approvingly. "Little Bear stumbled onto the pull and found the portal into our world. He fell in love with a Sohrig woman. She became pregnant and had a baby, William 'Smiling Bear' Robb. Our officials found out about the union and demanded that Little Bear make a choice between worlds. They did not want our world to exert any other influences on yours.

"Little Bear was a great chief in your world, which made our officials nervous. He made his choice, not wanting to desert his people during the hostile takeover by the white people in your world. He was killed at a peace treaty meeting, and Robb never recovered. He feels that the Sohrigs should have intervened to help him, but our people try to remain universally neutral. We stay out of the affairs of neighboring worlds, regardless of their current status."

My mouth fell open. The holes in Commander Robb's story were filled in nicely . . . except for one.

"But why can't you find each other's camps?"

The traveler shook his head.

"Robb is looking for one of our energy units, not our camps. We do not have camps, only cities and villages like yours. You see, our world is well beyond yours in regards to energy. We have an abundance of resources, so there are no wars over them. We have developed a technique to compartmentalize energy, or power, into pellet form. We keep these power pellets stored in units, which we now have to keep hidden, thanks to Robb."

Pellets—suddenly the conversation I'd overheard while exploring the camp popped into my head. I could distinctly remember the other soldier in the tent asking Commander Robb about pellets.

He continued, "Robb desires access to the power pellets. If he is successful in finding them, he will have the energy he needs to travel back in time and warn the native people of their bleak future. This would change your world's entire history. We *cannot* let that happen. It is not our way. His actions would throw your world onto a different path, obliterating your current lifestyle." He looked around, making eye contact with each of us as if he were pleading his case to a jury.

"If you are so advanced, then why can't you find this guy?" Mike asked tersely.

The traveler nodded his head. "As I said before, we are peaceful. We have no need for armies. We have a small handful of monitors, which are similar to the police in your world. They are looking for him and his followers, but he is always moving. We have not been able to find his camp."

"So where do we come in?" Brody asked.

"Robb had a connection with this world. The Sohrigs thought that by sending someone—me—to your world, we could find a back door into his camp. I would let the monitors know of his whereabouts, and they could detain him and his followers. That is why I came to you."

The pieces still didn't add up. "So you aren't looking for the Cleansing Pool?"

A look of bafflement flickered on his face before he answered. "Of course not. That is how I traveled here in the first place."

"But Commander Robb said if we led you to the pool, you would find them and it would cause a war."

The traveler looked aghast. "The pull leads to Trate, one of our cities. Commander Robb and his followers do not live there anymore. They are a rebel group of nomads, always on the move, and that is the reason we are having trouble locating them. Commander Robb is dangerous. If he succeeds with his plan, it would alter your world drastically, violating our neutral universal stance and beliefs. He must be stopped."

We all stood quietly with the same wide-eyed expression, trying to absorb and process all of this information.

Nausea swept over me, and I sat down. Brody quickly looked over at me, trying to assess my condition while keeping an eye on the traveler.

"I almost helped him," I said. "He would have ruined everything—destroyed us all. We won't exist if he succeeds. We have to stop him, Brody." Panic flashed across my face.

Brody glared at the traveler. "How do we know you're telling the truth?" he demanded. "How do we know you aren't the one who wants to change our world?" He stood up, stepping between the traveler and me.

I reached my hand out, grasping Brody's leg. "Commander Robb looked Native American: he had dark eyes and skin, black, straight hair, high cheekbones, and a strong jawline. Plus, I overheard Commander Robb talking about them"—I nodded my head in the traveler's direction—"with another soldier. They were discussing pellets, and whether or not I had access to any. He didn't have any intention of letting me go, and he was angry—incredibly angry—when he spoke of Little Bear's last visit." I shuddered at his fury.

My conversation with Commander Robb flashed into my head. I could see anger and sadness in his eyes as he explained his version of the story to me. In retrospect, it was obvious that Little Bear was his father.

"I think the traveler's telling the truth," I said softly.

Sarah spoke up for the first time. "But why did you give *us* the directions here?" she asked the traveler.

"I needed to find someone who had a passion about Native American legends, enough to go on the trip in the first place, and who knew the area well enough to find the cavern."

He pondered his next words, speaking carefully. "I went into the future looking for an expert on Native American legends who lived in this area." He looked directly at Brody.

Brody's eyebrows furrowed. "I'm hardly an expert." Although he argued the point, a small smile appeared on his face.

"Not yet, but you're well on your way. I knew that if I approached you directly, you would think I was a fool." A sly smile grew on his lips. "So I planted the seed in someone you would listen to. And as for why—I need you here to show me the door. I can only see pulls, not foreign doors." He could see our confusion growing.

"Pulls are stable passes through worlds," he continued. "We have studied them extensively, and we have most of them mapped out. A door is a randomly created passageway from one world into another. I knew there was a possible door in this cavern from our textbooks, but doors created in another world can only be created and recognized by someone from that world."

Rebecca joined the conversation. "So you can't see the haze?"

The traveler grinned. "Yes, of course I can. However, no one is aware of how a door will present itself until it is discovered. Doors manifest differently in each world. Plus, they will not appear without the ionic pull from local beings."

It was hard for me to focus on the traveler's explanation; I was still obsessing that the traveler had linked me to Brody—future Brody. My heart and mind began to race. How far into the future did he go? A month? A year? Ten years?

It seemed that Brody was thrilled with the information as well. He grabbed me, pulling me to my feet, and whispered into my ear. "I told you I wasn't going to let you go. You're stuck with me for good."

My heart raced and felt as if it could leap right out of my chest. I pulled in a jagged breath. "Perfect."

Brody chuckled and kissed my forehead before he walked over to the traveler and extended his hand to him. The traveler put his hand out apprehensively, and Brody helped him up.

"I'm sorry if we hurt you," Brody said.

The traveler shook his head. "I was not hurt."

"What do we do now?" Rebecca asked, still holding on tightly to Mike's arm.

We all turned and looked at the traveler.

"I am open to suggestions," he said.

Chapter

S I X T E E N

With Sarah leading the way, we rounded the final corner and entered the pink room. I unloaded my bag from my shoulders and placed it where it had spent the last day. I sat down and relaxed, curling into Brody's side.

Enjoying the company and the distraction, we conversed lightly. We touched on a few random topics, such as food and vacation spots. The traveler was a pleasant addition to our group, and he was knowledgeable on many travel destinations. He didn't care for our food, stating that it had "too much sugar and sodium." This made me giggle, because the Sohrigs' mush blocks were not my idea of a culinary masterpiece.

Everyone sat motionless and looked exhausted as they unwound from our adrenaline-filled evening. Tomorrow would prove to be another taxing day, what with trying to stop Commander Robb and save our world and all.

My fatigue grew stronger, overcoming me. I tried to keep my eyes open, only allowing one to close at a time. My head began to feel heavy, swaying, finding solace on Brody's shoulder. I felt content and safe as he leaned in and kissed my forehead. Finally, I succumbed to my exhaustion.

My eyes opened and I looked up at Brody's perfect face. He was leaning against the cavern wall with his arm around me, and to my surprise, he was awake. I rose up from his shoulder, looking into his cheerful eyes.

"What time is it?" I felt slightly disoriented.

"It's early. Everyone is still sleeping, and—"

"—Why are you awake?"

He flashed a grin at me. "I had trouble sleeping. So I thought I would keep watch."

I reciprocated with a smile, again appreciating his protective role.

I had never felt more content than in this moment: wrapped in the arms of the man I loved, feeling safe and wanted and adored. Add in the fact that I was surrounded by friends and it was as if I were in a bubble, untouchable by the outside world. This moment was perfect.

I looked at Brody and spoke without thinking. "I love this."

"Oh?" His eyebrows rose.

My face heated. I was glad the cavern was dimly lit with a pink hue, because it masked my reddened face. I instantly felt juvenile. "Are you going to make me spell it out for you?"

He sat silently, patiently waiting for me to respond. A slight smile teased his lips.

I wanted to blurt out that he was the most magnificent man alive, and that I was putty in his arms. His smell, his body, his sense of humor, his smile, and his strong hands all made me weak in the knees. I wanted to be with him—forever.

"This entire trip has been amazing, and you, well . . ." I paused, trying to build up the courage to tell him how I felt.

Before I could finish, he leaned forward and kissed me lightly on the lips. "You are the amazing one." He kissed me again. "And I love you."

"Me too," I whispered intimately in his ear. It wasn't what I wanted to say, but I was overcome with emotion. I wrapped my arms around him, smiling with satisfaction, and squeezed. I could feel the contours of his well-defined chest under his shirt, and the thrumming of his heart.

He pulled me in even tighter and stroked my hair. I had trouble catching my breath, unsure if it was due to his embrace or the fact that he had just declared his love for me.

He loved me. *He* loved *me*, and we had a future together. I almost pinched myself to make sure I wasn't dreaming.

We stayed engulfed in each other's arms. I heard the others begin to stir, but Brody wouldn't let go of me. I melted into him willingly.

Brody's body suddenly stiffened and I released him, having to push away slightly to see why. The traveler had woken up. Brody still seemed leery of him and looked faintly on edge. I leaned back into Brody. I had planned on keeping my own watchful eye on the traveler, just in case.

The traveler stood up, stretched, and walked over to join Sarah at the pool's edge.

"Why does it glow pink?" she asked.

He smiled at her. "It is due to the crystals in the rocks. They react with the water, producing a harmless gas that gives off the iridescent glow."

"Excellent." She smiled back at him, satisfied that the mystery had been solved. He seemed happy to comply.

Everyone was awake now. We sat in the same formation as the previous night, talking and dining on the last of my almonds. Our conversation focused on our plan to capture Commander Robb.

"We have to find the way back to their camp," the traveler said.

I reassured him. "When their camp moves locations, it creates a door in our world—the haze. We have to be patient and wait for them to relocate. Then we can enter your world . . ."

I faded off, suddenly perplexed by an unforeseen complication. "What about the blackout?" I looked up, meeting the traveler's eyes. "Both times I moved between worlds, I passed out and it took a while for me to recover. If we enter his camp, we're sitting ducks."

Everyone sat quietly, waiting anxiously for his answer. "I'll go—" he started.

"No!" Brody and Mike said in unison.

The traveler flinched at their tone and spoke quickly. "I am not going to *do* anything. I am far outnumbered. I will get a read on their location and come right back. Then I will go home through the pull—the Cleansing Pool as you call it—and report their location."

Fear flashed through my mind. "What if they follow you back?"

The traveler looked at me. "I already told you, they do not have the power to travel between worlds."

Rebecca looked at him with a frown. "How did Brit travel between worlds then? We don't have a power source either." She sounded skeptical.

He shook his head. "I am uncertain of the mechanics, but my presumption is that the door catapulted her into my world; therefore, Brit did not need power." He paused for a moment, contemplating before he spoke again. "I think it is a one-way entrance and exit—like a revolving door for your world, and your world alone. They would have to go through the pull, and the pull leading here is located in a major city."

"Trate," I added.

"Yes, that is correct. I do not believe they would attempt that route."

He turned toward me. "Whenever a person travels—except for a traveler—they need recovery time, and that was why you felt so ill, Brit. You do not belong in our world. The ionic pull of your body is made for your world, making your attraction to this world great—like a magnet. When you are pulled apart from your world, your body protests."

Rebecca looked at the traveler, sighed, and shook her head. "Okay, let me get this straight: the pool always opens a pathway between our worlds, without any issues."

The traveler nodded. "But only for a traveler. If you are not a traveler, you will need power, and you will have to recover. The pull's recovery should be less severe than that of a door's, however."

Rebecca continued. "The haze—or door as you call it—appears at random. So it tears you from this world and drops you into your world?"

The traveler nodded again. "The door in *this cavern* goes to my world. There are other doors, but I do not know where they appear, or where they lead."

"But you won't feel sick or black out either way because you're a traveler, right? Anything I'm missing?"

The traveler grinned as he answered. "I'm not sure. You see, I have never actually traveled through a door—but even so, I think it will be routine. Normally I travel only through pulls."

"Why don't you have to recover? What makes you different?" Sarah inquired.

"Remember when I was talking about magnets and ions?" He paused for us to respond with a nod. "Well, travelers do not have an ionic connection with their world. I do not need power to travel, as long as I use a pull. And because I am a traveler, I do not encounter the same side effects as a typical person."

One thing still puzzled me. "So a traveler is a profession and not your name, correct?"

He laughed and nodded his head.

"What's your name then?" Rebecca asked.

"James. James Edwin."

Mike sounded skeptical. "Exactly how many travelers are there?" he asked as he rose to his feet and walked away from the group. I assumed that nature was calling.

James smiled, speaking loudly enough for Mike to hear. "There are only a handful of us throughout the entire universe. One out of several trillion, maybe. We are incredibly rare."

My mind flashed back to Commander Robb. "Little Bear must have been a traveler then. That's why he could travel between worlds?"

"Yes." James beamed. "Travelers can be from any world."

"How did Little Bear—" I looked up and froze mid-sentence. Mike was returning from the shadows, walking toward us, unaware of the large wall of haze approaching behind him.

I wanted to scream, but I couldn't find my voice. Mike had no chance; the haze had caught him by surprise. The haze was inches from his shoulder, ready to smother his frozen body, which was rooted firmly in fear.

I winced when I heard Rebecca's single word, "No!"

I couldn't let Rebecca suffer. I reflexively stepped toward Mike; I knew I could talk Commander Robb into sparing him. We had spent time together and he trusted me . . . At least I think he did before I sprang free from the camp. Regardless, I had to do *something*.

Just as I took a step toward Mike, a hand grasped my arm and pulled me down, hard. I sat stunned for a moment and turned toward the offender, ready to lash out. To my surprise, it was James.

He looked at me. "No—stop. Look."

I flung my head around. I could see the cavern, the pool, the haze, and . . . Mike?

I was baffled. Mike walked toward us, tiptoeing through the last bit of the haze. His shoulders were hunched and his eyes were constantly moving, glancing at us every second or so. He emerged through the haze unscathed, and still in this world.

I looked at Mike and then back at James, who was still holding my arm. He had an astonished expression.

"What does that mean?" I choked out.

Still looking shocked, James said, "This can mean only one thing. You are a traveler."

His face turned blank, lost in thought. "This changes everything. I cannot pass through the door—I will get caught, just like you. Our great plan turned out to be not so great." He sounded defeated.

We all stood silently, waiting for the haze to pass and allowing our emotions to settle.

My mind raced. *A traveler . . . incredibly rare.* I was among the privileged few who could travel through worlds. I blushed at the thought of it. Brit: one in a trillion.

I instantly felt my confidence grow. This knowledge gave me the assurance to step forward. I always felt I was meant for leadership, but always succumbed to others' wishes. Now I had a higher purpose and the credentials to act on it.

I broke the silence. "I have a plan B," I said. "I could go back, gain Commander Robb's trust, and then lead him to your monitors— an ambush."

I flinched slightly with embarrassment as I looked at James. His brows rose with interest; he didn't seem fazed by yesterday's ambush on him. "I could tell Robb I know where you are, and lead him to the ambush party."

"No," Brody protested. "Robb will know it's a trap. There's no way he'll buy your story. Robb doesn't sound like an idiot, and he would have to be a gullible idiot to fall for that. It's way too dangerous." Brody looked deep into my eyes with a stern and unwavering expression.

Sarah sided with Brody. "I agree. It's too dangerous, Brit. There has to be another way. Your parents would kill me and Rebecca if anything happened to you."

My parents. I had totally forgotten about my home and my work. It had to be close to our expected return deadline, but I couldn't think of that now. I had to stop Commander Robb. I had to save our world from his plan. I had to save my parents, my friends, and my future with Brody.

"I'll be fine, I promise," I said. "But we'd better hurry; I would prefer to reach him before he gets to the mountains. I think finding his camp in the mountains will be too difficult."

"Mountains?" James stuttered with surprise. A smirk crossed his face. "There is only one small mountain range in our world, and it is conveniently located near Trate. This information narrows our search exponentially."

Confusion struck. "I was told that Trate was a ten-day hike, straight north from the camp's location."

James' face turned sour, yet slightly amused. "No, Trate is only a day's hike from the edge of the mountains. And even from the farthest point within the mountain range itself, it is only a five-day trek."

I mumbled, "I knew I couldn't trust him."

"Do you remember anything else about the landscape?" James asked animatedly.

"Sure," I answered. "Everything." I had sat there for several hours while the soldiers prepared for a "back-door" attack, giving me plenty of time to memorize the landscape.

I remembered the three highest peaks. Compared to Colorado's mountains, they would be considered hills. A stream snaked along their base, getting lost in the rolling hills that stretched out as far as I could see. In the other direction, there was a bluff; its odd arrangement of boulders looked like a face laughing. The landscape was full of green vegetation, but unlike Colorado, it was treeless.

James looked at Brody for a moment and then spoke. "Okay, I have an idea: Brit and I will go through the pull to Trate, and then Brit can lead our monitors to Robb."

Mike joined the deliberation. "Brit, are you *sure* you remember what the location looked like?" he asked.

I nodded. "I know I can find the camp if James takes me to the mountains."

James continued. "This might work, and it is the safest plan. No one will touch Brit—I promise." He looked at each member in our group as he pitched his plan. There were no more rebuttals.

"It's settled then. Let's go!" I said, bounding to my feet and grabbing my bag from the cavern floor. "Where's the Cleansing Pool?" I couldn't wait to see it.

Brody shook his head. "I don't know. I still don't like it, Brit."

I smiled at Brody as I offered him my hand to help him up. "Brody, it was your idea to help in the first place. We have to do something to stop Commander Robb."

A sigh broke through his lips as he grasped my hand and rose from the floor. "Fine, but I still don't like it," he grumbled.

James was already on his feet. "This way."

Everyone hurriedly reached for their bags, wanting to be prepared. James interceded. "You will not need those. The pull is not far."

I looked at James, shrugged, and dropped my bag in its usual spot in the corner. With an anxious smile pasted across my face, I waited for Brody as he returned his bag. He tossed the bag to the floor and paused, as if contemplating our decision, and then walked back to me. He took my hand and gripped it. Although his expression was emotionless, I could tell he was conflicted.

I, however, was completely resolved in our decision. I was going to stop Commander Robb and save our world. It was all too surreal for me to be nervous.

We followed James as he led us back to the split in the path and took the narrow left fork. He was obviously familiar with the cavern, which meant that he knew we were going the wrong way earlier, but he'd still walked into our trap. *Why would he do that?* I asked myself. Keeping an eye on us, most likely.

We followed him through the passage, which snaked around and then abruptly ended. I was confused. James walked up to the wall, bent down, and felt along it. He flashed a quick smile at us and disappeared through a large hole. Cloaked in darkness, it was well concealed.

Mike was the first to follow James, with Rebecca and Sarah close behind. I was next to crawl through the passage. As I took my approaching step, Brody pulled me by the hand, making me turn toward him. He brushed his free hand through my hair and brought his forehead to mine.

"Brit, babe, you don't have to do this," he whispered.

"Yes I do. I have to stop him, Brody. I can do this," I said, pleading for his approval.

He was silent for a moment, and then he leaned in and kissed me. His lips were full of passion, intensity, and urgency. He pulled away slowly. "You're right, you can do this. Let's go."

We continued for a few yards, crouching as we passed through the hole, until it opened into another large channel. James waited for everyone to catch up and then continued on. He led us for about five more minutes until he turned the corner and the passage opened up into another room. This chamber was large, and it held a shallow pool in the far corner.

I smiled. We would've never found this pool on our own. Both the Cleansing Pool and the moment were beautiful. I stood in awe for only a second before I approached the pool. It looked like a kiddie pool, shallow and perfectly clear, and it had a faint golden glow to it. My friends soon joined me, gathering at the edge of the pool.

"We should go," James said. "We need to hurry." He spoke calmly, as if trying to respect our moment.

"Okay then, let's go." I took a deep breath to steady myself. *Here goes nothing*, I thought, and then stepped into the water.

Nothing happened.

I looked down at the surprisingly warm water and then over at James.

"What are you doing? The pull is over here," he said, looking perplexed.

I looked over at the wall next to James and saw a slight golden glow emanating from the rocks.

James broke into laughter, filling the room. I could feel the blood rushing to my face.

"The portals are called pulls, spelled p u l l s. As in they *pull* you through worlds." He laughed again. "This pool—spelled p o o l, or the Cleansing Pool as the Arapahoes called it—does not have a function other than as a ceremonial hot springs. I believe that is how Little Bear found the pull to begin with. He must have been visiting the Cleansing Pool and saw the pull." He motioned toward the glowing wall.

I looked down at the water. Now that the pull had been pointed out, I could see that the pool was simply reflecting its light. I joined in with his laughter, feeling ridiculous standing in the shallow pool.

"Oops," I said, giggling. I stepped out of the pool and walked toward the pull.

James looked at me with a large, amused smile, and shook his head before he turned to Brody. "Ready?"

Brody's eyes widened with disbelief. "Who, me?"

James pulled an object from his pocket. It was small, the size of a jellybean, and dull gray.

He held it out to Brody. "Here, eat it. This should be enough power to transport you through the pull."

We all stood looking at Brody's stunned face. The prospect of having him by my side was thrilling, and comforting. I didn't know James well, and having a member from my group eased my mind.

Brody stood speechless for a moment before he glanced at me. The look of relief on my face was unmistakable. Without a word, he snatched up the power pellet and popped it into his mouth.

"Well?" Mike sounded skeptical. "How do you feel?"

He shrugged his shoulders. "I feel fine."

"We must go. The time has come," James said. He stretched out his hand and waited for me to grab hold. I reached for Brody's hand first, looking back at my friends and offering a reassuring smile. Then I turned back around and grasped James' hand.

The last thing I heard was Rebecca saying, "Be careful," as I stepped through the glowing door of rock.

Chapter

SEVENTEEN

The room was magnificent. It was light and refreshing and the complete opposite of the drab, gray sky. The front door was propped open, exposing the street. The room was large and open, and had no furniture. An exquisite, cream-colored, marble-like material lined the floor; it was smooth and polished to a reflective shine.

The walls were also cream-colored but they had a matte finish, allowing the floor to be the focal point of the room. The floor seemed to glimmer from the light of the pull, which was located on the wall behind us. The room smelled pleasant, reminding me of pumpkin pie—my favorite fall scent. I shut my eyes and inhaled deeply.

Wait. My eyes popped open. Brody wasn't holding my hand anymore. My heart skipped, and as I scanned the room I saw James hunched over Brody's body. My eyes widened in horror.

Reading my expression, James said, "Do not worry. With the amount of energy I gave him, he will recover quickly."

At that same instant, Brody moaned. I ran to his side and dropped onto my knees. His face was a pale, chalky color. I felt helpless. There was nothing I could do but sit there and wait for him as he made his way back to consciousness. I had been there twice before and only time seemed to help. I felt sorry for putting everyone else through this similar stress.

He moaned again and started to blink, trying to break through the fog. "Brit? Oh, my head."

"I'm here, Brody. You're okay. Give your eyes a minute and they'll clear up. Take your time and try not to move. It makes it worse—trust me."

I flashed back to my first experience with jumping worlds, when Commander Robb had to catch me after I moved too quickly. The thought of it made my stomach churn. I was thankful we had traveled through a pull this time so I didn't have to recover like Brody.

Only a few minutes passed before Brody recovered. I knew how bad it felt, and I was glad I was a traveler. James and I helped Brody to his feet once his eyesight returned. I also felt a little woozy, but it was nothing compared to Brody; I was positive of that.

Once Brody felt well enough to continue, James stepped forward and motioned at us to follow him. "This way," he said as he walked toward the door. Hand in hand, we followed him readily. I was eager to embark on our mission.

Suddenly, James froze. I ran squarely into him, almost knocking both of us over. Brody pulled my hand back and stabilized me as we both looked up to see why James had stopped so abruptly.

Three figures were standing in the doorway, cloaked by the door's shadow.

James took a step back, and the figures came closer. As we slowly retreated, the figures exited the shadows and stepped into the light. My heart pounded so hard that I could feel my pulse in my head, and my hands began to shake from the amount of adrenaline pumping through my body.

I glanced over at Brody. "Commander Robb," I whispered.

Commander Robb was accompanied by two of his soldiers. They were almost as large as he was, and they had similar looks of hatred plastered on their faces.

The three miscreants took one more step forward and then spread out, creating a barrier that blocked the door. We reciprocated by taking a few more steps back, placing a healthy distance between our group and theirs.

Sizing up his competition, Commander Robb looked at each of us with a calculating gaze. His eyes widened with surprise when he saw me, but he recovered quickly.

"James. Brit." Commander Robb stated matter-of-factly.

James replied firmly, "William."

He smirked. "I like what you have done to the place—my place."

My mind flashed back to my original conversation with Commander Robb. He told me Little Bear would take the pull directly to his home, which means that this structure must have been Robb's childhood home. I felt a jolt of sadness. I wondered how long it had been since he'd been here.

Commander Robb took a step in my direction. I noticed that he had something strapped to his back, securely fastened with a thick leather strap that crossed over his chest. The object on his back looked like a quiver without any arrows. *What is that?* Whatever it was, he was probably planning on using it against us.

"I knew you were working for them," Commander Robb spat out, looking at me with disgust. His piercing glare locked onto mine, not allowing me to escape.

James intervened. "She has nothing to do with this."

Commander Robb turned his attention toward James. Although they stood in silence, I could see an entire conversation occurring between them. I could see anger, betrayal, regret, and a hint of sadness.

I watched intently as my courage built up. "I wasn't helping them at first," I said. "But once we knew the truth, we had to help. You can't destroy our future." I had more to say, wanting to defend my actions, but Brody squeezed my hand as a warning and I stopped.

Commander Robb turned back toward me and laughed at my words as if they were a joke.

His face grew solemn. "Your people destroyed your own future when you turned your back on peace and balance and slaughtered the people who taught you everything." He fumed with every word.

Brody answered calmly. "You're right."

His words caught me off guard, but I knew he had a point.

"Our native people were mistreated—the people and their knowledge," he continued. "They were thrown to the wayside, but revenge won't make it right. What's done is done. Plus, you're speaking of the natives of our land only. There are millions of people living on neighboring lands that you are condemning unjustly. If you change the future of our land, it will be their demise as well. Then you'll be no better than the people who slaughtered your father."

Commander Robb's look of rage shifted into one of grief. "That was going to be his last trip to your world. He was going to make sure his people were safe, and then he was going to come home for good. Your people—*your* ancestors—murdered him at a *peace* treaty meeting. The native people were like the Sohrigs: they were so focused on respecting balance and life that they did not take a stand, and they were slaughtered like animals because of it."

His voice grew louder with each sentence. "I am going to change that. Your people are tainted and condemned!"

His anger was seeded deep; he'd had years for the hurt and sorrow to fester into a rage like this. I pitied him. To spend your existence focused on revenge and events that happened more than a hundred years ago would be enough to drive anyone crazy.

Brody tried to diffuse the situation further. "Killing is not the answer. Educate our world. Your knowledge is extensive, pulling from Little Bear himself. He was such a great, wise chief—"

"—What do you know of Little Bear?" Commander Robb interrupted callously.

"Well, he was a great chief of the Arapahoe nation," Brody said. "He was a spiritual person, always going on vision quests, trying to better himself and the world around him. His primary mission was forging peace among other tribes and the 'palefaces' alike.

"If you continue with your plan, you won't be honoring his memory. You won't be honoring everything he worked for—and died for. You're willing to go against your father's wishes and wipe out the present, only to hold on to the past?"

Commander Robb's face was cold and unresponsive. The years of hatred had made him irrational and almost inhuman, allowing him to step away from the core values of his father and the Sohrigs.

The Sohrigs believed that letting fate take its course would ultimately result in balance. They refused to participate in a quest for power or universal policing.

Revulsion filled Commander Robb's eyes. "How would you know of his wishes? Your people died with Little Bear when they stabbed him in the back and laughed as he took his last breath."

Commander Robb paused as he looked at his soldiers and then back at us. The corners of his lips turned upward in anticipation. I shuddered in fear.

"And now it is my turn!"

I didn't know who had acted first; it happened so quickly. I felt like a deer in headlights, knowing I was in danger but unable to react. One moment we were standing there, listening to Commander

Robb's monologue, and the next thing I knew, it had turned into hand-to-hand combat.

I surveyed the scene: Brody was fighting with one soldier and holding his own while James struggled with the other soldier. James was not faring as well. Commander Robb was off to the side, removing the quiver-like object he had strapped to his back.

I kept my distance, moving to avoid the action. I soon found myself near the door while Brody was along the far wall near the pull. I thought about running to find help, but I couldn't tear myself away from Brody. He looked as if he had the upper hand, but I wasn't willing to leave in case there was a change in the current.

Brody landed a blow to the soldier's jawline with a right hook. The soldier staggered and fell. Brody glanced at me, and then we both looked at James. He needed help. Brody took a step toward James as Commander Robb came closer.

I screamed at Brody, warning him of the impending danger. "Brody! Look out!"

Commander Robb took a step toward Brody and pulled something out from behind his back. I looked at the object, trying to solve its mystery. It was short, brown, and had a blade—it was a tomahawk! The quiver-like object was on the floor behind him.

Brody spun around and intercepted Commander Robb. I stood in shock as I watched the two of them struggle. I wanted to shut my eyes, but they were wide open with fear. Both men were fighting for their lives.

They struggled with the tomahawk, which was raised above their heads. Each man had one hand firmly on the handle as they exchanged blows with their free hands. It was an evenly matched fight. I held my breath, being eaten alive with panic.

Suddenly, Commander Robb threw an elbow and caught Brody off guard, making him step back and release his grip on the tomahawk. This made Brody vulnerable, and that split second was all it took. Commander Robb's lips curved into an evil smirk as he began to swing downward.

"No!" I screamed.

I sprinted toward the two men and tackled them with all my might. It felt like I was hitting a concrete wall, and the impact knocked the breath out of my lungs. I caught both men by surprise, and we all fell toward the wall and through the pull.

* * * * *

Darkness washed over my eyes. Even the stale, moist cavern was welcoming after our experience in the marble room. I landed hard on my back, looking up at the ceiling and trying to regain the air that had been forced out of my lungs with the blow.

Brody flashed through my thoughts and I started to get up, desperate to find him and make sure he was safe. I jerked upward for a split second, then collapsed in excruciating pain. I was hurt— seriously hurt.

The pain was crippling. I tried to move again, and cried out from its sheer force. I wasn't sure if it was the aftermath of hitting the human wall, the floor, or something else.

"Brit? Holy crap, she's hurt!" Rebecca yelled. I tried to focus on her voice, but the pain hindered me. I wanted to ask what had happened, but I was afraid that if I opened my mouth a scream would escape.

I tried to be strong. I kept telling myself *mind over matter*, but I continually fell back into the pain's grasps. It was ruthless, forcing my body to gasp for air. Finally, my body's coping mechanisms set in: the pain decreased, the room began to shrink, my eyes started to feel heavy, and the voices around me began to sound muffled. I tried to hold on, but I could feel myself slipping deeper and deeper.

Rebecca, Sarah, and Mike were hunched over me. Sarah applied pressure to my right shoulder . . . or was it my collarbone, or my chest? It all hurt, especially when I took a breath. Every time they caused any movement I winced reflexively.

Rebecca sounded calm, almost as if she were on autopilot. She never showed emotion during emergencies at the hospital, always holding the situation firmly by the reins. She was flawless at times like this, and I was thankful she was in my corner. Regardless, knowing she was in her zone added to my realization that this was serious.

I looked around, still fading in and out of consciousness, and couldn't see Brody. Anguish smothered me. Where was he? Did he get hurt? Was I not quick enough? Then it occurred to me that he probably hadn't recovered from traveling yet. And Commander Robb, where was he?

"Calm down, Brit, it's going to be okay. You've lost some blood, so try to stay still and relax." Rebecca's words instantly registered. I wasn't helping matters by increasing my heart rate.

Stay calm. Just breathe. I shut my eyes and focused on my breathing, trying to relax, but I felt cold and began to shiver. A sudden heaviness pressed against me: someone's coat or sleeping bag. Even with the blanket, I was still getting colder. This was not good. Between my pain decreasing, the shivering, the panicked looks on Rebecca and Sarah's faces, and my trouble focusing, I knew I was going into shock.

"Brit?" Brody's voice brought me back to the surface.

"Oh no! No! I'm so sorry!" There was a combination of alarm and guilt in his voice. "Oh, God . . . Please tell me she's going to be okay," he begged.

Brody's voice was shaky, but more importantly, he was here. He sounded fine. Actually, he sounded better than fine—he sounded perfect. Relief washed over me.

I did it! I stopped Commander Robb from hurting him. I opened my eyes, struggling through the fog, and looked up at Brody. I wanted to tell him everything was okay, but my body wouldn't cooperate. All I could manage was a small smile. He bent down and kissed my forehead gingerly, as if I were a broken porcelain doll and he was afraid to touch me. My smile faded and my eyes closed; they were too heavy to keep open.

I could hear Sarah explaining my condition to Brody. "She's lost a lot of blood. We need to get her to a hospital. I'm not sure how we're going to get her out of here."

"What happened?" Rebecca demanded.

Brody sounded angry. "She was hit by a tomahawk, trying to protect me. Dammit! Does she always have to be the hero?"

The word caught me off guard. Brittany Scott, a hero? I never imagined myself a hero. I'd been the hero of a game or had a heroic moment in the eyes of my parents, but I'd never been a hero in the truest sense: a person who is completely selfless, regardless of their own fate.

A hero would never shy away from the higher path, even if that path led to their demise. Yet here I was applauding myself and going so far as to call myself a hero—a true hero.

I felt disoriented, and writhed in pain. But for the first time in my life, I was exactly where I belonged. Pride filled me. My ultimate goal of self-discovery and self-acceptance had been achieved. Acceptance and love from Brady, and from my friends, was an added bonus.

I lay there peacefully. I felt complete, like I was in a mental bubble of utopia.

Brody's words broke my concentration. "He hit her, James! We need to get her to a hospital . . . she's lost a lot of blood."

Chapter

EIGHTEEN

Forcing my eyes open, I saw James standing over me, uninjured and smiling. I wasn't sure if smiling was the proper response, but I was too weak to care. He knelt down beside me and gently brushed my hair from my sweaty brow.

His expression was warm and loving. He held out his hand and opened it, exposing another pellet that looked like a bean. This one was blue.

He held my head up. "I am going to place this under your tongue, okay?"

Following his directions, I mustered all of my energy and opened my mouth. He placed the pellet under my tongue, and it dissolved quickly, tasting bland, like a wafer. I kept assessing myself for changes, but I felt nothing but pain. However, thanks to the shock, even that had subsided a bit.

Brody's voice was grave and full of trepidation. "James?"

"Give it few minutes, she will be fine." James spoke confidently.

Rebecca's curiosity was piqued. "What was that?"

"It was another type of power pellet—a healing pellet. It works by drastically accelerating her innate healing ability. Plus, it will work more quickly than it does back home because time moves faster here. She will heal nicely."

It took about ten minutes before I could feel a difference. My tunnel vision began to open and my breathing steadied. The pain was still there, but now it was manageable. I felt more alert and . . . alive.

All the eyes on me were wide with disbelief, except for James.' I felt good; so good that I was ready to push my limits. I cautiously began to sit up, and felt no pain.

I smiled at James. "I'll have to see about getting one of those healing pellets in case of a future emergency."

"That would be a wise idea." He grinned back.

Brody helped me up and continued to hold onto my arm tightly; I was still a little unsteady. I stood motionless while assessing my condition. Feeling stable, I turned toward Brody. I stepped into him as he simultaneously pulled me into his chest, wrapping me in his arms.

"You *really* gave me a scare." He sighed with relief.

"I know. I'm sorry, but—"

He didn't let me finish my sentence. His kiss was intense and fervent, making me feel light-headed. I took a step back, and he had to steady me once more. He chuckled as my cheeks flushed.

Smiling with gratitude, I looked around the room. I threw my arms around Rebecca first and then Sarah. I even hugged Mike, who returned my gesture by giving me a big bear hug. Lastly, I walked over to James.

"Thank you, James. I owe you one . . . especially for the saving my life part," I said sheepishly.

He placed his hand on my shoulder, smiling. "You did a great job, Brit."

I was flying. I wasn't sure if it was because of the pellet or because of our success. Suddenly, Commander Robb flashed through my head. I looked around the room and gasped. "Where's Commander Robb?"

Mike's smile disappeared. He spoke each word slowly, drenched with frustration. "He got away."

"What!" I exclaimed.

Mike spoke defensively. "He came through the pull right when you and Brody did. I checked on Brody and then helped Rebecca and Sarah with you. When I looked back at Robb, he was gone. I'm sorry."

A swarm of emotions smothered me as I looked down at the bloodstained rock next to the pull.

"No, I'm sorry." I felt ashamed of my initial reaction. "We're all safe, and that's all that matters. It wasn't fair of me to freak out. Plus, he doesn't have the power to get too far, right, James?"

We all looked at James for confirmation.

James nodded. "That is correct. He did not acquire a pellet to time travel."

"But how did Commander Robb come through the pull in the first place?" I questioned.

Puzzlement spread on James' face as he looked at me. "Well, between your traveling ability and Brody being full of power from the pellet he consumed, it is possible that you forced him through the pull when you tackled Brody and William." A frustrated sigh passed through his lips. "But honestly, I am not certain how he passed through."

James' voice had a troubled edge to it. This information could prove to be problematic. Could Commander Robb hitch a ride from someone who'd consumed a power pellet? Or even more chilling, could he hitch a ride from a traveler? My heart began to pound, and I looked up at James for reassurance.

His expression was one of chagrin. Suddenly he smiled, and relief smoothed out his furrowed brow.

"What? Why aren't you worried anymore?" I asked.

He chuckled under his breath. "You are observant, aren't you? I had forgotten that the pull's strength decreases when it is used continually. Our passage to Trate and our return here took place in such a short amount of time that it weakened the force enough for him to hitch a ride. If the pull had been given adequate time to *recharge*, for lack of a better word, I believe his passing would not have been plausible."

My nerves settled a bit.

"What happened to the other two soldiers?" Brody asked.

James face beamed as he answered. "We apprehended them. A monitor heard the commotion and came to my aid. We retained my soldier but left yours alone, letting him think that he had escaped. After he came to, we followed him, and he foolishly led us straight to their camp. It was ideal—we detained them all.

"The only person who escaped was William. Our monitors are still on heightened security until they capture him. I suspect he will return soon enough, wanting to obtain a power source. The only way he can return is through the pull, and when he does pass through it, he will have to recover. The monitors will be waiting for him."

The echo off the cavern walls was almost deafening as we celebrated our success. Smiles and hugs were given out like candy at a parade. We had reason to celebrate: we were alive, our future was safe, Commander Robb's camp had been apprehended, and Commander Robb would surely be seized. We all displayed similar expressions of elation and pride.

Finally, Sarah spoke, quieting the last remaining merriment. "We should probably get going. We have a four-day hike out of these mountains." She paused for a moment, looking slightly stressed. "James, do you think you could get some supplies for us? We're running a little low on food."

I froze as Sarah's words sunk in. I would have been worried, but I knew James would help us.

James searched for his bag, which had been tossed onto the cavern's floor during the chaos. He reached in and pulled out several small packages that looked like granola bars. I was famished, so I snatched one from the top, tore off the packaging, and took a big bite. It wasn't granola like I expected, but it didn't taste bad either. It reminded me somewhat of a bland protein bar. Regardless, it was a welcome meal.

The bars disappeared quickly; it seemed I wasn't the only hungry member in our group. Sarah looked uncomfortable as she ate her meal. "James . . . um, thank you and all, but I think we'll need a bit more than this to make it home."

James burst into laughter, as if Sarah had told a joke. I couldn't help but giggle at him.

"I'm sorry," he said. "We can get you home much quicker than that. There is a pull in the room where you trapped me and took me prisoner. That is why I followed you. You said you had found the pull, and I was curious to see what you *had* found. Plus, I had to make sure you did not go through the pull if you had really found it. That pull leads to Boulder."

Smiling at the irony and humor of his confession, I shook my head. "I enjoy spending time in Boulder. I find it . . . entertaining."

I snickered at his statement. The most entertaining thing I had encountered in Boulder was James and his bizarre behavior.

"Come, I will take you to the pull." We followed James away from the Cleansing Pool, crawling through the hole and making our way back to the pink pool.

After changing out of my blood-soaked shirt and washing up, I slowly gathered my belongings. I stood with my pack slung over my shoulder, double-checking to make sure nothing was left behind. It was time to leave. We started making our way back to the room we'd lovingly named the Ambush Room.

Brody and I were the last two to leave the cavern. I looked back at the room, the pink pool, the gleam of the polished-looking rock, and our sleeping corner. A sense of loss overcame me. I would miss it here—not necessarily the room, although I appreciated the intimate time we had spent in it, but the memories. Brody telling me how he felt, the laughs and stories and camaraderie we'd shared, the scares, and my traveling discovery.

Brody squeezed my hand, and I turned to face him. Trying to be comforting, he smiled at me, but I could see right through his attempt to hide the same expression of loss. He brushed my hair back and kissed my forehead. It was time to close this chapter. We turned our backs on the room and followed our friends.

We came to the familiar fork in the trail and turned right, heading back to the room where we had captured James. As we walked into the room, I chuckled at the turn of events. The room hadn't changed, except that this time James wasn't our target, but our friend.

A dim glow along the far wall caught my attention. "Look, a pull!"

Brody had a look of concentration and confusion. "What do you see?"

"The rock is glowing. What, you don't see it?"

James interrupted us. "His eyes will not be able to see it well, if at all, Brit. You have a genetic predisposition to see pulls, once you know what you are looking for. And the more you travel, the more in tune you will become to the pulls. Eventually, you will see them as clearly as street signs."

My eyes were wide, and my voice filled with excitement. "There are more pulls?"

James grinned. "Yes, there are many, *many* pulls."

"Do we need a power pellet, James?" Rebecca asked.

"No. This pull doesn't leave your world; it travels through it. Power is only needed to break through your ionic connection with your world when you leave. You do not need the extra power, only a guide. I will lead you through it. Who wants to go first?"

Brody answered hesitantly. "Will it feel the same as the last time I traveled?"

James nodded with an apologetic expression. "Even traveling through pulls within your own world is still cellularly violent, and it will most likely render you unconscious."

Brody rolled his eyes and sighed.

"Try not to be troubled. The pull opens to a pleasant area that is next to a stream; it is peaceful. Plus, because this is your world, the recovery time should be much shorter."

Brody looked around the room; there were no volunteers to go first. "Hmph," he pouted. "All right. Fine. I might as well get this over with."

I giggled at Brody, which made him flash a facetious smirk at me.

He walked over and stood next to James. They looked at each other and Brody nodded. James placed his hand on Brody's shoulder and they walked through the pull, disappearing into the rock.

One by one, James escorted each member of the group through the pull, until I was the only one left. James reemerged alone with a perplexed expression.

"Brit, you don't need a guide—" he stopped speaking once he processed my accusatory expression. I had questions that needed answers.

"James, I saw the exchange between you and Commander Robb."

James' face fell into a look of sadness before he nodded once. "William and I were childhood friends. We were inseparable." He smiled for a moment, but the smile quickly faded. "I found out that I was a traveler at about the same time his father was murdered."

"How did you know you were a traveler?"

He flashed a sheepish grin. "I leaned against the wall in William's house and fell through the pull. It was quite shocking—conversing one moment and sitting in the cavern the next."

"I bet."

"I spoke with our authorities and they connected me with the traveler assigned to my world. His name is David, and he was my mentor. I began traveling with David when I should have been by William's side." The guilt seemed to smother James like a thick blanket.

"Robb felt abandoned by you?"

"Yes. First by his father, and then me." He exhaled a long sigh.

I wanted to say so much, but didn't know where to begin. Sympathy wasn't what James wanted, but I was at a loss.

"I'm sorry," I said.

He didn't say a word. Only allowing the corners of his mouth to turn up, he nodded once. It was evident that hunting Commander Robb was heartbreaking.

"James, will I ever see you again?"

His smile was warm and encouraging. "Of course, Brit. Traveling is part of who you are. You are one in a trillion. You have been given a master key to the universe, and I suspect you will want help maneuvering through it. Am I correct?"

I nodded.

A bigger smile broke across his face. "Travelers are a rare breed, so we have to stick together. My guess is that you will see me again soon."

"When?" I pressed.

"Very soon. I must first return to Trate. I have a few items to discuss with my superiors."

I returned the smile and gave him a warm embrace. "Thanks, James."

"Thank you, Brit."

I released James and walked toward the pull. I glanced back, flashing one last smile of appreciation, and then stepped through the pull alone.

I stood in a small clearing. Looking behind me, I saw that the pull was located on the side of a walking bridge's concrete pillar, whose wooden rungs spanned the stream. The clearing was circled with aspens and a babbling stream was only a few yards away. James was right; it was serene. The sun was brilliant. I shut my eyes and turned my face toward it, taking in its warmth. It was a welcome change to breathe fresh, crisp air instead of the stale air within the cavern. I turned around and saw my friends lying peacefully on the grass. I sat there enjoying the tranquility of the clearing as I waited for my friends to recover.

Brody started to stir, letting out a small moan. I knelt by his side, waiting patiently for the fog to lift so I could help him sit up. He moved slowly, holding his forehead as he finally rose to a sitting position. I felt sympathetic to his situation, knowing exactly how crummy he felt.

"How are you feeling?" I whispered.

He looked at me and shook his head with disgust.

I couldn't help but snicker. "I know. I'm sorry . . . that just sucks." I leaned into him and kissed his forehead.

A jesting smile appeared on his face. "Show-off." He grabbed me and pulled me into his chest, making my heart flutter. Still unsteady, Brody lost his balance, tumbling back, and I fell onto him. We laughed and kissed tenderly, enjoying the intimate moment.

Soon, the rest of the group slowly started to wake, all feeling equally as bad as Brody had. I tried to help each of them the best I could, but I knew that time was the only antidote for their symptoms. We rested for twenty minutes until everyone felt well enough to continue.

"I vote we go get some food; I'm starving," Sarah said.

The group agreed, and we started walking. We broke through the row of aspens concealing the stream and could see civilization a few hundred yards away. Once we reached the road, I regained my bearings—we were only a few blocks from Pearl Street. I remembered parking on the same road when we were here earlier during our road trip.

I was eager. "We're near Pearl Street. Let's go there to eat. It has a lot of cafés." What I actually wanted to do was go back to the coffee shop. I wasn't sure why, but I needed to. I knew it wasn't rational, but I already missed James and longed to see him again.

Too hungry to search for other options, we settled on the first café we came upon. We ate quickly and barely talked, far too exhausted and ravenous to put any extra energy into chatting. I ordered a large turkey and spinach panini and ate it all. I still wasn't satisfied, and wanted more. My yearning to go to the coffee shop was great.

"It's been *forever* since I had a good cup of coffee." Since they all knew I was a coffee addict, convincing the group to soothe my cravings wasn't difficult. "And I know the perfect coffee shop," I said, speaking in an upbeat tone. Everyone agreed to join me, not wanting to burst my bubble.

We entered the coffee shop and I looked around, sighing with slight disappointment. I knew James wouldn't be here, but I'd still hoped. I had discovered a new direction for my life, and I wanted to speak with the only person who could answer the questions accruing in my mind.

Rebecca and I ordered lattes, the men ordered drip coffee, and Sarah opted for tea. I waited impatiently as the steam wand added the final touches to my latte. Its nutty aroma overtook me, making my mouth water, and I asked the barista for an added shot for good measure. The barista finally handed me my drink. I took a sip and paused, allowing my body to celebrate the return of this precious, savory treat.

After pulling two tables together, we sat down, happy to be off our feet. Time poured by as we discussed our trip, recapping each day and the adventures they held. I was enjoying myself, but I felt conflicted. I was elated to be out of the mountains, sitting here with my friends. Our trip had been a success, and we'd walked away unscathed. However, something occurred to me—it was over.

My chest felt heavy, shortening my breath. *Now what?* I looked over at Brody, and my helpless expression caught his attention. We needed to talk about this, and soon, or I was going to go crazy with worry.

He grabbed my hand and kissed it, looking at me with an optimistic expression.

"Well, it looks as if you'll be moving to Colorado," he said, flashing me a grin.

My heart leapt, but I tried to sound nonchalant. "Is that so?"

"Well, someone is going to have to watch your animals while you're jumping through rock walls. I spoke with Rebecca and Sarah, and they aren't willing to do it. They're too busy. Sorry." He tried to make his voice sound disappointed.

Sparing a glance across the table toward them, they each displayed a huge smile. Sarah shrugged her shoulders while Rebecca shook her head emphatically and added, "Nope, sorry!"

And that was it—I was moving to Colorado.

My future was full of potential: a new place to call home, a new love, and new traveling adventures. I beamed as my bubble of utopia appeared once again.

I turned to Brody. "I love you."

He leaned over and kissed my cheek before resting his forehead against mine. Looking relieved, he smiled at me. "Me too."

Chapter

NINETEEN

he drive back to Breckenridge was a blur. We had rented a car for the day to make our way back to Mike's truck; Brody drove and I sat next to him, holding his hand. I repeatedly glanced over at him, enjoying the view.

Descriptive words flashed through my mind and my heart raced with each peek. He caught me staring at him several times. Never questioning my gazes, he squeezed my hand and smiled with satisfaction each time he caught me. By the third time, I blushed and he chuckled under his breath.

My mind felt like it was lost in the clouds, dancing with thoughts of him and of us. I was on a high better than any runner's high I had ever experienced. It was far superior to when I passed my boards or graduated from vet-tech school. I decided that this was the highlight of my life so far.

We took the interstate, mirroring our previous route, which felt like a lifetime ago. I leaned my head back, resting on the headrest. I could hear talking in the back seat, and I tried to focus on it. Rebecca, Mike, and Sarah were debating which was the wiser purchase: a registered purebred dog or a mixed-breed. My eyes were heavy, causing me to blink in between giggles. The topic was silly.

I blinked one too many times. When I reopened my eyes, Mike's Cherokee was coming into view. Somewhere in that blink, I had lost several hours.

"How was your nap?" Brody asked, smirking.

I gasped in horror, hoping I didn't do anything too embarrassing.

He responded with a soft chuckle and a wink.

Brody pulled over alongside the truck and turned off the engine. We sat in silence for a moment, realizing that our journey was complete. It had been a week full of highs and lows, tapping out our emotional reserves.

Sarah was the first to stir. "Okay then, let's meet at Mike's house tomorrow morning—let's say eight?"

Rebecca and Sarah looked over at me and I nodded my head in agreement.

A sly grin crossed Rebecca's face as she spoke. "You have a good night, Brit."

"You too." I grinned and shook my head at her.

As Mike, Rebecca, and Sarah climbed out of the car, a sense of gloom overcame me. I knew that good-byes were inevitable. I also knew that I wanted be with this man forever. Unfortunately, he lived a thousand miles away from these two astounding women, and I had to make a choice. I loved them both and would miss them terribly when I moved.

Brody and I began our drive back to Breckenridge. I plugged in my iPod, resurrecting it from the dead, and played my favorite songs. Our taste in music was similar: a good sign. We laughed at some songs, while others catapulted us into the past. We discussed memories associated with each song, sharing stories of our childhood and some more recent tales. It was fun to hear him speak so freely. He truly loved life and wore rose-colored glasses.

Brody's demeanor shifted, looking at me with a hint of sympathy. His expression seemed misplaced for our current conversation. "Is there something wrong?"

"We're almost to the interstate, so you may want to call your folks. They're probably worried."

"Crap! My parents." The blood drained from my face as I thought about their reaction.

Brody's laughter broke my concentration. "You look like you're going to be sick. Are you afraid you're going to get grounded or something?"

I pouted. "*Or something* is about right." I took a deep breath before I confessed. "I don't do this."

"Do what?"

"*This!*" I wailed.

"I don't understand."

"I usually do exactly what my parents expect. Even taking this road trip was unusual for me. Then add the hike, jumping through pulls, trying to save the world, and moving to Colorado . . . my parents will probably have me committed," I grumbled.

Brody grabbed my hand, trying to calm my hysterics. "I'm sure they'll understand. Give them a little credit."

I frowned at him.

He grinned. "They're not going to commit you. You called them before you left. They knew you were out hiking. And this little hiatus of yours was good for them, too. They need to learn to give you some space so you can live your own life."

I nodded and plucked my phone off the console. He was right. Regardless, the phone felt like a brick. I looked at it, still feeling ill.

I took a deep breath. "Well, here goes nothing," I mumbled and dialed the number.

The conversation went relatively well once my mother calmed down. I explained to her that when we went hiking, we were out of cell phone range, and we had just returned to civilization.

"I told your father that this road trip was a bad idea," she griped.

"Mom, I'm an adult and I have things under control. I told you that you didn't need to worry."

"Hmph," she replied.

I ignored her and continued. "We've met some really great people out here. In fact, I met someone. His name is Brody, and he was our guide. He's fantastic." I paused, gathering my courage. "I want you to meet him."

The other line was instantly silenced by my news. Although I hadn't told her about my feelings for Brody yet, she could hear the intonation in my voice. My decision was made and unwavering, and she knew it. The discussion ended quickly when I told her we were all leaving for Portland tomorrow. What I hadn't told her yet was that I was moving. *Baby steps*, I kept telling myself.

I hung up the phone and exhaled. I was proud of myself for accomplishing my final challenge: proving that *I* was in control of my life.

I looked over at Brody and he was beaming with delight. Feeling the same way, I giggled.

"See, that wasn't so bad, now was it?"

I shrugged, smiling.

We passed through the large tunnel opening to the breathtaking view. The sun hitting the peaks made them look almost purple. My mind flashed to the lyric "purple mountain majesties." I'd always wondered about that line, and now I knew where it came from. The sight of purple mountains was delightful.

We dropped into the valley below, passed through town, and turned onto Brody's street. As his house grew near, my nerves began to rise. This would be our first night alone together, and I was consumed with anticipation. I tried to suppress my anxiety, but failed.

Brody looked over at me and his expression went somber. "Brit—" I could hear conflict in his voice. "I'm not sure what you're thinking, but I want you to know that I love you."

"I love you, too."

"I know," he said with a grin. "I wanted you to know that I'm not going anywhere . . . and that I don't have any expectations for tonight. I just want to hang out with you."

My eyes grew wide with surprise and my anxiety instantly ceased. Would this man never cease to amaze me?

"I want you to"—he paused for a moment, choosing the right words before he continued—"to be comfortable."

"Thanks. That means a lot to me." I felt like my heart was full and running over with happiness. Never had I placed myself into a more vulnerable position than now, and never had I felt so secure. The contrast was exhilarating.

Obviously pleased with himself, Brody's childlike expression glowed with satisfaction, making me laugh.

Finally, we pulled up to a large, A-frame log house. Nestled into the side of a hill, its windows reached up to the roof's peak, and it boasted a wrap-around deck.

"Your home is beautiful."

Brody shrugged a shoulder. "Thanks."

My excitement instantly spiked. I was looking forward to a shower, a home-cooked meal, and sleeping in a comfortable bed— all a welcome change.

We hauled our packs inside and I looked around. The open floor plan highlighted the wooden beams spanning the ceiling. A stone fireplace continued upward into an exposed chimney. A large, pine table was tucked into a nook adjacent to the kitchen, and the stairs leading to the bedrooms were on the opposite side. The house was decorated in earth tones, embracing its mountain heritage.

"I'll show you where you can clean up."

I nodded and followed Brody up the stairs and down the hall. He stopped in front of a door and motioned toward the bathroom. "Clean towels are on the shelf. Take your time. I'm going to unpack and then I'll get dinner started."

Hot water ran down my back. My muscles relished the heat, releasing more than a week's worth of stress and tension. The scent of the shampoo was a fresh and invigorating change compared to the musty smell from the cavern floor. I spent extra time brushing my hair and teeth, both luxuries that I had taken for granted until now. I slipped on one of Brody's large T-shirts and a pair of sleeping shorts, and then walked down the stairs.

Brody was standing over the stove, stirring what looked to be spaghetti. He had changed his clothes and his hair looked damp. He looked away from the meal in progress, his eyes meeting mine and widening.

Feeling self-conscious, I responded defensively. "What?"

"You're beautiful," he said with a small smile.

He left the stove and met me at the bottom of the stairs. He grabbed my waist and pulled me into him. I wrapped my arms around his shoulders and tucked my head into the crook of his neck. He smelled incredible, with his typical sweet essence highlighted by a touch of aftershave.

Admittedly, I'd taken my sweet time cleaning up, but I felt a little silly that he had showered and cooked dinner in the same amount of time.

Regardless, he looked incredible and my willpower was quickly diminishing. I lifted my head, meeting his eyes. The softly lit room seemed to intensify his allure. He leaned in slowly, and my heart started to pound. His lips pressed against mine once before he pulled back and smiled seductively.

He placed one hand around the back of my neck and started kissing my collarbone. He followed the contour of my neck, ending at the hollow under my ear. I tilted my head, exposing more of my neck and inviting his lips to explore. I tried to show some restraint, but my body screamed with desire.

A sizzling sound from the kitchen broke my concentration. Without pause, Brody broke away from me and ran into the kitchen.

The water was boiling over the rim of the pot and flooding onto the stove. He grabbed the pot, pulling it off the burner and revealing the puddle of water underneath. He looked up at me, flashed his radiant smile, and shrugged.

"Oops."

"Need to brush up on your culinary skills?" I raised my eyebrows. His lips curved. "I was a little distracted."

I grinned. "What do you want me to do?"

"Nothing. Just sit there and distract me some more," he said, adding a wink.

I shook my head and giggled. I pulled out a kitchen barstool and sat down, watching as he worked swiftly and efficiently to finish our meal.

"Where did you learn to cook?"

"My mom loves to cook. I would sit right where you're sitting and watch her for hours as she worked her magic. I paid attention, and picked up a few tricks along the way." He smiled warmly; his affection for his mother was unmistakable.

"That's nice," I said approvingly. "Where is she now?"

He cut the last piece of bread, popping a small chunk into his mouth. "My mom and pop got tired of the snow, so they moved to southern California. They're enjoying it there, so I'm happy for them."

"Why didn't you move?"

"And leave Breck? No way, this is home. Plus, someone has to hold down the fort."

My eyes widened with surprise. "Was this your childhood home?"

He shook his head. "No, not exactly. We moved into this house when I was in high school."

"Do you miss them?"

"Who? My folks?"

I nodded.

"Sure, of course. But my older sister Jenna and her kids live in San Diego, and my younger brother Mitch isn't too far away. He's in Arizona. My parents have a lot of company. Plus, a little space is a good thing . . . it keeps me out of the family drama."

He smirked. "Except I'm the one stirring the pot now."

My eyebrows furrowed in confusion. "You? How so?"

He shook his head. "Really, Brit? You have to ask?"

162

I looked at him blankly before it dawned on me. I gasped—he had told them about me. I was suddenly petrified of their opinions. Would they like me? I had never dealt with siblings before, and the idea was nerve-racking yet exhilarating all at once.

He began to snicker. "Don't look so stressed. I had to tell my folks I was back from our trip. As soon as I spoke, my mother guessed—she has a sixth sense about these things. They can't wait to meet you."

I gulped. "O—okay."

Brody's lips curved into a smile. "They'll love you, Brit. Trust me."

I blew out a shaky breath. I hadn't thought about his family before. I prayed that they would like me.

Brody scooped noodles and sauce onto two plates. After adding a slice of bread, he carried them to the table. "I sure hope you're hungry. I went overboard."

"I am. Thanks." My appetite seemed to be unappeasable, having a week's worth of skimpy meals to make up for.

We didn't speak a word for the first few minutes. I ate quickly, even though the spaghetti was hot and burning the back of my throat. I didn't care. Finally, satiation started to set in and I slowed down.

"Have you ever thought about leaving here?"

He shrugged a shoulder. "Perhaps, but it would have to be for a good reason. I have everything I could want here: a good job, skiing, hiking, friends, and now, you." He flashed a large smile. "Thank God you said you would move here, or I would've had to seriously think about moving to Portland."

I beamed as I relished the fact that he would have moved for me, too. "You don't like Portland?"

"No, it's not that. Portland's nice, especially in the summer. I'm not a huge fan of the rain because it's boring. You can't play in the winter there. At least I can ski when it snows here."

I nodded. "Yes, but the rain makes it green back home."

"It's green here, too."

"But it's a different kind of green there. The vegetation is way thicker and more diverse."

"True," he conceded.

I looked down at my plate and realized I'd finished most of my meal. I felt full, warm, and clean.

"That was great, thank you. I can't believe I ate all that food." I grimaced at my gluttony.

He smirked at me, picked up both plates, and dumped them into the kitchen sink. Then he walked back over to me and lifted me from the chair and onto my feet.

"So, where were we?" he asked as he wrapped one arm around my waist and unexpectedly picked up my legs with his other arm, holding me tightly. I was caught by surprise, letting out a small shriek. He proceeded to the couch and sat down with me on his lap.

His eyes gleamed as he leaned forward slowly. My anticipation built, making me feel like a dam trying to hold back a tidal wave of emotion. His lips, full and warm, brushed along my jawline until I crumbled and kissed him back.

His lips were the perfect dessert. We kissed until I had to break away, gasping for air. He laughed lightly, flashing a triumphant smile.

I placed my head on his chest and he wrapped his arms around me, engulfing me, and leaned back on the couch. I was relaxed, too relaxed, and I felt at home enfolded in his arms. I shut my eyes and inhaled deeply. This evening was encroaching on perfect.

I felt his fingers brushing across my cheek. Thinking about the last few moments made me smile.

* * * * *

I opened my eyes and had to blink twice. The fireplace was directly in front of me, located across from the couch. Disoriented, I almost jumped up into a seated position.

"Good morning, sleepyhead. I'm sorry if I startled you."

His voice was music to my ears. I turned, instantly melting at the way he looked at me. His expression was a mixture of contentment and amusement; it had been a common look from him, especially in the morning. He was standing on the other side of the couch, his thick hair in disarray.

His words caught up with me. "Morning?" I paused, thinking about last night. Disgust washed over my face. "I'm sorry. I must have totally crashed last night."

He smiled and kissed me on the forehead. "You needed sleep. I'm just sorry you fell asleep on the couch instead of the bed. I know how eager you were to sleep on an actual bed."

My smile widened. "Yes, but the couch was still better than a sleeping bag in the middle of nowhere."

"Very true."

"What time is it?" I felt stiff, and was pretty sure I hadn't moved all night.

"Six thirty."

"Ugh, mornings are brutal." I pouted in protest.

He chuckled at me, like he did every morning when I recited a similar line.

"I'm surprised you aren't used to getting up at this hour by now."

"Not everyone's born with a built-in alarm clock, Mr. Six A.M.," I mused as I stretched.

Brody reciprocated with a smirk. "Mornings are my favorite time of day. Know why?"

I shrugged. "No."

"Because you're the first person I get to hang out with before the day has had a chance to wreak any havoc. Mornings are perfect—especially when I know I get to spend the entire day with you."

My mouth dropped in astonishment. He laughed as I gained my composure and shut my mouth.

He leaned forward, brushing his lips to mine. "Are you hungry?"

"Yes." I wasn't sure how that was possible after last night's gluttony. Nonetheless, the thought of a real breakfast made my mouth water.

"I already made coffee. Wait here. I'll get some for you."

My face instantly lit up as he walked into the kitchen, grabbed a mug off the counter, and poured a healthy cup of coffee. He returned with my cup of joe and kissed the top of my head as he handed it to me.

"Does a cheese omelet and toast sound good to you?"

"Yeah. That sounds great. Do you want some help?"

"Sure. You can make the toast."

I rose off the couch, rearranged my clothes, smoothed out my hair, and padded across the room to the kitchen. Brody told me where I could find the bread and butter, and I began my task. A sudden contentment washed over me. We'd spent several mornings together, but this was the first time it was only the two of us.

Plus, this morning seemed different: here we were in our PJs, looking mussed, working together in the kitchen. I could see myself doing this for the rest of my life.

Once I'd completed my job, I sat on the couch, wrapped myself in a green fleece blanket, and ate. My taste buds celebrated the fact that they didn't have to process another breakfast of almonds or protein meal bars. I was sure that it would be some time before I'd be able to eat either of those things and actually enjoy them.

After breakfast, Brody went upstairs to clean up and I remained on the couch, contentedly finishing my coffee. I felt at home. Brody's company, the smells, and the decor suited me, right down to my coffee mug. My apartment was cold and lonely compared to his haven. I thought of the trip home and sulked; I didn't want to leave. That's when it hit me—I would be back here soon, permanently. My mood instantly elevated, taking me near ecstasy.

Brody walked down the stairs with a small suitcase. "You should probably get ready. We have to be at Mike's at eight, and he likes to make good time. Plus, Sarah might have a conniption if we're late."

His words confused me. "Mike's going too?"

Brody laughed as he answered me, shaking his head like I had missed something important. "I'm pretty sure you're not the only one moving out here, at least if Mike has anything to say about it."

My heart instantly rejoiced. Knowing that Rebecca might embark on this journey with me was like a breath of fresh air. I was mentally prepared to face opposition, but her presence would give me added strength. It already made me feel invincible. I was anxious to hear her decision.

"Really? Let's go!" I popped off the couch, trying to control myself enough to place my dishes gingerly into the sink instead of hurling them.

Nearly stumbling, I sprinted up the stairs, clearing two at a time. I tossed on the first clean outfit I came across and shoved the dirty clothes in the side pocket of my bag. I quickly brushed my hair and teeth, both a courtesy for Brody's sake, but was too preoccupied to worry about the trivial vanities of makeup.

I jogged down the stairs with my bag in tow. Brody chuckled at me and opened the front door. He snatched my bag out of my hand as I scampered through the door, kissing him with delight as I passed.

Chapter

TWENTY

$\mathcal{W}$ ith Brody by my side, the trip back to Portland felt quicker than the ride out to Colorado. My euphoric state was to blame; I could hardly contain my happiness and contentment. Sure, my parents wouldn't be pleased about me relocating, but I was ready to move forward with my life. They would understand. How could they not? I needed independence, and I wanted to be with Brody.

Our first stop in Portland was my apartment. Sarah and Rebecca loaded up their cars, which were parked in the lot around back. With Mike in tow, Rebecca was the first to leave. She hugged all of us and said she'd talk to us soon. She was bubbling with excitement, and she waved as they pulled out of the parking lot.

Sarah also hugged me good-bye. "That was the best trip I've ever been on. I'm glad you wanted to go."

"I couldn't agree more," I said, beaming.

Sarah got into her car and left, leaving Brody and I standing alone in the parking lot.

"Let's take our suitcases up before we head over to my parents' house."

Brody nodded. We grabbed our bags from out of the trunk and climbed the stairs to my apartment. I maneuvered through the front door and dropped my bags on the floor of the cramped great room. My apartment wasn't huge, but it was home: a tiny kitchen, one bedroom, and a bathroom. It had been ample, until now.

Although my apartment was always immaculate, now it felt cold. The white walls and sparse decor spoke volumes about my life pre-Brody.

Brody entered behind me. "So, this is home."

"Yeah. It seems pretty bland, especially compared to your place."

A black-and-white blur caught my attention. I set my bag down where the kitchen and hallway met, walked over to the couch, and picked up Edie. I squeezed her until she let out a small meow. I'd missed her. "This is Edie-Mumu," I said as I scratched her head.

"She's cute." He looked around for a second. "No dog?"

"Having a dog is too difficult with my work schedule. Cats are less maintenance, but one day I'll have lots of dogs. And cats too."

He grinned.

I hesitated, "I mean—you want dogs and cats one day, right?" I tried not to sound panicked, but I couldn't imagine my life without animals in it.

"Yes, of course."

Relieved, I nodded and put Edie on the couch, petting her one last time.

"You can drop the bags over there, and we'll worry about them when we get back."

Brody placed the other bags with mine.

"I'm excited for you to meet my parents. You'll like them."

Smiling, he grabbed my waist and pulled me into him. "Of course I'll like them. They raised you, didn't they?"

He didn't give me a chance to reply. His lips brushed over mine so lightly that it gave me the chills. The corners of my mouth curved before I kissed him back. I couldn't believe this was happening. Here he was in Portland, ready to meet my parents.

Trying to avoid temptation, I drew away slightly. "We should go."

He flashed a small smile and grabbed my hand. "Okay, let's go," he said, pulling me toward the front door.

During the car ride my nerves suddenly spiked, getting the better of me. I knew my parents would love Brody, but my heart began racing. Little nagging *what ifs* crept into my mind. What if they didn't approve? What if Brody didn't like my parents? I would have to be strong and assertive. I'd made my decisions and my future was set; there was no going back. I was anxious about taking these next steps, but confident with my choices. I glanced over at Brody and he looked

168

completely relaxed and poised. I took a deep breath, smiled with resolve—clearly I was being paranoid—and drove on.

Fifteen minutes later we pulled up to my parents' brown, Cape-Cod-style home that looked like a storybook cottage. Its perfectly manicured lawn and colorful flowerbeds were the envy of the neighborhood.

As we got out of the car, I wasn't surprised when my parents walked out the house accosting us before we even reached the front door. My mother was wearing her typical summer outfit: khaki shorts and an orange golf T-shirt with her hair pulled into a low ponytail. Dad was in his khaki slacks and black golf polo. They'd been on the golf course that morning; a good sign. If they were playing golf, they couldn't be too concerned about my actions.

"Hi, Mom! Hi, Dad!" I gave them each a big hug before I turned toward Brody. "Mom. Dad. I want you to meet Brody. Brody, this is my mom, Mary, and my dad, Jed."

"It's nice to meet you," Brody said as he shook their hands.

Brody and I followed them into the living room. It hadn't changed much since I'd moved out: crisp tan walls, and a chocolate-brown leather couch and chair that faced the fireplace. The burnt-orange rug and matching pillows accented the room nicely. My mom had placed a plate of cheese, crackers, and green grapes on the glass coffee table in front of the couch.

I tried to relax as we all sat down, but it was hard at first. It wasn't every day that I brought home the love of my life to meet my parents. Ten minutes into the conversation, however, I reached for a handful of grapes, eased back in the chair, and smiled with satisfaction. My dad and Brody were talking sports. My parents seemed content, and Brody appeared to be enjoying himself. Between my dad's engagement in the conversation and my mother's smile, I could tell that my parents approved of him.

An hour later, as the conversation slowed and the snacks disappeared, I decided the time had come.

"I have some news," I said cheerfully.

My mom's brows furrowed and my dad looked at me with a serious expression. The room went eerily quiet.

I plastered on a stiff smile. "I've decided to move."

My dad frowned. "Move?"

I took a deep breath and blurted, "Yes. To Colorado." Before I gave my dad the chance to refute my decision, I continued. "Rebecca and I want to get an apartment together. With us splitting the cost, it will be comparable to what I'm spending now. I've found three clinics that are hiring techs, so getting a job won't be hard. I have enough in my savings account to move, and my lease is up next month at my apartment anyway."

My eyes widened and I blew out the breath I'd been holding in. I did it! I was taking control of my own life and securing my independence. I glanced toward Brody; he was leaning back on the couch with a satisfied smile on his face.

My parents looked stunned and didn't say a word for several seconds.

Finally, my dad spoke. "I don't know, Brit," he said sternly.

I squared my shoulders. "Dad, I'm an adult, and I want to move. It would be a lot easier on all of us if I had your support."

"At least she's not going alone, Jed," my mom interceded.

He sighed and nodded his head in defeat.

"But I'm *still* going to worry myself sick," she said sadly. My mother's gloomy expression made me feel edgy. At one time I would've cared enough to let it change my mind. Not anymore.

"You worry too much," I rebutted firmly. "I'll be okay."

Her chin jutted out into a pout. "Fine. But I expect you two girls to stick together."

"We will, Mom. We're going to be roommates, remember?"

"And I expect you two to sign a year-long lease."

I rolled my eyes. "Yes, Mom." What she was actually saying was that she didn't want me moving in with Brody, which was fine for now. But really, she was too late—my mind was made up. I would be with him forever. Rebecca and I being roommates was merely a formality for their sake.

She grinned at my compliant answer.

After a few hours, I announced it was time to go. Although my parents wanted us to stay for dinner, I was ready to have some alone time with Brody. We left and headed back to my apartment. The afternoon was a success: my parents loved Brody, and they were onboard with my big move.

As we pulled into my parking lot, Brody's stomach growled and we both chuckled.

"What should we do for dinner?" I asked.

"How does Thai food sound?"

"Perfect. I'll call and have it delivered."

After ordering dinner, I plopped onto the couch next to Brody. He wrapped his arms around me and pulled me into him tightly. We sat silently for a minute.

"What are you thinking about?" he asked.

"Oh, a few things actually. I can't believe how smoothly it went with my folks today. I figured they'd put up more of a fight. And I was thinking about James. He said he would contact me. I guess I'm anxious to begin traveling."

Brody didn't respond.

I looked up, meeting his eyes. "What?"

He seemed conflicted, as if he didn't want to tell me what was on his mind. Finally, his expression shifted into resolution. "I'm not sure if I like the idea of you traveling."

My jaw dropped. "What? Why?"

"I think it could be dangerous. You saw what happened the last time you traveled."

"Yes, but that was an unusual case. Plus, James is going to teach me. He won't take me anywhere I could get hurt."

Brody frowned. "Yes, I know. But that's why they're called *accidents*. I'm still not sure I like it."

James had said traveling was in my blood, and I felt it too. I couldn't wait to travel, see new worlds, and meet new people.

"I don't want to have regrets one day because I didn't try something that *could be* dangerous. If that's the case, we should stop skiing or hiking. A tree could accidentally fall on our heads."

Brody squeezed me. "I know. It just makes me nervous. I'd feel better if I could go with you. I came close to losing you once, and it felt like I was getting a chunk of my heart ripped out."

I flashed back to when I thought Brody had been in a car accident. I remembered how scared I was, and I never wanted to feel like that again.

"I understand."

I blew out a breath of frustration. This was a conversation I would expect from my parents. Once again, I was being placed in a constrictive box. *Was I willing to give up traveling for Brody?* I shook my head.

"But Brody, traveling is something I *need* to do. I promise I'll be careful and use good judgment. It would be a lot easier with your support."

He exhaled and nodded. "And you have it. Just remember that I'll be a nervous wreck until you get back safe and sound and are next to me where you belong."

I giggled. "I'll leave a note, and I'll be back before it's dark. Promise," I said, making an "X" over my heart.

"Ha, ha, very funny," he said as he began to tickle my side. I shrieked and kicked, trying to escape his grasp.

The doorbell rang. I sprang off the couch, snagged the money we'd placed on the counter, and opened the door. Our food had arrived. We sat eating Pad Thai on the living room floor, laughing and talking as we tried to eat the noodles using chopsticks.

* * * * *

Brody and Mike had to return to Colorado. Mike was needed at work; he'd used up all his vacation time. Brody promised to fly back in three weeks to help us load the moving truck and drive back with us. In the meantime, he and Mike were going to try to find Rebecca and me an apartment in Breckenridge. I knew it would be hard not seeing Brody every day for such a long time, but I needed the time to pack and get organized for the move.

Rebecca and I put in our two-week notice at work. I was surprised when they threw us a going away party, but Rebecca wasn't; she had expected it. Dr. Straight came, which made me happy. Feeling indebted to her, I smiled and gave her a hug. It was interesting how nice and normal Dr. Straight seemed once I returned. I wasn't sure how or why I'd put her on such a large pedestal. Regardless, if it weren't for her, I wouldn't have met Brody or discovered that I was a traveler.

Between packing and wrapping things up at work, the three weeks flew by. Brody came back to Portland to assist with our move. Between the three of us, and with my parents' help, the packing and loading process was relatively painless.

We spent the night at my parents' house, wanting a full night's rest before we embarked on our adventure. Of course, I slept terribly. I was far too excited to sleep. After a small breakfast of bagels and cream cheese, it was time to go. I was thankful that Sarah and Kat came to my parents' house to see us off. I was blessed to have friends like them.

We gathered in my parent's driveway to say our good-byes. I hugged Kat first, thankful for her help. I embraced my parents next; it took all of my emotional composure not to totally break down.

"You call as soon as you stop for the evening," my mom demanded.

"And take your time. Don't run that truck too fast," my dad said to Brody.

"I won't. We'll take it easy, I promise."

With tears running down her face, my mom nodded and then pulled me into her arms again. I would miss my parents terribly, but this was something I had to do. It was time to leave the security of home and make my own way.

Lastly, I hugged Sarah. A few tears escaped, and I wished that she could join us on this adventure, too. I would miss her sassy presence.

"Don't cry, Brit. You'll see me soon—and I expect to be a bridesmaid."

I sniffed as I giggled. "Of course. And you'll probably be my wedding planner, too." I squeezed her tightly, thankful for her friendship.

"Are we ready to go?" Rebecca asked. She hated good-byes.

I nodded, hugging my mom one last time.

Brody drove the moving truck, and Rebecca and I drove our own vehicles. With Edie secure in her traveling crate in the front seat, I waved to my parents, Sarah, and Kat as they faded into the distance.

I was ready to forge my new path—*my* way.

Chapter
TWENTY-ONE

I glanced around our new apartment, listening to Rebecca ramble on about her date with Mike the night before. The place was small, but I didn't care. It was cute, cozy, and surprisingly reflective of both Rebecca's and my style.

Our khaki loveseat sported bright green-and-purple pillows that matched the polka-dot picture we hung over it. There was a media center holding a tiny TV across from the loveseat. A chocolate-brown leather chair was nestled by the window. It was already my favorite spot to sit, think, and lose myself in the view.

Tucked into the opposite corner was a small, rectangular kitchen table just big enough for two. The narrow kitchen was separated from the living room by a breakfast bar. Down the hall were two small bedrooms separated by a single bathroom. This was the hardest thing about living with another female: sharing a single, small bathroom.

I returned my focus to Rebecca.

". . . and then he held my hand in front of everyone. It was so sweet." She paused before she blurted out, "I love him."

I rolled my eyes. "Of course you love him. We can all see that."

She beamed. "Yeah, but I think I'm going to marry him one day."

My eyes widened and I smiled, thrilled to hear Rebecca commit to something so wholeheartedly. I knew this was a big step for her. I had never envisioned my free-spirited friend settling down.

Rebecca stood up and stretched. "I think I'm going to take a nap."

For some unknown reason, I felt antsy. "I think I'll go for a nice long run."

"Overachiever," she said and then walked down the hall toward her room.

After changing into my running clothes, brushing my hair into a ponytail, and grabbing my iPod, I was ready. I opened the front door and took a step back in surprise.

"James. How did you know I was here?"

His lips curved. "Nice to see you as well."

My face heated from embarrassment. "Sorry . . . Hi, James."

His expression turned serious. "How I found you is not significant. I am here to train you. It is time to start traveling."

"Now?" I asked incredulously.

"Yes, now. I have been assigned as your mentor."

"Assigned? Who assigned you?"

"Travelers are overseen by a group of appointed directors. They are, for lack of better words, the governing body of our group. Plus, they act as a checks-and-balances system for travelers. They are voted into service, serve a six-meeting term, and then step down. The directors have acquiesced to my request and granted your entry into the training program."

"Which means what exactly?"

"Which means it is time for you to hone your skills as a traveler. Are you ready?"

I looked down at my outfit. "I was going to go running."

"Your clothing is adequate for your lesson today."

I shrugged. "All right. Let's go."

I closed the door behind me and took three steps before I stopped. James looked at me curiously.

"Should I leave a note for Rebecca and Brody?"

He frowned at me.

"She's taking a nap and I don't want her to worry. And I'm supposed to meet Brody for an early dinner."

He let out a small sigh. "I'll have you home before dinner."

"Okay, I'll leave a note for Rebecca then." I ran back into the apartment and scribbled a quick note saying that I'd be home before dinner. I came back out and found James waiting patiently for me, although I could tell he was slightly irritated with my delay.

"Are you ready?"

I nodded. "Yes."

He began to walk away from my apartment, toward the street.

"Do you want me to drive?"

He shook his head. "No. The pull is only a few hundred yards away, and it is a nice afternoon. We can walk."

I quickened my pace and fell into step beside James.

"I am going to show you the basic pulls first," he said. "These worlds are similar to yours. Once you feel confident with those, I will show you more. During this time, you need to memorize the safe pulls. It is imperative that you *never* enter an unknown pull. It could be exceedingly dangerous. Do you understand me?"

I nodded. "Yes."

"Good. I have heard of overzealous travelers who entered unknown pulls and did not fare well."

"Will I get to meet other travelers, too?"

"Of course. We are an intimate group with massive responsibilities."

"Responsibilities?"

"Yes. Each traveler is assigned worlds to watch over and make sure that they are in balance. We cannot have worlds influencing each other; it could be devastating to one of the worlds."

"So you watch over Earth? And you had to protect it from Commander Robb's influence?"

James nodded. "Our goal is to allow worlds to run their natural course. Sometimes it is hard to watch, but it is not our place to interfere."

"Will I have an assignment one day as well?"

"Naturally."

My eyes grew wide. I would oversee worlds. It was hard to wrap my head around the idea.

We followed the street down the hill and around the corner. James took a sharp right and began to climb the embankment. We made it halfway up the hill when I saw it. The pull was located in a chunk of exposed rock. It was small, and it glowed slightly.

"This pull leads to Ireland."

"Ireland?"

"Ireland in early September is nice. Their foliage is starting to change, and it is beautiful there."

I was disappointed. Sure, Ireland sounded great, but I was antsy to see new worlds. "I think I'd rather go to Mars."

"There are local pulls you should be aware of, and many of them lead to universal pulls. Plus, Mars is a poor place to visit; it cannot sustain life," he said, amused.

"Have you been there?"

James flashed a smile at me as he jumped into the pull as if he were jumping into a puddle, and disappeared.

My stomach knotted slightly. I took a deep breath and jumped into the glowing circle. I saw a blinding light, like I did with the other pulls, and then it was gone. I landed with a thud, jarring my knees slightly.

After I caught my breath, I looked around. It was a cool, partly cloudy day. Thankfully, it wasn't raining. The landscape was green— not Breckenridge green, but Portland green. The grass was plentiful and the trees were sparse, but the few I saw were an array of colors, looking like murals. Rolling hills surrounded us, and there was a long, stone fence on one side. I didn't see any buildings or people.

"I am impressed that you landed on your feet." James commented from behind me. I turned and saw James standing there with a large smile on his face.

"Most people don't land on their feet?"

He shook his head. "No, most travelers do not land on their feet."

James turned and began to walk up the small swell of a hill. I quickly followed, trying to memorize our path. We crested the hill and I saw a small town in the distance, with the ocean in the horizon.

"That's Dingle," James explained. "It's a great little town. I'll take you there someday, but not today. You have to be home for dinner."

I wasn't sure, but I thought I saw him scowl as he turned and continued north. I followed him down the hill to a set of boulders scattered under a large tree. He walked to the back side of the massive tree and I saw another pull.

Confusion struck. "A pull in a tree? I thought they were always in rocks?"

"The pulls are located in the ground. This pull is located beneath this tree, so it filters through the tree."

"Oh, okay. Where does this pull lead?"

"We are going to a world called Raymon, which is quite lovely. I think you will enjoy it." James held out his hand, and I took it. "Are you ready?"

I nodded feverishly. I'd spent most of my life wanting to explore, but I'd always gotten talked out of traveling: it was too dangerous, too expensive, or I would be gone too long. Now there were no excuses.

We passed through the pull and stepped into a fairy-tale-like land. I gasped from sheer delight and surprise. I thought Portland and Ireland were green until I saw Raymon. There were deciduous trees in every direction with green moss hanging from them. Beautiful white flowers hung off the moss, looking as if hundreds of flowers were dripping off the trees, shimmering in the moonlight.

An abundant assortment of strange-looking flowers blossomed on the ground around us. I bent down to get a closer look. These flowers looked like a mix between a lily and a mushroom. Only fifty feet from us was a pond. In the moon's reflection, the pond seemed iridescent. The landscape was surreal; it looked fake, as if someone had painted it.

"What do you think?" James asked, interrupting my moment of awe.

"Oh, James. This is beyond beautiful."

He smiled triumphantly. "I thought you would like it here."

"Where are Raymon's people?"

"Most of them should be sleeping; it is the middle of the night here. There is a town about a mile and a half down this path. Come, I'll show you." James led me slowly through the magical-looking forest.

"What do you think of their people?"

"They are friendly and welcoming. You will enjoy them."

After strolling for ten minutes, James stopped and pointed to a village nestled down in a small valley.

"There is the town. Do you see it?"

I nodded. "Yes. Are we going down to it?" I was anxious to visit the town and meet the people.

He shook his head. "Time moves faster here than in your world. If I am to get you back in time for dinner, we cannot visit the town today."

Disappointed, I frowned. "How much faster?"

"If we went to town and socialized, it would be the next day on Earth."

My eyes widened. "The next day?"

James nodded. "Time is relative, especially when you are traveling. That is why traveling should be a priority. You should not have obligations holding you back."

I grimaced at his reference to my friends—I would hardly call Brody and Rebecca obligations. But there *were* obligations that I had to focus on. "That's great in theory, but I have to pay for my apartment, which means I have to work."

He opened his mouth as if he were going to speak, but shut it quickly. After a moment of silence, he continued. "You could have dinner with Brody tomorrow," he suggested.

James was right; I could have dinner with Brody any night, but I could also come back to Raymon with James anytime. I couldn't wait to see Brody and tell him about Raymon. Plus, this would give Brody a chance to warm up to the idea of me traveling. During our last conversation he'd seemed unsure because he feared for my safety. If I was going to visit docile worlds like Raymon, Brody had nothing to worry about.

I shook my head. "No, I would like to come back during the day. Plus, I don't want anyone worrying. We *can* come back here, right?"

Defeated, James responded with a solemn, "Yes." Without a word, he turned and began the trek back toward the pull.

James walked a few paces ahead, which gave me a chance to study him. He was competent and proud. It was obvious that he loved to travel and had made that the center of his life. I wondered if he'd ever had anything or anyone that was more important than traveling. Sensing that the answer was no, I felt sorry for him.

Chapter

TWENTY-TWO

he snow on the windowsill shimmered in the sunlight, looking like thousands of diamonds. I sat in the leather chair, wrapped up in my warm, fuzzy blanket. It was a beautiful, early spring morning.

"Ugh! It's not *normal,* Rebecca."

"Oh please, Brit, it can't be that bad. The boy is head over heels in love with you. I don't see what the problem is."

"There is *never* a problem, and that's the problem. I'm telling you, he's perfect. He's like a mutant or something."

Rebecca burst into laughter, holding her side. I could feel the blood rushing to my face.

"Rebecca," I whined, pleading for her to focus on the issue at hand.

I exhaled as I mentally reviewed the six months since we had moved to Breckenridge. They had been the quickest and best months of my life.

The first month was a blur. The apartment Brody and Mike found for us was small, but perfect for our needs. We both found jobs at a local animal hospital, and it was a great gig. I worked three twelve-hour shifts a week, which were mostly swing shifts. This gave me plenty of time to spend with Brody and go traveling.

Brody had become my best friend. At first I didn't want to admit that I'd moved to Breckenridge for him. I told everyone that it was for me, to establish my independence. Now I could readily admit that my main lure out here was Brody. He was everything I'd hoped for and more.

Besides hanging out with Brody, traveling was my new favorite pastime. It made me feel centered and competent; plus, I was a natural. I traveled several times per week with James, trying to hone my skills. Within a short period of time, I was familiar with several pulls and their worlds.

James kept telling me that traveling was in my genes, and I think he was right. He'd become a close friend and confidant. His presence was calming, even when we were going through a new pull. Actually, experiencing a new pull was my favorite part; it reminded me of chocolate truffles—you never know what delicious surprise will be hidden within.

Rebecca broke my concentration. "Brit?" She sounded frustrated.

I smiled sheepishly at her. She must have been talking to me while I was lost in my own saga.

"Sorry."

"Brit, don't you think you're being a bit dramatic?" She shook her head and sighed with irritation. "You two are perfect for each other, and you're just being silly."

I paused. "Tell me something, Rebecca . . . do you and Mike ever fight?"

She flashed a puzzled look at me. "Sure, we've bickered, who hasn't?" she said defensively.

"*We* don't, that's who! He's so nice, it's almost frustrating. I've even gone as far as to try and pick a fight, and he *apologized*. Rebecca, he didn't do anything wrong. No matter what I do, he only smiles at me. I feel like he's placed me on a pedestal, which only highlights my flaws."

"You pick fights on purpose?" Her eyebrows rose with disapproval.

I could feel tears starting to build from my frustration. "Yes. I know it's ridiculous, but he's not normal. I want him to fight back."

"You want to fight?" She was still confused.

"Yes, anything. He's always so . . . so perfect."

Concern crossed Rebecca's face. "Don't you want to be with him anymore?"

My eyes grew wide and my heart skipped a beat with protest. I gasped at the thought of his absence. Brody was my soul mate. I needed him, but I also needed him to be emotionally vulnerable and real. I wanted to bask in his idiosyncrasies too: the good and the bad, making us equal—a partnership.

"Of course," I scolded. "I want to be with him forever. I just want to have a fight or two. I can't keep up with his perfection. He's always so composed and I'm a frantic nut."

Rebecca smiled, sarcasm brewing behind her words. "You know, it's not a contest. Have you told him any of this?"

"Oh, that's great, Rebecca. I can hear it now: 'Brody, I'm not happy with the fact that we have never had a fight.' He'll think I've cracked."

Laughter broke through her words. "I think it's too late for that."

A flicker of brooding crossed my face. "Don't get me wrong, it's not like I want to fight all the time. But how will we ever make up if we've never had a fight?" I glowered at the thought.

Rebecca ruptured into laughter once again. "Brit, you're too funny. My advice for you is to suck it up and tell him what's bothering you."

My chin jutted out into a pout. I could discuss it with him, but he would think I was being ridiculous. Of course, he would never allude to it, and he would smile and kiss me. Regardless, the thought of confronting him caused anxiety to swarm through me.

Stretching as she spoke, Rebecca stood up from the couch. "I'm starving; want to go grab a bite to eat?"

"Sure, but let me change out of my sweats." I stood up and tossed my blanket to the side.

Suddenly, a familiar voice yelled from the hallway outside our apartment door, sounding distressed. "Brit!" Something was seriously wrong.

There was an aggressive pounding on the door, making me jump. Rebecca took a step toward the door right as Mike came crashing through it.

Rebecca's alarmed voice matched the expression on her face. "Mike? What's wrong?"

His words were breathless, but he forced them out. "He's gone!" Still gasping, he said, "He's got him!"

A puzzled expression crossed both of our faces while Mike attempted to communicate.

"Mike, I don't understand. Who's got who? And who's gone?" Rebecca asked.

"Brody!" A pained grimace spread across his face.

I fell back onto the chair, completely speechless.

Mike crossed the room and thrust a piece of paper in my face. *A note—how cliché*, I thought as I snatched it from him it and read it out loud. The writing was scribbled.

> *Bring five power pellets and meet me at the coffee shop in Boulder at three, or he's gone.*
>
> —*Robb*

My mind started to race as panic washed over me. I jumped up from the chair and ran down the hall toward my room.

"Where are you going?" Rebecca asked, alarmed.

"I have to do *something*. I'm going to go get James," I yelled back to her as I entered my room.

I threw on the first clothes I could find and my tennis shoes, grabbed my car keys and a flashlight, and ran back down the hallway toward the front door where Rebecca and Mike were waiting for me.

"I'll be back," I panted, trying to catch my breath.

Rebecca took a step in front of me. "Oh no you don't. We're going with you."

I took a step back.

"I'm going to go see James; how are you going to go with me?"

She looked irritated. "Go get James and bring him back. Then we'll all put our heads together and figure out the best way to stop Robb and save Brody. You're not doing this alone, Brit."

Flooded with gratitude, I managed to squeak out a thank-you while Mike held the door open. We filed out of the apartment and headed toward the car. All I could think was *here we go again* as I tried not to sink into despair.

Mike drove while I was lost in a trance of misery. I felt terrible about my earlier conversation with Rebecca. If this ended badly, I would spend my life treading in guilt. My heart pounded and tears began to swell. I fought them back by focusing on my breathing, reining in my mind and not allowing it to wander.

After a couple of hours, we pulled up to the stream where the shortcut to the Cleansing Pool's pull was located. The two-and-a-half-hour drive felt like it took two and a half days. I jumped out before the car came to a full stop and ran toward the pull.

I could hear Rebecca yelling behind me. "Bring him back here! Do you understand me? Brit, I mean it—don't do anything stupid!"

Her voice vanished as I passed through the pull. The bright sky disappeared, replaced by rock and darkness. The stale cavern air pierced my lungs, almost making me choke. I stood motionless as I fumbled for my flashlight, allowing my eyes and lungs to adjust. Once I turned on the flashlight, I sprinted toward the path leading to the pull.

I'd taken this path many times, and could practically do it blindfolded. I ran swiftly down the tunnel, only slowing through the narrow passage leading to the pull. As the passage opened, I sprinted the last leg. The pull came into sight, and I leapt through it without even a pause.

The marble room was unusually well lit compared to its typical drab lighting. It was summertime in Trate, allowing residents to occasionally relish in light and warmth. Sweat began to bead on my brow; I was dressed too warmly, coming from the snow-covered mountains. It had been bitterly cold the last four months in Breckenridge. Nonetheless, I was still grateful for Trate's beautiful day.

I tore out of the room and into the street. The surrounding greenery was bright, looking vivid as it reflected the sky's illumination. The rolling hills had depth I'd never seen before, appearing several layers deep before being engulfed by the horizon.

I began the short trip toward James' home. It was close by, equivalent to the distance of five city blocks. I ran as fast as I could, but expectantly, I hit a wall as stabbing pains made me groan, halting me in my tracks. I placed my hands on my knees, trying to catch my breath. Pressing on, I held my side and walked toward his house as quickly as I could.

I looked up and saw my target. The tall, oddly shaped, asymmetrical house was light gray with charcoal trim. It had a modern edge, but it still felt welcoming. It reminded me of a row house found in San Francisco, narrow and trendy.

I ran up to the house and pounded on the door. My hands found their way back onto my knees as I waited patiently for the footsteps to grow near. I heard the door open.

"Brit? Brit! What is wrong?"

James' voice instantly soothed my hysteria, bringing me down to only a frantic state.

I strained to look up. As usual, he was dressed perfectly in a pastel shirt and gray slacks. I affectionately called the ensemble his "uniform."

"Robb's . . . taken Brody . . . I need your help," I said, gasping for air as I spoke.

Alarm flashed across his face. He disappeared for a moment and then returned, shutting the door behind him.

"Come. You can explain on the way." He spoke swiftly, grabbing my hand and pulling me along behind him.

We walked quickly back to the pull while I filled him in on the events that had occurred this morning. He paused only once when I mentioned the power pellets, and then continued on. I knew exactly what he was thinking: power pellets were completely out of the question, regardless of the circumstances. If Robb had access to the power he needed, our world would be devastated. I ended by telling him that Mike and Rebecca were in Boulder, waiting for the two of us to return.

We entered the marble room and James stopped abruptly. "You realize we cannot involve Mike and Rebecca," he said cautiously.

I was stunned. "Why not? They want to help us."

He spoke sternly. "They could get hurt."

I glowered at him, not satisfied with his rationale. "It's never stopped them before."

He spoke softly, trying to calm me. "Brit, this is something that *we* have to handle. Travelers are the protectors of the universe—that is why we exist. We have a higher purpose and cannot risk their lives."

Anger brewed to the surface. "We owe them for all they've done."

He shook his head with disapproval as he stepped through the pull. I followed closely behind, still irritated at his attempt to exclude my friends.

Once we'd both cleared the pull, he continued our conversation. "Precisely—and that is why they must not be involved. I do not want anyone else to be injured because of Robb."

I knew they would protest at James' decision. "They deserve an explanation at least."

Still bickering about their involvement, we followed the same path I had previously traveled, heading back to the stream. Rebecca and Mike were sitting down next to it, basking in the sunshine. I was sure they were enjoying a break from the relentless spring snow up in the mountains.

James and I must have had sour expressions on our faces, because Rebecca looked at both of us suspiciously. Rebecca was my best friend, and she could read me like a book. I tried to keep my emotions concealed, but there was no use around her.

"What's going on? Are we having issues?" she asked.

The words spilled out of me. "James thinks it's a bad idea for you and Mike to help. He thinks this should be dealt with by travelers only."

Rebecca flashed a fierce scowl of disbelief and betrayal toward James as he defended himself.

"If our interaction goes amiss, Brit and I can escape through a pull. You could be vulnerable. And who knows what weapons Robb has found in your world. I am not trying to be difficult. I cannot have anyone else getting hurt because we could not control Robb in the first place," he said, frustrated.

We stood in a silent standoff for a moment before Mike spoke. "James is right."

Confusion flashed on my face. Incredulity blazed on Rebecca's.

"No—" Rebecca began to protest.

"—I'm sorry, but I can't have you getting hurt. We'll take James and Brit to the coffee shop and let them handle it." Mike sounded determined.

"Mike, we can—"

Mike interrupted her again, standing his ground. "Rebecca, I am *not* going to let you risk either of you—and that's that."

Something caught me off guard. "Either of you?"

Rebecca looked at me, flashing a quick smile.

"No way!" I shrieked while I threw my arms around her. "Why didn't you tell me?" I demanded, protesting at her secrecy.

"I only found out yesterday. I wanted to make sure before I told anyone."

Mike walked up to join in our celebration. I released one arm from Rebecca and pulled Mike in, giving him a big hug as well.

I stepped back so I could look at Rebecca's face, raising my eyebrows. "Mike is right, you aren't going anywhere."

Rebecca sighed. "Fine." Both Mike and I smiled at each other with victorious grins.

I threw my arms around Rebecca once again as the happiness bubbled within me. I was momentarily overcome with joy when James broke through my merriment.

"Quit hoarding the mother."

I released Rebecca, beaming at her while I let James squeeze in.

He embraced Rebecca and then shook Mike's hand. "Congratulations. This is wonderful news."

James broke away from the joyous moment, focusing back to the matter at hand. "It is settled then, and I have an idea."

We watched James as he began to walk toward the car. We quickly caught up with him and crawled into the car. Mike drove as James explained his plan.

"Mike and Rebecca will give a note to a barista, who will then deliver it to Robb. The note will tell him to meet us at a place I know of—it is isolated and it has several pulls. We will deliver the pellets to him when he delivers Brody. I will drop the pellets on the ground, and when Robb picks them up, you and Brody can escape through a local pull. I will deal with Robb."

I didn't like his plan; it was riddled with holes. "What if I can't get to Brody? And how are you going to handle Robb, exactly? Plus, I thought we were keeping Rebecca and Mike out of our plans. And power pellets? Are you kidding?"

James smiled, lowering me from the cliffs of panic. "You said power pellets remind you of jelly beans, and that is exactly what he is going to get. Everyone will be fine. Robb is not going to do anything to compromise his chance of obtaining pellets—trust me. And let us just say that Robb will be shocked at the turn of events . . . literally."

I flashed him a confused expression.

James fumbled in his bag and pulled out a Taser. At that moment, his plan sounded solid to me.

I smiled with enthusiasm and hope. "Mike, let's find a grocery store. I have a sweet tooth."

Chapter

TWENTY-THREE

James directed Mike to an area at the edge of town, only a mile or so from the foothills. We followed the road to a dead end off the beaten path. It was quiet, even desolate, although we were only a few blocks from civilization.

There were older brick buildings on one side and a small bluff on the other. The bluff had an unusual shape, looking top-heavy, and was covered in small rays of light. It took me only a moment to realize that the rays of light were pulls, decorating the bluff like spots on a Dalmatian. Relief crossed my face as I mentally celebrated our bounty of exits.

I quickly turned toward James with an approving grin.

James had a smug smirk on his face. "I told you this was an ideal meeting place."

Mike came to a stop, and we stepped out of the vehicle. Both Rebecca and Mike's expressions were identical: consumed with worry and a touch of guilt.

"Please be careful, you two. Call us as soon as you have him," she pleaded.

"We will, Rebecca. Don't worry, okay? Everything will be fine, you'll see." I said softly, trying to calm her anxiety.

I shut the door and waved. Rebecca forced a small, reassuring smile, but the worry in her eyes exposed her lie. I watched them pull away and was relieved that James had won this time, and that we weren't risking their safety.

Mike and Rebecca had the harmless role of couriers. Once they'd delivered the note to a barista at the coffee shop, they would go home. Describing Commander Robb to the barista should be easy: he was an enormous man with black hair and a short temper . . . although they would probably leave out the temper part. James and I would handle the rest.

I sympathized, knowing that the next few hours would be much more difficult for them as they waited and wondered, unaware of the outcome. It was neither Rebecca nor Mike's personality to sit on the sidelines.

The car faded out of view, and I turned around. James was already retreating with his short-stepped gait. He walked over to the bluff and waited for me. Once by his side, he began to educate me on some of the pulls. Two were local pulls: the lower one led to Iowa, and the other pull high up on the bluff led to Florida. He pointed out a few other pulls leading to worlds that were safe, but that I hadn't been to yet.

Finally, he turned and sat down. "Okay, we need a plan." He patted the ground beside him. "Come join me."

I nodded, grateful for any distraction.

For over an hour, James and I strategized our plan of attack. Once we came to a consensus, we reviewed our plan repeatedly.

James was going to distract Commander Robb while I grabbed Brody and jumped through the local pull leading to Iowa. James was going to drop the fake pellets, and when Robb went for them, James would strike. After dropping off Brody and making sure he was recovering safely, I would return to assist James with Commander Robb. He was going to be contained once and for all.

After the fourth review of the plan, I protested. "I think I've got it."

James refuted, "Brit, being well prepared is essential—it is the key to a successful outcome."

"Okay," I agreed with a sigh, letting my face droop downward to make my sentiment known. My pouting worked, and he let me change the subject.

James laughed as I told stories of Brody and my adventures together: my first botched mountain climbing expedition, his attempt to help me with my mediocre skiing, and me sinking in powder while snowshoeing. After the third story where Brody had to swoop in and save the day, I paused.

Bitterness seeped into my words. "I'm in love with Superman, and I feel like Lois Lane—helpless and weak."

James scolded me. "Brit, you are being ridiculous."

"I wish you were right, but he's good at *everything.* It's hard to keep pace."

He smiled at me. "You do not give yourself enough credit."

"I couldn't even handle this on my own. I had to run and get you."

He shook his head. "You would have saved Brody fine on your own, and there is nothing wrong with being wise and recruiting reinforcements." He paused for a moment. "Actually, you are the superhero."

"Yeah, right." My head dropped as his words pierced my heart. I wished Brody thought of me like that too . . . but how? How could he when I was nothing but irrational compared to his perfection? He was good at everything, always avoided conflicts, and treated me like a princess.

"What? Was it something I said?" James questioned the sudden shift in my expression.

"No." I tried to mask my frustration with a weak smile. "I'm just worried about Brody, that's all. I need to talk to him. I feel like a jerk."

He looked at me with a puzzled expression. "I have no idea what you are talking about, but you are hardly a jerk. You are completely selfless. Might I remind you that you are in the midst of *saving* Brody? I am sure whatever is troubling your relationship is inconsequential."

James was not only a true friend, he had become like a big brother to me. My lips curved with appreciation as I reached out my hand to him.

He smiled at me and grabbed my hand in return. "You know I am here for you unconditionally, correct?"

"Yes, I know." My smile widened. "Thanks, James. I don't know what I would've done without your help."

"I would have asked for assistance in this situation as well. As I have said repeatedly, your instincts are exceptional. What you lack is confidence." His advice was often a mix of authority and friendship, convincing me of my abilities.

I sat quietly, reflecting on our prior conversation, when James suddenly jumped to his feet. I spun my head around and saw a white sedan closing in on our location. My heart sped as I sprang to my feet.

"All right, Brit, they have arrived—proceed as we rehearsed, okay?"

I nodded my head. "It's showtime."

* * * * *

The white car approached us slowly and then turned and parked at a perpendicular angle to us. Commander Robb stepped out from the driver's seat, shielding himself with the car. His hair and clothes were unexpectedly clean and pressed.

He glared at me with a look of annihilation when his gaze met mine. His eyes were as black as onyx, looking lifeless and empty. I shuddered as my attention was diverted to the back seat of the sedan—it looked empty.

Betrayal crept into my thoughts and stole my breath. I was petrified that Commander Robb had fulfilled my greatest fear: not holding up his side of the bargain.

Robb's voice was cold. "Where are the power pellets?"

James' tone matched Robb's. "I have them." He pulled the beans out of his pocket. "First, we want Brody."

Commander Robb stood for several minutes without speaking, allowing the tension to thicken. Without warning, he opened the rear door. His quick, fluid movements made me flinch. Commander Robb reached down and Brody's head appeared. Relief inundated me as Robb pulled him out of the car by his upper arm and onto his shaky feet.

"Brody!" Seeing him made my heart dance and break simultaneously.

Brody's hair was messy and his clothes were dirty and tattered. A mixture of dirt and blood concealed his face. His hands were bound behind him. He flashed a grim smile at me, but exhaustion overtook his expression.

Robb threw Brody to the ground without even a glance as he marched toward James. I cautiously walked around Commander Robb as he approached James. Once I realized that we were on the

192

bottom of his priority list, I ran over to Brody. I grabbed his arm and helped him to his feet.

"Are you okay?" I whispered, never taking my eyes off Commander Robb.

"Uh-huh. I think so," he whispered back, still hunched over in pain.

As tenderly as possible, I grabbed him securely by his upper arm and wrapped my other arm around his waist. I lead him to the pull. Although I struggled under Brody's weight, I pressed on. I couldn't stop.

I heard James and Commander Robb arguing. I tried to keep an eye on their activities in my peripheral vision, but it was challenging with Brody in tow.

Suddenly James' voice spiked with panic. "Brit! Watch out!"

Several events occurred simultaneously: I took the final step before we entered the pull, I saw Robb turn and face our direction, I saw James spring away from Robb, and I heard a loud *pop*.

I passed through the pull with Brody by my side and stood in the middle of a young cornfield, absorbed in a sea of green. The sun was bright, providing warmth, and the clouds were wispy, unlike the billowy clouds in Colorado. Luckily, the stalks were only a few inches high. I quickly looked around and found Brody at my left side.

Brody lay peaceful and motionless. I knelt down, untied the rope binding his hands, and rolled him onto his back. His beauty was enchanting, forcing me to pause and stare at him for a moment. I kissed his forehead, stood up, and refocused as I approached the pull.

I stopped and took a calming breath to gather my courage. I couldn't leave James unattended with Commander Robb; he needed my help. I squared my shoulders and stepped back through the pull.

The familiar dead-end road was quiet. I scanned the road in both directions, but it was lifeless. However, the car remained. Was it abandoned? There were no signs of Commander Robb or James.

My nerves spiked as I yelled, "James?"

There was no answer. My worry intensified, but I stood my ground and tried to yell for him again.

The ground shifted behind me and a pebble bounced off the heel of my shoe. The pain was instant as I fell onto my hands and knees. Although I didn't see the blow, its messenger was unmistakable. My head spun and I spat out the blood that had pooled in my mouth.

Thankfully, it seemed like my teeth were all intact. I blinked, trying to refocus my vision.

"Who do you think you are?" The rhetorical question was filled with rage.

I looked under my arm, still slightly disoriented, and saw a pull tucked under a bush only a few yards away.

Commander Robb had walked over to my side. I tried to avoid Robb's boot but couldn't, and his kick hit my ribs. The force of his blow rolled my body toward the pull. The stabbing pain increased as I gasped for air, and my coughing added to its knifelike intensity.

"I'm sure I can get those pellets out of James now that I have his new pet," he spat, laughing.

I decided this would be my only chance to make a run for it. A mixture of determination and self-preservation filled me, allowing me to spring to my feet. I dove toward the pull and his laughter stopped abruptly.

Most of my body had disappeared into the pull as I felt something lock onto my ankle. I kicked and fought, trying to ward Robb off. I heard him struggling to maintain his grip, which fed my motivation and aggressiveness. Triumphantly, I broke his grip and scrambled the rest of the way through the pull.

I lay motionless on my stomach, trying to catch my breath now that I was untouchable. Thoughts flashed through my head like a strobe: the world was safe for now, Brody was safe, and I was safe. But where was James?

Not daring to move from my location, I sat in the new world. I was afraid I would get disoriented and wouldn't be able to find my only known way home. This strange world was different from any other I had encountered. I felt like I was sitting on a cloud, and pools and streams of light were everywhere. It was Northern-Lights-meets-the-sixties. *Trippy*.

After watching the lights' mystical performance for a few minutes, I decided to go back. Now that I knew I could pass a selected body part through a pull, I was going to peek and make sure Robb was gone. The bush concealing the pull would screen me momentarily, keeping me safe.

I popped my head through the pull and looked around. The sky was gray and it was raining, unlike the sun-filled day I had left. There was no sign of Robb, and the car was missing. The clearing seemed safe, yet something gave me the chills. I walked through the pull, exhaling a breath of relief. I smiled at my victorious escape. Now it was time to attend to Brody.

I walked through the Iowa pull and stepped into . . . dirt? The sky was dim, the corn was gone, and so was Brody. My eyes grew wide and my heart began to race.

I jumped back through the pull and started running toward town, needing to find a phone, answers, and Brody.

Chapter

T W E N T Y - F O U R

*M*y lungs screamed as I rounded the second corner that led to the main road. I froze in shock. Boulder looked strange and foreign, not holding the same familiar characteristics it had had only hours before.

At a glance, the surrounding buildings appeared the same, but I wasn't fooled. The storefronts were too new, too clean, and too commercialized. Although attractive, their auras had changed. I was unsettled and misplaced in this new Boulder.

The cars were also edgy and unfamiliar. They seemed to be floating as they passed by. A car turned, humming past me. I heard a female monotone voice highlighting its movements. It reminded me of something you would hear on an answering machine or at the self-checkout counter in a grocery store.

A cute couple, both dressed oddly, walked toward me. They tried to act like they weren't staring, but I clearly didn't fit in with this new environment. My clothes were dirty, bloody, and torn in places. Besides looking like I'd recently walked away from a fight, my style in fashion was plainly out of place in this new Boulder.

The man was dressed in a glossy black suit. It had a touch of punk rock, which matched his spiky blond hair. The female was in a snug, short red dress, highlighted by thick ribbons of material sporadically layered over the waistline. She highlighted the plunging neckline with chunky platinum jewelry. It reminded me of something you would see on a runway in a high-profile fashion magazine: the one outfit so over the top that no one would actually wear it.

I startled the couple when I spoke. "Where am I?"

They looked at me with a number of emotions written on their faces—sympathy, confusion, but mainly fear.

The male stepped forward, shielding his counterpart from me as he answered.

"You're in Boulder, Colorado."

I was bewildered. "But how? That's impossible."

At this moment, something glimmered through my mind—*time passes differently in different worlds.*

My eyes widened and my breath stopped. "What year is it?"

His answer made me take a step back, like he had smacked me. I quickly calculated the difference in my head. My face paled and I felt ill as I realized that sixty years had passed while I was in the Northern Lights world.

* * * * *

I pounded on James' door. The journey to his house was tricky with the new scenery, but I'd managed to make it through the foreign obstacles. Still breathless and with dried tears streaked through the dirt on my face, I stood patiently, waiting to see if I had any hope at all. My anticipation grew as the footsteps increased in volume. The door opened to a face I was accustomed to.

"James!" Relief flooded over me.

"Brit?" His dumbfounded expression made me uneasy.

I couldn't restrain myself, and I threw my arms around him. He stood motionless as my tears started to flow once again. I held onto him tightly while my heart swam through a pool of emotions. I finally broke away, exposing my red, waterlogged face. I felt as if a huge weight had been lifted, and the abundance of emotions I felt all merged into one: relief.

"Surprise!" I laughed, due to a combination of his reaction and my nervousness.

His puzzled expression seeped into his words. "What happened to you? I searched everywhere. I thought Robb . . . there was blood," he whispered, cringing. I understood his assumption.

I looked at him. I thought that he would have aged significantly, but he seemed immune to the passing years that tormented his world. He looked as if only five years had passed. Even so, there was something different.

"You look well—too well," I accused, smiling. I held one of his arms as if I were holding onto him like a lifeline.

"Traveling can significantly slow down the aging process. One of the perks, I suppose."

"Really? It'll slow my aging?"

Smiling, he didn't answer but instead embraced me again. He held onto me tightly, not releasing me for several moments. I could tell that my absence had been tough on him.

"I'm sorry," I started as tears started to swell once more. "I tried to escape from Commander Robb through a pull I was unfamiliar with. I did exactly what you warned me never to do."

James stepped back so he could look at my face, grasping each of my shoulders. I hung my head in shame knowing the grief I'd caused.

"Everything is fine now—stop tormenting yourself," he said as he shook his head. "Did you enjoy the light show?"

Surprise washed over me. "You've been there too?"

James laughed under his breath. "Yes, I have. But I had power pellets to get back to my current time. From this point forward, you need to always have one on you. My nerves cannot handle losing you again."

"Sorry," I mumbled, embarrassed that I had caused so much heartache.

He lifted my chin, looking at me with a depth I did not recognize.

"What?" My stomach began to feel queasy.

"Where else have you been?"

"Nowhere. I came back to this world, looked in the pull I had left Brody in, and then came directly here."

His expression didn't change. I became uneasy, dreading his news.

"Tell me, James," I begged. I could tell he was trying to soften the blow. The heaviness returned to my chest.

His posture straightened. "I must show you."

His back turned to me as he shut the front door and paused, still grasping the handle, contemplating his decision. Then he turned back around and held his hand out, waiting for mine. His touch made me feel safe, although I suspected he was about to show me something unpleasant.

We left his house, walking in the opposite direction than I was accustomed to. He led me to a new pull, and we passed through it. Lush greenery overwhelmed the landscape, choking out everything in its path. It was dense, like a rainforest. We walked a few yards and came upon another pull. We passed through it and came to the bank of a river.

The river was wide and serene, instantly making me feel peaceful. I looked up the bank where the river wound around a hill, highlighting its contours. The river spoke to me—I knew this river.

I spun around and gasped with surprise and enthusiasm. Portland! We were home! I had spent many hours on the grassy lawn adjacent to this bank.

A smile filled my face, but it quickly faded when I looked over at James. His expression was still solemn. My mood crashed into anxiety.

"Okay, James. Fess up." I couldn't handle the suspense.

"I will tell you everything. But first we are going to see one of my friends. He lives down the road."

James looked down at his watch, an odd-looking contraption that was universal in a literal sense.

We walked a few blocks into town. I tried to focus on James and our conversation, but I was distracted. I'd missed the rivers, the bridges, and the neon green of my childhood home. With every sight I flashed back and was overcome with memories.

James walked purposefully until he turned onto a sidewalk leading up to a low, elongated building. It looked slightly misplaced among the skyscrapers.

The building was brown with white trim. It had a neatly manicured lawn with flowers trimming its edges. The tulip bed stole my gaze; it was a colorful and vibrant contrast to the lush grass. There was a fountain near the porch, which added a serene touch. It was pleasant here, wherever here was.

Looking tense, James spoke. "Here we are."

We walked through the front door and up to the front desk.

"Well, good afternoon, James." The lady spoke in a deep Southern drawl. She was pleasant but unremarkable, with short brown hair, brown eyes, and a husky stature. She wore a teal vest with a badge showing that her name was Betsy.

"He's not here right now—he's gone for his daily walk. But I expect him back in thirty minutes or so."

James nodded. "Thank you, Betsy. I will wait in his room, if that is all right with you?"

She smiled and laughed. "Well of course, James. You don't have to ask me, honey."

We continued into the building and entered an oversized room. It was open and bright and full of people. Some moved busily, creating a slight buzz, while others sat peacefully. Only a second passed before I realized that this was a retirement community.

James walked through the large common area and then took a sharp left turn that led down a wide hallway. We walked to the second door, number nine, and entered.

The room reminded me of a hotel room, slightly impersonal except for the pictures on the dresser and the homemade quilt on the bed. It smelled of a sweet musk that was masked by commercial cleaning products. Along the far side of the room there was a glass sliding door leading to an outdoor patio. The sunlight shone in, making the room bright, at least by Portland standards.

After a moment of hesitation, James walked over to the dresser displaying the pictures. His hands hovered above the photographs until he picked up two lucky winners. He took a deep breath while looking at them, turning his head between the two, and eventually set one of them down.

James tentatively walked over to me and placed the picture into my hands, unable to look into my eyes.

Although the picture was older, it was still in good shape. It was a charming picture, like something you would see in a magazine. It was taken at a zoo, and there were bears in the backdrop and a family in the forefront—a mother, father, and three beautiful girls. I smiled. The little girls mesmerized me.

One had long brown hair, gray eyes, and a soft smile. I was drawn to her, feeling calmed by her essence. The second had long blond hair and wore a huge, expressive smile; she glowed with charisma and life. The last had short reddish-blond hair with bright blue eyes. She reminded me of Sarah, hiding something tenacious underneath that sweet facade. I chuckled under my breath.

I was momentarily pleased, until my eyes moved to the father.

My legs felt weak and I couldn't breathe as the knife dug in deeper. I felt James brace me until he could gently sit me down on the bed. My head spun, and my stomach followed suit.

"I think I'm going to be sick."

James knelt down in front of me and held onto both of my shoulders firmly.

"Breathe, Brit. You're going to be okay."

I looked up at him, begging for answers with tear-filled eyes.

He brushed the hair out of my face before he began. "We couldn't find you anywhere, Brit. We looked and looked. Brody decided to move to Portland in case you came here, while Rebecca and Mike kept watch in Colorado. After a few years . . ." He paused, and pain struck his face. "We thought you were dead," he whispered.

"Brody waited for you, but it was not healthy. Eventually, we all encouraged him to move on. He met Eileen, and she was good for him. It took some time, but eventually he continued on with his life."

I winced as I said her name. "Dr. Eileen Straight."

James nodded. "Brody met Eileen through Sarah."

I flinched as memories of her perfection seeped into my head.

"She helped him with the healing process." James was trying to make me feel better, but I could feel myself sinking into a pit of despair.

James' words quickened. "They had a good, long life together. Eileen passed away a few years ago, and Brody moved here."

The room began to spin more quickly. I leaned over and placed my head between my knees, but it was no use. I fell into blackness.

* * * * *

My head pounded as the light pierced my vision. My eyes remained unfocused, hiding the person in front of me behind a mask of disorientation. I groaned in anguish as the latest events replayed in my head. The grief was intense as I imagined my life without Brody. My frustrations with our relationship were insignificant and minute compared to the magnitude of the current events. I shut my eyes as tears started to roll down my cheeks.

"Brit?" I could hear pain behind his voice. I was trying to be strong, but this was too much, even for me. The tears came quicker. I rolled onto my side and curled up in a fetal position.

"Brit, you are going to be okay." James stroked my hair gently. "We will get through this." He paused momentarily. "Actually, it is better this way."

Instantly full of rage and incredulity, my eyes flew open, but I didn't say a word. James looked uncomfortable, trying to gather his words carefully.

James flashed a look of resolve and he squared his shoulders. "Brody has had a great life, and you should be happy for him. It is your destiny to travel. We are loners, fading in and out of others' lives like a dream. I know it hurts, but the time has come for you to embrace your destiny. You were put in this universe to protect."

Feelings of helplessness started to overcome me. "Why can't I be with Brody *and* travel? I don't want to be alone. It's not fair!"

James sighed. "You do not have to be alone, Brit." He paused, speaking guardedly. "You could stay with me. We would be a team, traveling the universe together and protecting it." His words were suddenly aggressive. "Brody has had a happy and fulfilling life. Are you sure you want to change that?"

The corners of his mouth turned down. "Would you be going back for him or for you?"

His challenging words quieted me. I needed a minute to think without James reading the emotions plastered all over my face. I slowly rose off the floor and picked up the picture. After a deep, calming breath, I walked over to the dresser and set the picture down gently. It easily found its place next to three other pictures all showing people filled with happiness, love emanating from their faces.

I wanted Brody to be happy, and from the looks of it, he had found happiness with Eileen. I should walk away and ignore my needs, but I wasn't sure if I could. Even the thought of it made me want to jump off a cliff. I *was* selfish, and I wanted a life with both my soul mate and my destiny.

But deep down I knew that James was right.

Brody's life was full of beauty, laughter, love, and family. That was my definition of the perfect life. The only thing more important than my happiness was Brody's.

Maybe I, too, could recover and move on. I would travel and protect, distracting myself from the gaping fissure forming in my chest. Plus, traveling would be a helpful diversion from the knowledge that I had lost it all—my parents, my friends, Brody. The only things left were traveling and James.

After contemplating his proposal for several moments, I looked up to meet James' eager eyes. The tears threatened to escape again, filling my eyes to the brim, and I could feel my spirit draining as I said, "You're right. If I went back, I would only be thinking about myself. All I want is for Brody to be happy."

James nodded. "And he is." His eyes moved to the pictures, reiterating.

James tried to maintain a neutral expression, but it was clear that he enthusiastically approved of my decision. He was barely able to suppress his excitement. He held out his hand, and I reluctantly took it. I followed James, allowing myself to be led away from the only man I had ever truly loved. We walked out of the room, shutting the door behind us.

Chapter

T W E N T Y - F I V E

I opened my eyes, trying to squint past the swollenness. I lay still, staring at the lifeless white wall in front of me. As far as I was concerned, it could have been a mirror. My heart was a deflated balloon and my body was heavy, like it was full of lead. I couldn't move. I didn't want to move.

A knock at the door broke my trance.

Go away, I thought. A sigh broke through my lips. "Come in."

My eyes traveled along the wall and made their way to the door. I didn't move my body, only my eyes. James walked in, looking perfect as usual. Another disgruntled sigh broke through my lips.

Frustration and sympathy were written on his face. "I have a treat for you today—a new pull," he said, trying to sound optimistic.

I didn't budge.

He looked confused. "I recall you enjoyed exploring new pulls. Am I incorrect?"

"No, you're right." I paused for a long moment, hoping he would change his mind by giving me the day off.

He stared at me—no such luck.

"I'll be up in a minute," I grumbled.

"Great. You will enjoy this one, Brit." He sounded upbeat.

It was time to get a grip. James was trying, and honestly, I couldn't feel anything anyway. I was numb and empty.

"Can't wait," I muttered.

This was best for Brody. I pictured his face and let his scent fill my memory. A smile crossed over my face. Like a cruel joke, the picture in my head transformed so I could see him laughing and holding his child.

Suddenly furious, tears filled my eyes. That should have been our child. Mine—his—ours!

"Brit? Are you all right?"

I jolted back into the present, and I could feel the dampness on my face. My cheeks filled with blood, exposing my humiliation. "I'm sorry, James." I struggled with each word.

A soft smile appeared. "You *will* heal. What you need to do is clean up and tend to your traveling duties as soon as possible. Go ahead and get started, and I will make you a meal."

"Okay," I sniffled, wiping the tears away with the back of my hand.

He turned and walked out, shutting the door behind him.

It was time to face my new destiny. I rolled out of bed, plunking onto my feet. I stood motionless for what felt like an eternity, trying to summon some motivation and energy.

"Move!" I ordered myself. I heaved one leg in front of the other.

It took a long time for me to get ready. When I finally emerged, James was annoyed. I gave it a flicker of thought and sat down at the table mindlessly.

The meal James had prepared was a bland heap. It made my stomach turn just looking at it. There was no way I could eat, so I stirred it around on my plate as James tried to distract me. He spoke far too quickly for my blurred brain to keep up.

"I thought we would start in Raymon"—one of my favorite worlds—"and then move to the new pull. I think you will appreciate the new world, Huron; it is bright and colorful."

"Hmm." He could've taken me to heaven itself and I would've been indifferent. I couldn't feel anything, and if I did tap into my feelings, the pain made Commander Robb's tomahawk slash feel like a paper cut.

He continued, "Plus, you are going to meet Violet today— another traveler, and a good friend of mine."

My eyes ascended from the mush, meeting his.

"I get to meet another traveler?"

He nodded. "Yes. It's a big universe to protect without help. We have divided the worlds up to keep watch, and we meet every fifth moon—about every five months or so—to discuss our observations.

It is comparable to a conference; it is a travelers' convention of sorts." He smiled at the analogy. "You will also be assigned worlds to watch."

"I know. You already told me that," I answered blankly.

He stood up and removed both plates of food as I sat in a trance. Ignoring me, he continued. "Naturally, we never interfere. We make sure others do not intervene in neighboring worlds—preventing universal domination and the mess that comes with it."

I didn't respond.

"Brit?" His voice was a mixture of annoyance and impatience, sounding exactly like my father when he was cross with me. He shook his head. "It is time to go."

I nodded and stood up, following him like a shadow, unaware and uncaring of the destination.

* * * * *

The hard chair only added to my body's discomfort and amplified my exhaustion. The day had been full of traveling: exploring worlds, both new and old, and their pulls. I was introduced to new sights, sounds, and people. But I had nothing. I didn't have the ambition to invest any time into any of them.

Violet seemed nice, but I had hardly noticed her—my head had been hidden under a blanket of misery, blurring the entire encounter. The whole day had been lost; a faded memory.

I sat at James' table watching him conjure up another meal, feeling like I had been dragged through the mud. James' attempt to divert my attention by keeping me busy had failed miserably. A battle was brewing: a duel between grief and anger.

I had been ripped away from my life, love, and everything I had ever wanted. My priorities had been stolen from me and replaced by something superficial in comparison. I felt cheated.

I enjoyed traveling, but it was nearly impossible to now. The hole in my heart had grown, encompassing my entire chest. No matter how I tried to evade it, the numbness was beginning to wear off, and the pain was incapacitating.

Brody—I had to remain focused on his happiness. Plus, he had three beautiful girls: I couldn't take that away from him.

I could go back in time and reclaim my life, but at whose expense? I would be ending three lives. Brody's girls would no longer exist, and

I couldn't have that on my conscience. I would be playing God by deciding who existed and who didn't, and that wasn't an option. I had to live with my mistake and the fact that my hopes and dreams had been extinguished.

It had only been forty-three hours and twelve minutes since I'd come back from the Northern Lights world, but it had felt like perpetuity. This was the longest we'd been apart since I had moved to Breckenridge. I missed him and his optimistic approach on life. Brody's boisterous laughter flashed through my mind, making me long to hear it. I missed his touch, his sweet cologne taunting my senses, the warmth of his eyes, and his radiant smile.

I bounced up onto my feet, needing to divert myself from my haunting memories before I had a breakdown. I walked over to James. "What would you like me to do? If I'm going to be staying here, I might as well make myself useful." I flashed the largest smile I could muster.

James let out a small chuckle. "You may set the table if you wish. I am happy to do it if you do not feel up to it, though."

I nodded, instantly flashing back to Brody. Meals in James' world were more of an annoying necessity. Eating in our world was festive, social, and a time of connection. Brody and I would eat meals casually, on the couch or on the floor while watching our favorite TV shows. When we dined at the table, it was romantic and intimate. The thought of it made me cringe as the overwhelming grief consumed me.

I needed affirmation of my decision. "James?"

He looked up with a smile.

"Tell me about them—Brody's girls."

Confusion crossed his face. "Brody and Eileen chose not to have children."

I froze. "What? What about the girls in the picture?"

"They are Brody's nieces. His sister's daughters, I believe."

"Oh," was all I could sputter out.

I was confused and ecstatic all at once. Brody and I had had several discussions on family. I was positive that he wanted kids, and a lot of them. Family was Brody's life, and he chose *not* to have a family with her. He loved her, but not as much as he loved me. Of course, there could have been other circumstances, but I chose to hold on to my self-absorbed theory.

In any case, this knowledge changed everything. If I did go back in time, I wouldn't be destroying lives. Eileen would meet someone else, of that I was sure. The beautiful children would exist regardless of my actions. Hope filled my heart as I began setting the table.

James' kitchen was small, only used to store a few prepackaged meals and the tools to prepare them. I walked over to retrieve the plates and utensils from the storage rack. The plates were square and practical, making them easier to stack. The few eating utensils were neatly stored on the same rack, placed in a compartment that was tucked into the corner.

I robotically picked up two white plates and matching utensils. As I turned toward the table, I bumped firmly into James. He grabbed my arm to steady me and grinned.

"Oh, I'm sorry," I mumbled.

He stood motionless, looking at me with a mixture of concern and . . . desire? My stomach instantly knotted.

"Brit, I have always been content with my life and the choices I have made. I am even content being alone—I enjoy the solitude," he admitted. "But after today, I realized how much I miss having someone to share it with. Thank you."

"James," I started, reflecting his smile. "You're such a good friend—" His expression fell, catching me off guard and halting my words. Had I missed something?

I quickly replayed his words in my mind. Had his feelings grown for me? James was my colleague and my friend, but I had had more with Brody. And unselfishly—foolishly—I had walked away.

Love was possible with just about anyone, but when you found the one person made specifically for you, it was profound. Losing that bond was like losing a piece of your quintessence. Consumed by my desperation, I was willing to do just about anything to get it back. My heart knew my brain would give in—it was only a matter of time.

The corners of my mouth turned up. "You are important to me, too."

His movement was swift and direct, making me freeze with surprise and shock. His lips pressed onto mine, full of passion and warmth.

I didn't reciprocate, but I didn't reject him either. I loved James. I was *in love* with Brody. Kissing James was nice and warm and safe. But my whole life had been safe. I didn't need safe.

Selfish or not, I knew *exactly* what I needed.

James pulled away slowly, assessing my reaction. Rejection crept onto his face as he saw my expression.

"James—" I paused. There were no words to soften the blow. The truth was what he needed to hear.

"I need him."

James sounded abrasive. "I am sure you will survive without him."

James was a good man, but Brody was like an obsession. My hands began to tremble just thinking of another day without him.

The last forty-four hours had been hell. I felt as if I'd been chiseled at—picked away piece by piece. All that was left was a huge hole in my chest, and despair. I was lost, after just having been found. All the work I'd done finding myself and living my own life had slipped through my fingers like water, leaving me with nothing but memories and heartache.

I paused, trying to gather the correct words. James waited patiently, looking at me with a challenging glare.

"Brody brings me balance. He gives me a healthy perspective on life, and he makes me laugh. I feel complete as a person with him because my priorities are kept straight."

James looked frustrated by my explanation.

"James." My voice flushed with admiration. "Perhaps I'm not explaining it properly."

I paused for another moment. The words I had spoken were true, but I had still not nailed it. Suddenly, the reason was as clear as glass. A smile of gratification spread across my face as I spoke. "I *want* to be with him."

James eyes went blank.

"You see, before Brody, my life was dictated by my need to please other people. I did exactly what others asked of me, because I was basically a coward. It was easier to succumb to their wants than to my needs. I would pretend to be tough by momentarily standing up for myself during a conflict, but it was only a show. I cared too much about what others thought, and the guilt of not pleasing them would eat at me. Eventually I would give in, and everyone knew it.

"It was okay though, because they were happy, which made me happy. However, I eventually lost control of my entire life by trying to please my parents, my bosses, my friends—everyone.

"But now, things are different. For the first time in my life, *I* am dictating my life. Brody helped me achieve that. I don't care if he's what I *need* or not—he's what I *want*. And I'm willing to fight tooth and nail to be with him. Selfish or not, I want him and he wants me."

A smile broke through my lips. "Not to sound corny, but he's my soul mate . . . actually, he's more. He has taught me what it is to love, and he's shifted my entire perspective on life. When someone comes around and has that kind of impact on you, you'd be cutting yourself off at the knees if you didn't commit. I deserve that. He deserves that."

James drew back while my words registered. A flash of disappointment crossed his face, and then he nodded.

"Okay then, we had better get you back to him," he said, smiling, trying to wipe away the look of defeat. "And to the correct time. But first you need a meal. I am not going to send you into battle hungry. You will need your energy."

I placed my hand on his shoulder. "Thank you, James. I appreciate all your help."

He smiled slightly before he turned toward the table.

I placed the plates on the table, and within seconds James served the meal. Uncharacteristically, and thankfully, it wasn't mush: it looked like a fruit salad filled with foreign fruit. I wasn't hungry, but I knew James would object if I didn't eat. I took a few bites, stirring the rest around on my plate.

James eyed me with disapproval, obviously not fooled, before he spoke. "We need to discuss your tactical approach so you are prepared."

"I agree."

We discussed the logistics of my upcoming trip. Focusing on James' directions was nearly impossible now that I knew I would get to see Brody soon. I would get to see and touch him—the anticipation of holding him nearly sent me over the edge.

"Okay, so let us review the plan—"

"—Ugh, not again, James."

"Brit, it is imperative we get this right the first time."

"Okay," I succumbed. "I stand on the traveling ring, focus on the event, and—"

His words were drenched in irritation. "Not the event, Brit, or you will end up right in front of Robb. You have to be safe while you recover."

I cringed. "I'll have to recover?" My body protested at the thought.

"Yes. Time travel is similar to a door, catapulting you and forcing a short recovery even for travelers."

"Aw, man . . ."

James looked at me intensely, redirecting our conversation. "You will have to focus on a location *close* to where Robb will be—but not the place itself—during the time of the incident. Once you have recovered, you will need to get there quickly. Make sure you do not change the events too drastically. Stop Robb—that is it. If you do too much, you might alter the future even more."

"Okay, it sounds easy enough."

The corners of James' mouth turned down. "You should be fine. But if you fail, your world could end up in shambles—especially if Robb succeeds with his plans. Please, *please* be careful."

I nodded my head as the weight of his words sunk in. My hands became unsteady as I thought of the possible negative repercussions. This mission was for my own selfish reasons, so failure was not an option.

James cleared the table and then grabbed his bag. "Ready?" he asked, sounding determined.

"Yeah, let's do this." My voice cracked.

James walked to the front door, held it open, allowing me to exit first, and then closed it behind us. It took all my effort to suppress my excitement and not tear into a sprint. I was going home to Brody! We walked swiftly and silently as he escorted me away from his house. I followed James for a short time before I began to wonder where the ring was located.

My curiosity won out. "Are we almost there?"

Still not speaking a word, James looked at me, nodded once slightly, and then stopped in front of a nondescript building. The silence was making me uneasy. I was certain James was still conflicted about allowing me to time-travel. He took a deep breath, pausing for only a second, and walked toward the building.

We entered the building, and James flashed something badge-like at the monitor. The monitor's expression was a mixture of authority and awe—James was greatly revered in his world. The monitor moved his gaze to me. His eyes darkened with suspicion.

"This is my apprentice," James said.

He looked back toward James and nodded his head with approval. "Please proceed, sir."

We walked down a cold, narrow hallway and turned left, entering a room. Instead of a beautiful, open room like that of the Cleaning Pool's pull in Trate, the room was dark, small, and drab. It was closed off and under constant supervision. The only thing in the room was a lit ring emanating from the floor: the traveling ring.

James stopped and looked at me with concern before holding out a power pellet.

Ignoring the stress radiating off him, I popped the pellet into my mouth and then gave him a hug. "Thank you, James."

He returned the hug. "My pleasure, Brit. It is good to have you back."

I released his embrace and cautiously walked onto the lit area. My hands shook with adrenaline, knowing that both my love and my nemesis would be waiting for me. I looked up at James, smiled nervously, and then shut my eyes.

"Oh, and Brit?"

My eyes flew open, taking in James' nervous expression. "Yes?"

"Don't let your other self see you, okay?"

"Why?" I squeaked.

"Please trust me on this one, okay?"

I nodded and shut my eyes again. I had to focus. It took every ounce of discipline to keep Brody out of my thoughts.

* * * * *

I jerked awake. Feeling woozy, I forced myself onto my feet and began staggering toward the clearing where Robb, James, and Brody would be. The prior events played repeatedly through my head like a movie as I tried to decide when I should make my move. I had to find a window when both Brody and James were safe and my other self couldn't see me. I paused as the perfect moment popped into my head.

Walking quickly, I found my weapon of choice—a large branch from a tree. It was the same width as a bat, and I knew it would do damage, even to someone Commander Robb's size. I picked it up and moved forward.

I continued until I could see the white sedan. Trying to approach undetected, I crouched down and moved in cautiously. Once I reached the car, I sat and peered underneath it, intently watching the show happening on the other side.

I saw everything playing out as it had before. I watched myself save Brody, disappearing through one of the two local pulls. James escaped Robb's clutches while Robb was distracted, and Robb fired his gun at Brody and me as we passed through the pull. Then James leaped into a pull that I had never been through.

Commander Robb flew into a fury as he stood there alone. His rage halted abruptly and he smiled slyly; undoubtedly, this was the moment he figured out that my return was imminent. I saw Robb take his position above the pull I had disappeared through, patiently waiting to attack.

My stomach knotted, but I remained hidden. I knew when I had to step in, but watching wasn't going to be pleasant. I cringed at the recollection of the forthcoming events.

My heart stopped when I saw myself step out of the local pull. I wanted to turn my head so I didn't have to watch, but the timing of my attack had to be exact, so I forced myself to observe. Robb punched my other self and my stomach twisted, bringing the pain of that blow to the surface of my memory. It was easy to remember since I still sported the bruise that accompanied it.

His voice boomed. "Who do you think you are?"

I knew the time had come. My heart pounded as I moved out from behind the car and took my position. Commander Robb had turned his back to the sedan, ready to kick the other me while she was recovering on all fours. I knew this would be a safe time to intervene because my other self couldn't see anything but spots.

"I'm sure I can get those pellets out of James now that I have his new pet," he spat, laughing.

The other me made a mad dash to the pull that led to the Northern Lights world. He lunged for me, there was a short struggle, and I disappeared. Commander Robb screamed out of frustration. "*No!* I *hate* travelers!"

I pulled the branch back, ready to strike. I gathered all of my might—this was for Brody, Rebecca, Mike, Sarah, and James, but mostly it was for me.

"Trust me. The feeling's mutual."

Commander Robb's head spun around. I could see shock and confusion written on his face before I stepped into the swing.

I heard the wind from the makeshift bat cutting through the air, and an earsplitting *snap* as the branch cracked across his jawline. He dropped instantly.

I did it! I was back where I belonged, and Commander Robb was incapacitated.

After I caught my breath, with Robb lying at my feet, I stumbled to the Iowa pull and crossed through it.

Brody lay motionless, still recovering. I knelt beside him, smiling in celebration as I kissed his forehead. His face was calm and serene, and once again he was mine. I wanted to lie by his side and listen to the beat of his heart, but I still had business to take care of. I took the rope Robb had used on Brody and left to go back to the clearing.

Commander Robb lay peacefully, and I kind of pitied him. He'd been kind to me when I was at his mercy. Regardless, I bound his hands tightly behind his back before I stood there silently.

Several emotions hit me simultaneously: happiness, relief, pride. Our world was safe. Brody was safe. And *I* was the superhero of the day.

"Well done, Brit!"

I jumped at the praise-filled voice and spun around. "James!" I threw my arms around him.

He returned the hug before stepping back. "Go take care of Brody, and I will see to William."

"Will you keep me updated?"

"Of course."

"Okay." I began jogging toward the pull as I yelled back, "Thanks, James."

I entered the pull leading to Brody. He began to stir lightly, waking from his travels. I knelt beside him, trying to exercise patience while he woke. Finally, his eyes opened and he smiled softly.

Without warning, I threw myself onto him and kissed him with fury. I couldn't control myself. I felt like a puppet, at my heart's mercy. I'd gone too long without his touch and smell. I relished the moment.

He kissed me for a minute and then pushed me away, holding on to my shoulders. He gasped, catching his breath. An ornery smile spread across his face, and he pulled me back into him. We kissed passionately, celebrating both our successful escape and our reunion.

After several minutes, I backed away from our intimate moment and rested my head on his chest. "Don't ever do that to me again! You have no idea what I have been through," I reprimanded.

He chuckled. "I think I have a pretty good idea; I went through it, too, remember?"

I smiled, letting him believe that he'd won this miniscule argument. He wasn't the one who had almost let true love slip through his fingers, being tortured in the process, and at the cost of sacrificing the known for the unknown. I felt selfish but settled about my decision—we belonged together.

I suddenly realized how incredibly close I'd come to losing him. My breath caught and sadness reflected in my eyes.

"What's wrong?" he questioned.

I quickly tossed the sadness by the wayside while I thoughtfully gathered my words. "I'm never letting you go. You're stuck with me—forever," I said, speaking in my most intimidating voice.

He laughed at my threat. "Good. I wouldn't want it any other way."

I exhaled a sigh of relief, appreciating his unknowing approval of the decision I had made for him, and for us.

Chapter

TWENTY-SIX

*O*ur first stop was Mike's house, where I knew both he and Rebecca would be waiting. I knocked once and the door flew open.

"Brit! Brody!" The relief on their faces was unmistakable, making me smile.

"I was so worried! You both look terrible. What happened?" Rebecca asked.

I giggled at her candor as I hugged her, grateful to be in the arms of this incredible friend.

I shared most of the events that had occurred, leaving out a few of the gory details, especially the ones that could lead to a conflict between Brody and me. It was an ironic turn of events.

I gave everyone a blow-by-blow of what had happened. I shivered at how close it had come to being deadly. I told them how Brody and I jumped into the pull, barely escaping Robb's speeding bullet. Skipping over how Robb had attacked me, especially when I saw Brody flinch in my peripheral vision, I told them about my grand escape to the strange Northern Lights world. It was fun describing the captivating light show. I spoke of how I had ended up in the future and had to find James. My story ended with me "immediately" traveling back in time, and my batting practice on Robb's face.

Brody wrapped his arm around me, beaming with pride while guilt festered inside me. I felt dishonest, but I couldn't share my ludicrous initial decision to walk away and let Brody think I'd died. So I conveniently left that entire part out.

It was time to change the subject. I looked at Rebecca. "So?" My eyes were wide with enthusiasm.

"So, what?" She smiled, knowing exactly what I was asking.

I sighed. "Does *he* know yet?" I asked as I nodded my head toward Brody.

The three of us looked at Brody.

His face tensed. "Do I know what?"

I blurted out the answer, unable to contain my excitement. "You're going to be an uncle!"

It took only a moment for him to process my words. He immediately looked up at Mike, who was wearing a huge grin.

"Hey! That's great, man. Congratulations!" He stood up, giving Mike a big bear hug first and giving Rebecca a delicate one. "I'm really happy for you both," he said cheerfully.

Brody looked at me and winked. "I think we need to let Mom, Dad, and Baby Perry get their rest. Are you about ready?"

I nodded. I was thankful for the nice visit, but I was ready to spend quality time with Brody.

Rebecca smirked, understanding that he and I needed to talk. Little did she know that my earlier frustrations were null and void after my days of miserable solitude. I acknowledged her nonverbal accusation with a smile, avoiding any interrogation, and turned toward the door. If I wasn't careful, she or Brody might realize that I had left out a few details.

We soon made it to Brody's. I walked through the side door, entering from the garage, and looked around. Brody's house was warm and welcoming; it was a house that could easily be called a home.

A vision suddenly flashed into my head. I could see children, more specifically the three little girls from the picture. I could hear their laughter and the pitter-patter of their feet on the hardwood floors. They were beautiful and happy as they ran past. The little blond stopped, flashing her charismatic smile at me before continuing on behind the others. My heart leapt with happiness.

Brody interrupted my vision when he wrapped his arms around my waist. I turned so I could look at him, wanting to see him as I spilled my feelings for him. I had decided earlier that conflict was overrated and that he could put me on any pedestal he wanted, just as long as he was in my life. All I needed was him. I was astonished at how quickly my perspective had changed.

"I love you."

He chuckled as he nibbled on my ear. "I know."

"No . . . I am *so* in love with you, and—"

A knock on the door pulled our focus. Brody's eyes had an anxious edge to them; he was obviously still jumpy from his earlier encounter with Commander Robb.

"Hold that thought. I'll be right back." He flashed his breathtaking smile before he kissed my forehead.

Brody walked to the door and opened it, slightly blocking my view.

"Hey, James. Come on in."

James shook his head. "Thank you, but I am afraid I cannot stay. I wanted to stop by and let you know Commander Robb is in containment, and he is being constantly observed by our monitors." James was almost giddy while delivering his news.

The stress associated with Robb's free rein in our world was gone, making me glow with satisfaction. Earth was finally free from his plans.

Brody nodded in agreement. "Containment—and a lot of counseling—is exactly what he needs."

I walked over to James and embraced him. "Thanks for everything, James. You're a lifesaver."

James grinned. "Will I see you soon?"

I giggled in response to his obvious question. "We have a whole universe to explore and only a lifetime to get it done. Plus, it's our job to keep an eye on it."

He placed a hand on my shoulder, flashing a huge smile. "I would not miss it."

James looked over at Brody and extended his hand. Brody accepted James' gesture with gratitude, and they shook hands.

"Take care of her, okay?"

Brody nodded. "I will, James. You have my word."

James turned to walk away.

A question popped in my head. "Hey, James?"

He turned, meeting my perplexed face with curiosity. "Yes?"

"I was wondering . . ." I paused, trying to word my question properly so he would answer it. "Exactly how far did you go into the future to find Brody and me?"

A large, mischievous grin spread across his face. "Far enough. Take good care of each other," he said, adding a wink before he turned to leave.

He passed from the house's shadow into the sunlight, almost glowing from the sun reflecting off his pastel perfection. I giggled at his angelic appearance. We stood by the door and waited until James was no longer in sight.

Brody shut the door and grabbed my waist, pulling me into him. He stroked my hair, trying to smooth out the mess.

"Now where were we?"

I wrapped my arms around him and squeezed. He squeezed me back and I flinched. The pain from Commander Robb's boot was still present, screaming in my ribs.

"Oh, babe, I'm sorry."

I flashed a smile of reassurance. "It's fine. I'm okay."

He shook his head, clearly frustrated. He released me and ran his fingers through his hair.

"Brit, I need to know you're going to be safe. I can't handle you traveling if I have to worry about you." He sounded like he was trying to suppress his anger.

I shook my head in disagreement. "The only thing that worries me is that you can be used as leverage against me. If something happened to you—" Tears started to swell. "I was terrified."

Brody flashed an agonized expression. He quickly pulled me in and held my head to his chest, running his hand down my hair. "I know. Shhh. I know." He took a deep breath. "I'm sorry, babe."

"Don't be. It's my fault," I sobbed.

His body stiffened. "Brit, how could you say that? If it weren't for you, I don't know where we'd all be. You're the most selfless person I know." He looked down at me and smiled sheepishly. "It's almost intimidating."

I laughed as I wiped the tears with my arm. "Me? Intimidate you? You're kidding, right? You're Mr. Perfection."

His smile grew. "You have a warped perception." He began to count on his fingers. "Let's see . . . you saved that little girl who was choking in the park, you saved me from Commander Robb, you saved the world, you saved me again, and you save people's pets on a daily basis. And I'm the perfect one?"

My jaw dropped as the realization of his words struck me. Perhaps the playing field was more level than I'd thought.

Brody burst into laughter. "I win." He released my waist and pulled me into the kitchen by my hand. "I don't know about you, but I would do just about anything for a shower and a hot meal. I'm starving. Let's eat."

* * * * *

I sat across the table from Brody, gazing at him and the picturesque horizon forming behind him. The sun was starting to set, and it accentuated the snowcaps on the peaks. The dark blue was slowly absorbing the pink that was painted across the sky.

I felt content. Not only from being full of stir-fry and taking a piping hot shower, but from the events of the past two days, and how they'd been resolved. Brody looked at me with loving eyes, sitting quietly. I knew he was thinking about something, although he didn't share.

I wrestled with my inquisitive side and lost. "What are you thinking about?"

He smiled. "I was thinking—wondering, really—what you would've found if you and James had searched for me in the future."

I sat like a deer in headlights, unsure of how to answer.

He eyed me suspiciously. "You found me, didn't you?"

I looked down at my feet, trying to hide my shame. I had conveniently left that part out of my story, and I didn't want to revisit those feelings of grief.

He sounded stern. "What happened, Brit? I mean it, tell me everything."

I looked up at him and began filling in the missing details—all of them. "Um, well, I jumped into a pull where time moves much quicker than here and ended up sixty years in the future. I tried to find you in the pull I'd left you in earlier, but you were gone." I looked into his eyes, which were clearly telling me to get to the point. I took a deep breath. "I guess you already knew that part."

"Quit stalling."

I paused as I gathered the courage. Brody wouldn't be happy with me, I was sure of it. "I ran to James' house and he took me to you—except you were old."

Brody's eyebrows rose as I gulped.

"You were married to Dr. Eileen Straight."

The surprise plastered across his face was quickly replaced with awkwardness. "I'm sorry you had to see that. Dr. Straight? Wasn't she the entire reason you went on the road trip to begin with?"

I nodded.

A chuckle left his lips. "And the reason we met?"

I nodded again.

"Well, there's some irony for you." He spoke almost to himself. "So how did you get back here?"

My voice hardened. "I stayed with James for a day or two and then traveled back in time to the clearing."

His eyes narrowed with suspicion. "Or two?" It was obvious that he could tell I was holding back. I took another deep breath.

The words popped out of me quickly, being pent up under a guilty cork. "I thought you'd had a long, good life, and I didn't want to take it away from you. I was going to focus on traveling, but I couldn't do it. I was miserable, and I came back to find you."

Brody's irritation was obvious. "You actually thought of leaving things the way you found them?"

Blood rushed to my face. "You looked happy, and I *thought* you had kids—three beautiful girls. It was just a . . . a miscommunication."

Brody stood up abruptly, pushing away from the table. Obviously infuriated by my answer, he turned his back to me and looked out the window.

"But I didn't," I tried to argue, unsuccessfully.

Brody turned to face me, clearly still heated, and began to speak. "I can't—who do you—" He halted his argument in its tracks, glaring at me. "I can't talk to you about this right now." He turned on his heel and stormed out of the room.

I sat in remorse and awe. I knew he would be upset, but I'd never expected this reaction. He was hurt and insulted, and it was my fault. He expected my full commitment, regardless of the situation. After this experience, I had never been more committed to a person in my life.

Stewing in guilt, I sat at the kitchen table and looked out the window. Eventually I couldn't handle it any longer and decided to find Brody. We had to talk. I gathered my determination, stood up, and turned. Brody was standing behind me, making me jump.

"Brody—" I began to apologize, but he held up a single finger, stopping me before I finished.

He spoke slowly. "Brit, my life is complete with you and you alone. I don't *want* another future, no matter how great you think it is. Do you understand me?" he asked. "It isn't your decision to make."

"I'm sorry. I thought you had kids. I wanted what was best," I pleaded.

"What's best?" Disbelief crossed his face. "What's best is that you and I are together. Don't you understand what you mean to me?" He paused, adding a loud sigh.

"Since the first time I saw you in the restaurant, I knew I had to be with you." He laughed as his mind flashed back to our first encounter. "It took all my self-control not to stare at you all night. I was going to join Mike and introduce myself, but I was afraid I wouldn't be able to form a coherent sentence. I slept like crap the night before our first hike . . . I couldn't wait to see you again. After that night in the club, I knew that you were the one. We aren't perfect, but we're perfect for each other."

I looked at him with a dumbfounded expression. "Really?"

"Yes, really," he scolded. "We belong together, Brit." He stepped back, looked at me with intensity, and then flashed a smirk at me. "Wait here."

He walked away, and I heard him shuffling in the other room. I was baffled by the sudden turn in our discussion.

He walked back into the room, grabbed my hand, and pulled me into him. His intense gaze pierced me deeply. My nerves grew when I saw the mix of emotions in his eyes. He guided me into him, kissing me with the same intensity, and then broke away.

"Brit, you don't seem to grasp how deeply I feel for you. Perhaps I should show you instead."

He brought up his hand, which was balled into a fist. He opened his hand as he dropped onto one knee. My heart skipped a beat as I realized what was happening.

"Hopefully this shows you what you mean to me. I want to have children with *you*. I want to grow old with *you*. I only want to be with *you* for the rest of my life. Please say you'll make me the happiest man alive. Marry me?"

Overwhelmed, I couldn't speak so I nodded and pulled him up by the hand. He immediately stood up and I threw my arms around him.

I cried, embraced by my fiancé.

Printed in the United States
By Bookmasters